Max Davidson was born in 1955 and now divides his time between London and Cheltenham. His first novel, *The Wolf*, was published in 1983 and was followed by *Beef Wellington Blue* in 1985 and *Hugger Mugger* in 1986.

By the same author

The Wolf
Beef Wellington Blue
Hugger Mugger

MAX DAVIDSON

Suddenly, in Rome

GRAFTON BOOKS

A Division of the Collins Publishing Group

LONDON GLASGOW
TORONTO SYDNEY AUCKLAND

For

Grafton Books
A Division of the Collins Publishing Group
8 Grafton Street, London W1X 3LA

Published by Grafton Books 1989

First published in Great Britain by
Hodder and Stoughton Ltd 1988

Copyright © Max Davidson 1988

ISBN 0-586-07478-3

Printed and bound in Great Britain by
Collins, Glasgow

Set in Baskerville

MAX DAVIDSON

Suddenly, in Rome

GRAFTON BOOKS

A Division of the Collins Publishing Group

LONDON GLASGOW
TORONTO SYDNEY AUCKLAND

Grafton Books
A Division of the Collins Publishing Group
8 Grafton Street, London W1X 3LA

Published by Grafton Books 1989

First published in Great Britain by
Hodder and Stoughton Ltd 1988

Copyright © Max Davidson 1988

ISBN 0-586-07478-3

Printed and bound in Great Britain by
Collins, Glasgow

Set in Baskerville

For Kathryn

Part One

1

Geoffrey Danes wasn't obviously mad. You could talk to
him for hours at a time and be left with the impression of
perfect normality. He didn't transfix you with a fierce stare
or sway nervously from side to side, and his conversation
was measured, sensible. He was politically a middle-of-the-
roader and religiously an agnostic; he had all the same
prejudices, the same dreams, the same bugbears as all the
other Englishmen in Rome. He was generally well-informed
but, unless you wandered on to his favourite subject, he
never went out on a limb conversationally. He was softly
spoken, a bit reticent. He might have been a civil servant if
he hadn't been an accountant.

Again, to look at, he was normality itself. There was
nothing in his appearance to frighten people off and his
quiet, conservative clothes faithfully protected his anonym-
ity. A purist might have found his ties too loud and his
shirts too quiet, but he didn't dress for the purists, and
there were no purists in his circle anyway. More noticeable
was his head, which was large in relation to his body and
had a concentrated stillness that some people found discon-
certing. But it wasn't a madman's head. The cranium
didn't bulge unduly and there was no facial hair in unexpected places. The nostrils were slightly flared, but you
didn't expect flames of fire to come belching out of them
and, unless you wandered on to his favourite subject, they
never did.

But he was mad. I had always had to take Helen's word
for it, and I did take her word for it because we were, had

been, close. Then, much later, years after I'd stopped taking her word for anything, I found out for myself. It was far worse than I realized. With Helen it had been a joke, something we laughed about when he was out of the house as a way of keeping him at a distance, making him seem less immediate than a husband. But face to face it was only three-quarters funny. The little men in white coats should have taken him away long before he arrived on my doorstep that April night and greeted me with a single, unintelligible word: 'Camillo.'

I stared at him uncomprehendingly. We hadn't met at all for nearly eight years and it took me a second or two to recognize him. Over his shoulder, the piazza was still and deserted, patiently soaking up the rain which drifted down from a darkened sky: I could barely make out the great dome of Sant'Andrea half a mile away. Even the couple in the flat above, whose record-player normally throbbed away while the rest of us slept, had put up shop for the night. I rubbed my eyes and looked at my watch. Two-thirty: too late for riddles.

'Camillo,' he whispered again, his eyes gleaming like a dog's in the light of the street-lamp. He was shivering and I noticed he was wearing pyjamas under his raincoat.

Is there anyone more laid-back than an expatriate Englishman? My head was a whirl of questions ('Why you? Why two-thirty? Why pyjamas? Why Camillo?') and I remembered a time when his appearance on my doorstep in the middle of the night might have had a different significance. But all I said was: 'Come inside, Geoffrey. You're soaking.' Upstairs, I sat him down and gave him a whisky. The gleam in his eyes reduced to a glow and the shivering stopped. We even made a little small-talk. How was he liking Rome? Where was he living? Did he find the traffic worse than London? The usual things. I asked him about his job – he was working for some obscure international body: IBIS, IRIS, ISIS, something like that – and he then enquired about my writing, more out of politeness than interest. He was still distracted and kept darting glances round the room like a nervous animal. It was an edgy, deliberately superficial, conversation. He didn't ask why I hadn't been in touch since he arrived in Rome (though it was now more than six months and a less naïve man would have suspected) and I didn't ask why he persisted in calling me Camillo when my parents had christened me Mark Henry Jonathan. Rome is Rome: you take life at a leisurely pace and, when it gets complicated, you don't ask questions. Just as I thought his fit had passed, he suddenly leant forward and started gibbering. The gleam in his eyes became a laser-beam.

'You're my only hope, Mark. Bill can't do it and Tony won't do it. I've tried Dr Martin, but he says Sally would have a fit if he had anything to do with it. That only leaves me and, if I did it myself, there'd be chaos. Besides, I'm too short and my voice is all wrong. I know you're busy with your writing, but I'm sure you could make a decent job of it if you made the effort. Do please say yes.'

I nearly said yes immediately because I'm that sort of person: someone who rushes into things, then spends his life picking up the pieces. In restaurants I enjoy choosing dishes with mysterious names without asking what they are; in love I buy first and look at the price-tag later. This time caution prevailed, just.

'Go back to the beginning, Geoffrey. What is it you want me to do?'

He stared. 'Haven't you heard?'

'Heard what? I keep myself to myself. I don't follow the gossip the way I used to.'

'You must have seen the posters.'

'Posters?'

'And I've advertised in all the newspapers. Everyone knows about it. You're the first person I've met who hasn't heard about the production.'

'Production? You mean you're putting on a play? Which play?'

'*The Winter's Tale.*'

'Really?'

'By Shakespeare.'

'I know who wrote the damn thing.'

'Yes, of course you do. I'm sorry.' The apology was almost genuine. He'd always patronized me relentlessly, ever since he discovered I wrote books people actually read, but he still had a residue of English decency, a horror of giving unnecessary offence. At the mention of Shakespeare, my interest quickened. So it was his favourite subject which had reduced him to this feverish state. Helen had told me about the symptoms, but I had never seen them at first hand before. A dull memory of school English lessons jogged my brain.

'Wait a minute. Isn't Camillo one of the characters in *The Winter's Tale*?'

'Yes, that's right.'

'Does he exit pursued by a bear or is that someone else?'

'No, that's Antigonus. Camillo is Leontes' courtier, the one who refuses to poison Polixenes because he believes in Hermione's innocence, so he runs away to Bohemia where, sixteen years later, disguised as a – '

'Yes, yes. It's all coming back. Glorious stuff. And you want me to play the part, I suppose?'

'Mark, I'm depending on you. Do please say yes.'

'When's the first night?'

'May 10th.'

'That's only three weeks away.'

'That's why I'm so desperate. The rest of the cast have been rehearsing since February. If I don't find a replacement soon, I'll have to cancel.'

'Replacement? What happened to the last Camillo?'

'He had a car accident yesterday. Some idiot ran into the back of him in the Piazza del Popolo.'

'Is he badly hurt?'

'I'm not sure.' He stopped and blinked. Again I could see remnants of decency in his face, as if part of him realized that this wasn't a trivial detail to be quickly sidestepped. Then the fanatic took over again. 'We have rehearsals every evening at eight in my flat. You could miss tomorrow's if you needed time to learn your lines.'

'It might help.'

'And you'll need to be measured. There's a woman in Trastevere doing the costumes: I could fix a time with her. How about tomorrow at nine?'

'Hang on, Geoffrey: one thing at a time. I haven't said yes yet. How many performances are there?'

'Four. Thursday to Sunday.'

'And where's it on?'

'Near the Pantheon. Someone's lent us a room in an old *palazzo*: it's perfect for the first three acts, but we're going to have to improvise for the pastoral scenes. It can seat a hundred and fifty.'

'You'll be lucky to get ten.'

'Don't be ridiculous, Mark. This is Shakespeare.'

'That's the problem.'

'What do you mean?'

'Never mind.' I glanced to see if he really didn't know what I meant and saw that he didn't. Apart from marbles, what madmen lack is antennae: they don't sense things that are obvious to the rest of us, in this case the lack of an audience for Shakespeare in Rome. Not since a loopy

13

second secretary at the British Embassy had mounted a Gilbert and Sullivan evening had I had such a powerful premonition of disaster. I was hypnotized. The unreality of the venture, the neglect of essential details in the excitement of the grand idea, was mind-boggling. Throughout the whole conversation, Geoffrey *never asked if I had acted before.* If I'd told him the last time was in a school nativity play, when I gave a competent rather than inspired performance as Fourth Candidate for Circumcision, would he still have badgered me so persistently? Would he still have begged and coaxed and pleaded until his voice wobbled with emotion and his eyes seemed to start from his head and reach out towards me? I honestly believe he would: I don't think I ever saw such desperation in a human face.

Madmen make those who deal with them cautious. It was four in the morning when I finally asked the question which had been smouldering beneath the surface from the moment Geoffrey arrived.

'How's Helen?'

Helen Danes wasn't mad at all. When people said she was insane to marry Geoffrey or she was crazy to lead the life she did, they only meant it figuratively. She could raise eyebrows sometimes, but she also commanded the trust and affection of the eccentric who is still on the right side of the fence. She had a lot of common sense: too much, I sometimes thought.

The world would say I had reason to hate Helen, but the world doesn't always get these things right. For eight long years, I did half hate her, muttering my private execrations and nursing my bitterness like a schoolboy resentful of an unjust teacher. But the hatred didn't burn or fester or explode, like those other, sweeter emotions. I don't have the energy to be a good hater – or I didn't then.

And, hatred apart, what is there to say about the only woman in your life you've ever really loved? How do you introduce other people, people you've never met, people who may never have loved or been loved, to that strange landscape of the mind in which there is only one moving figure – the rest are lifeless and without meaning? In one of my own novels I would feel obliged to describe what Helen looked like, what clothes she wore, where she bought her jewellery – all the things my agent insists sell books and for all I know do sell books, though I've never understood why a beautiful blonde in a Harrods negligée should be worthier of interest than a dumpy housewife in curlers. But I can't package her in that way. I've seen her in expensive negligées and I've seen her in curlers and to me she's adorable in both. You can't describe the essence of someone you love to a third person: you can only appeal to their own experience, their own imagination. She's a blonde, but that's all I'm telling.

We met at a party in Notting Hill in 1977. The party must have been given by somebody, some dear, sweet, generous person who bought the drinks and invited the guests and brought me the greatest happiness I have known. But I couldn't now tell you who it was. I'm not someone who commits that sort of detail to memory as if it were of telling importance: I remember faces, gestures, words, those little moments when time stands still. Besides, I went to a lot of parties that summer. A critic who mattered had written something complimentary about one of my novels in a magazine read by other people who mattered, and the other people who mattered wanted to meet me. I also wanted to meet them. Once I'd met them, they stopped mattering, but I didn't know that until I had met them and the thing about people who matter is that they mix better cocktails than people who don't matter. I liked cocktails then

15

too. I was brash and thirty and on the threshold of being somebody and I must have asked thirty clever women in a week which way they thought the post-structuralist novel was heading, when I met my match in Helen.

'You must know that's all crap.'

'Well, yes, I suppose it is crap, on one level.' Immediately I was on the defensive. My mother had warned me about women who used language like that and, if her bluntness was titillating, it also alienated.

'Not just on one level: on every level. I suppose you're a writer?'

I confessed. To think I had come to the party to boast about it.

'What do you write?'

I confessed that too. How mincing the word 'novel' sounds when it's spoken without conviction! To save face, I dropped the title of my latest book, the one that the critic who mattered etc., then summarized the story. She interrupted my limping resumé halfway through.

'And presumably the man with cancer ends up marrying his sister-in-law?'

'Yes, that's right.' I went crimson. My little masterstroke, the unexpected twist that had so wowed the critic who mattered, exposed for what it was: a device so threadbare it had become a party joke. Finally she took pity.

'I read the book.' Then, with an amplitude and a sweetness more thrilling than any superlative: 'I liked it.' She had won me.

Later I saw a darker side to this playfulness in her. She was so anxious to stay a move ahead, to keep me guessing the whole time, that I realized she was frightened of any emotional repose between us. With Geoffrey she did enjoy a kind of repose, the snoring, passionless inertia of an indifferent marriage; but with me she always seemed to be

16

on the run, as if from some vague spectre she was afraid to confront. I should have been suspicious of the feverish energy of her flirtation, but I was too young: it just seemed so superior to the usual tired repartee that I fell for it utterly. The darkness only closed in later.

And what about me? Was I mad? Did I imagine myself as another Helen, always poised, always in command, or another Geoffrey, driven to absurd and demeaning lengths by an ungovernable passion? The world would have said I was one of the sane, but the world would have got it wrong again. I wasn't sane, not really. I had the sane man's sense of perspective, but I wasn't a genuine traveller on the middle road: I was much too fascinated by the view from the edge of the precipice.

Some kinds of behaviour are simply stupid. A man going out in heavy rain without an umbrella is stupid. Teenagers sleeping together without contraception are stupid. A politician is stupid if he disregards the necessity of winning votes. A businessman is stupid if he invests in the wrong commodity at the wrong time. Most people do stupid things, regret them, survive them, even learn from them. But stupidity can also be sinister: it can become a wanton and dangerous addiction, driving otherwise normal people to do stupid things even when the consequences are staring them in the face. At its most self-destructive, it stops being simply intellectual laziness and becomes a kind of lunacy. That night I acted like a lunatic.

For consider my behaviour. No reasonable man would have agreed to act in that production of *The Winter's Tale*: it was doomed to disaster. I could already see my Roman friends chortling that the *Inglesi* had made fools of themselves again. Not only would I waste valuable writing time, I would suffer public humiliation. So, if there was no future in it, why did I say yes? Because I wanted to see Helen again? Yes, but *why* did I want to see Helen again? Hadn't I come to Rome largely to get away from her? Since she arrived in Rome herself, hadn't I studiously been avoiding parties at which I might meet her? The truth is, there was no future in Helen either, and the rational part of me knew that perfectly well. It can only have been madness that made me so desperate to turn back the clock.

2

I expected to see her at the rehearsal in Geoffrey's flat the
next day. She wasn't acting in the play, but she had always
been an assiduous hostess, the kind who doesn't trust her
husband to receive visitors alone. So I arrived ten minutes
early, having prepared various opening lines: 'Well, Helen,
it's been a long time', 'How nice to see you again after all
these years', 'Fancy our paths crossing again like this'. Pre-
scripted conversations are usually disastrous, but I've never
trusted to spontaneity in moments of crisis. I even worked
out my first joke: 'Isn't Shakespeare wonderful at bringing
people together?' – a reference to our torrid nights of love
while Geoffrey was out at the theatre, getting his weekly fix
of the Bard. We used to pace ourselves according to the
play: if it was *Hamlet* or *Richard the Third*, we could make
love two or three times without straining; if it was a briskly
paced *Macbeth*, we had to race against the clock. Once we
got it wrong and were almost caught out by a heavily cut
version of *The Two Gentlemen of Verona*; but Geoffrey was so
incensed by the truncated text that he noticed nothing
amiss. I remember him storming up and down the living-
room shouting 'No director in his right mind would have
cut that speech', while I sat quietly on the sofa putting on
my shoes and socks. I almost came to love Shakespeare
myself.

My prepared lines had to wait: Helen wasn't there. I
assumed she was avoiding me and wasn't convinced when
Geoffrey said she had gone out to dinner with friends. I
should have felt rejected, but my heart leapt: I was worth

avoiding, therefore I counted for something. What a twisted logician love is.

'Have you learnt your lines yet?' Geoffrey asked sharply.

'Only the first scene. It's a bigger part than I thought.'

'You can use a book today, but I'll expect you to be word-perfect tomorrow. Time's very short and we've got to get the staging right. Every second of rehearsal time is vital.'

'Yes, Geoffrey.' I touched my forelock ironically, but was chastened. The pathetic groveller of the previous night had turned into a martinet. I could see the madness underneath and was nervous of it: the one thing you can't do with a madman is argue.

The rest of the cast must have had the whip cracked over them too. They all appeared at eight o'clock exactly, in a quite un-Roman display of punctuality. One or two of them I knew: Tony Barclay, who owned a little print shop on the Via Babuino; Dick Shepherd from the Embassy and his wife Joanie; and a small man with a beard I had seen in the cheap seats at the opera. Geoffrey clapped his hands and said, 'This is Mark Barham, everyone: he's taking over as Camillo', and they all smiled welcomingly. I smiled back. Someone called out, 'Well done, that man', as if I'd held a difficult catch at cricket, and somebody else said, 'I hope you can act better than poor Harry', at which everyone laughed. I laughed too. The falseness was unbearable. Why is it always the people you leave England to get away from who keep turning up abroad?

A fresh-faced girl with large earrings came bouncing up to me. 'Don't you write?' she asked. Her lips pouted and I could tell at once we would end up sleeping together. There are women for whom second-rate novelists have an irresistible allure: they tend to be the sort of women second-rate novelists deserve. My loins stirred a bit, but I was depressed by my lack of discrimination: she was only mildly pretty and her efforts to bubble made me wince. 'Your name's awfully familiar and I've seen you sitting at a café in the Piazza Navona scribbling away. Do tell me you're a real writer.'

'I'm a real writer.'

'How amazing. I've never met a real writer before. You must have incredible will-power to be able to concentrate on your writing with that Bernini fountain right in front of you.'

'It's just practice.'

'I love Bernini. All the most beautiful things in Rome seem to be by him. Did you know he also did that obelisk with an elephant next to the Pantheon?'

'Yes, I think so.'

'What an amazing man, though. He must have had incredible energy, like all geniuses do. Does writing take a lot of energy? I know it looks easy enough, just sitting there and scribbling the first thing that comes into your head, but what you actually put in your books probably isn't the first thing that comes into your head, is it? It could be the second or even the third: it must be awfully fun choosing. Daddy, do say hullo to Mark. He's a real writer.'

'Daddy' shook hands glumly: he had the wary melancholy of an overprotective father who knows his daughter is beyond protection. 'Pleased to meet you, Mark. What is it you write?'

'Novels.'

'Really?' His face went even greyer: I think he had hoped for better. Clumsily he changed tack, in an effort to head me off. 'Vanessa's only here till the end of July, then she's going back to England.' His naïveté was pitiful. Did he really think we would be inhibited by the shortness of the time available? Didn't he understand the modern world at

21

all? Intrigued, I started to question him. He was called Peter Jansen and worked for the same international body as Geoffrey; he had been there two years and had had his contract renewed for another five; he was a widower; Vanessa was his only child . . . As the pieces of the jigsaw fell into place, his paternal anxiety became more explicable and I wanted to say something to assuage it. But I don't think he would have understood. The greyness on his face never lifted.

'Right, everyone, let's make a start.' Geoffrey's rasping voice cut the atmosphere like a knife. Everybody stopped talking immediately and turned to face him. Again I was struck by the power and authority he generated. This wasn't the mild-mannered weakling I had cuckolded so contemptuously, but a man transformed. When he started to speak, his whole body seemed to align itself behind the words.

'Tonight I want you all to concentrate on the language. This first act is complex in its wording because Shakespeare is describing violent emotions and the tortuous logic that accompanies them. Clarity is essential if we're to get that across. Remember: with Shakespeare *every word counts*.'

He carried on in the same vein and suddenly I was frightened. I had thought I was dealing with English amdram at its most preposterous, but instead there was a deep seriousness. Shouldn't I of all people have realized that love is a perfectionist? Geoffrey wasn't just doing a production of *The Winter's Tale*: he meant it to be the greatest *Winter's Tale* in history, however unpromising the cast, however unhelpful the conditions. What if my Camillo was bad? Would he shrug and be grateful that he had a Camillo at all or would he be angry? And how angry? For the first time I felt nervous.

Part of the trouble, was that *The Winter's Tale* isn't my

22

sort of play. To be precise, Shakespeare isn't my sort of writer, though it embarrasses me to admit it and I've been giving the old phoney a chance for the last twenty years, trying to find out what people like Geoffrey get so steamed up about. It's not that I'm a philistine. The novel of mine that caused such a stir when I was younger was really quite high-brow: there were semi-colons and echoes of Joyce and the heroine had some sensitive insights into the structure of modern society as she stuffed the Christmas turkey. If I've moved downmarket since, it's mainly because *la dolce vita* in Rome doesn't come cheap: I paid six thousand *lire* for an espresso in Trastevere the other night and you need sex in every chapter to keep up that sort of lifestyle. No: the real trouble is that I find his plays – not all of them but most of them and not all the time but most of the time – just the tiniest bit – what's the word? – well, you know, *boring*. There, I've said it: I feel better already. And, when it comes to yawns, *The Winter's Tale* takes a lot of beating.

Take my part, Camillo. His first line is: 'I think this coming summer the King of Sicilia means to pay Bohemia the visitation which he justly owes him'; his second line is: 'Beseech you'; and his third line is: 'You pay a great deal too dear for what's given freely.' Then he really launches himself and says: 'Sicilia cannot show himself over-kind to Bohemia. They were trained together in their childhoods and there rooted betwixt them then such an affection which cannot choose but branch now. Since their more mature dignities and royal necessities made separation of their society, their encounters, though not personal, have been royally attorneyed . . .' and so on and so forth. It doesn't exactly fizz, does it? You can see why people read Agatha Christie and Dick Francis on aeroplanes and not the Complete Works. Why on earth Geoffrey imagined the good people of Rome would come flocking to hear such stuff, I can't think. Oh yes, I remember: because he was mad. There's usually a simple explanation for these things.

Geoffrey waved his arms for Act One, Scene One to get under way: a little introductory section in which, as luck would have it, Camillo features prominently. There was nowhere to hide: furniture was pushed to one side, an acting area was cleared and I found myself standing centre stage with the small bearded man who was playing the other character in the scene, Archidamus. Geoffrey said: 'Now remember: I want to hear every word,' and someone else whispered: 'Good luck, old man.' The others remained silent, watching curiously. I froze. Were there really people who enjoyed doing this sort of thing?

'If you thall chance, Camillo . . .' On top of everything else, the man with the beard had a lisp and his opening speech was full of words he couldn't pronounce properly. When he got to 'Sicilia' and it came out as 'Thithilia', I couldn't help smiling. Geoffrey stamped his foot on the floor.

'What's so funny, Mark? This is a serious scene.'

'I'm sorry, Geoffrey. I thought there was quite a light-hearted moment then.'

'Don't be ridiculous. The purpose of this scene is to get information across to the audience: it's not a comic scene at all. When I want you to be light-hearted, I'll tell you.'

'Yes, Geoffrey.'

'Start the scene again from the beginning. A little faster, Walter.'

'If you thall chance, Camillo . . .' This time Walter bolted through his speech like an express train, his lisp degenerating into farce. Geoffrey tapped his pencil impatiently on his knee. Then it was my turn.

'I think this coming summer . . .'

'Louder, Mark.'

'I think this coming summer the King of Sicilia . . .' I was away. My first line was passed without comment; so was my second. With my third I even tried a little emotional colouring, the sort of trick real actors make their money from. Geoffrey seemed to like it: I could see him nodding approvingly out of the corner of my eye. With only the lisping Walter for competition, it was easy to believe I was acting well. My confidence boomed and I began to thrill to the sound of my voice as it resonated round the living-room. It couldn't last, of course. In the middle of my first big speech, Geoffrey tore into me again.

'Mark, are you feeling all right?'

'Yes, I'm fine, Geoffrey. Why?'

'You're flailing your arms about as if you were feeling very emotional about something. What's got into you? This is a low-key scene, giving information to the audience. I don't want to have to tell you again.'

'Sorry, Geoffrey. I thought, as there was nothing much happening, the acting should be pepped up a bit.'

'What the hell do you mean, *nothing much happening*?' He took a step forward and, for a second, I thought he was going to hit me. The angry concentration in his face was terrifying: the only time I saw anything comparable was at a dinner party where I told a professional violinist I preferred Monteverdi to Mozart. I backed down hurriedly.

'I only mean there's nothing much happening in terms of *action*, Geoffrey. In terms of language, of course, it's different: Shakespeare's so rich, so dense . . .'

'That's better.' He was so relieved to hear me toe the party line that he missed my irony. 'Now do the rest of the scene properly.'

I did as I was told, bolted through my lines and escaped on to the balcony for a cigarette. With ominous speed, Vanessa joined me.

25

'Don't worry,' she whispered. 'He treats everyone like that. He's a real task-master. God help anyone who forgets their lines.'

'Has he ever shouted at you?'

'Only once. I suggested cutting some lines from one of my speeches and he went totally berserk; said I didn't deserve to be acting in Shakespeare if I took that attitude. It was awful. And he seems such a mild person when you first meet him.'

'Yes, it's odd. He's not the Geoffrey I used to know.' How cruel memory is, how unfeeling in its associations. As soon as I spoke the words, I remembered the time eight years before when Helen said: 'He's not the man I married' – and the great leap of hope in my heart as I attached an unintended meaning to her words. And yet I didn't want to remember hope: I wanted to feel it.

'Isn't it funny how people are different on the inside from the outside?' Vanessa's bouncy platitudes offered no hope: they only led to despair. I sometimes think there are women men only sleep with as a form of punishment, to exorcize their desire to sleep with other women. 'You must enjoy writing about that sort of thing in your novels, having characters say one thing and all the time be thinking something different – you know, like Proust. Do you find it easy to make your characters behave convincingly? Or do you just concentrate on getting the plot right? How many words a day do you write?'

'About twelve hundred.' It was like school exams: I always answered the easy question first.

'Gosh, that sounds like an awful lot. How many pages is that?'

'Five of typescript, three of print.'

'That's amazing. You must be incredibly dedicated. I wrote a ten-line poem once which took a whole day.'

'Ah, well, poetry's different. Rhyming, scansion . . .' I fumbled for another cigarette. Literary groupies fall into two categories: the ones who just ask you where you get your ideas from and look wide-eyed whatever you say; and the ones who bide their time, waiting for an opportune moment to ask you to run a professional eye over the two-hundred-page manuscript which they wrote to come to terms with their unhappy adolescence. Had I assigned Vanessa too unthinkingly to the first category? To get her off literature, I started to flirt: the plodding, half-hearted foreplay of early middle age.

'How long have you been in Rome? Your arms are very brown already.'

'Thank you. Only since Christmas, but I spend a lot of time outdoors. It's an amazing city for just walking about. You live here, don't you?'

'Yes, that's right. If you're going to be a writer, you might as well do it somewhere pleasant. How do you find Italian men?'

'Self-centred. They don't exactly make you feel wanted.'

'Oh, I'm superb at that. I want women so badly it shows.'

'You're not telling me you're single?'

'Only half the time.'

'And the other half?'

'I improvise. You're not the only pretty girl in Rome, you know.'

'I never said I was.'

'I know you never said you were but, with your looks, you probably thought it. Has anyone ever complimented you on your ear-lobes? They're stunning.'

'Thank you.'

We meandered on, swopping coded information about our mating habits like used-car dealers, but all the time I thought only of Helen and whether I would see her that night or not. I hoped to catch a glimpse of her from the balcony as she returned home; but, not for the first time with Helen, I was outmanoeuvred. A curtain rustled behind me and there she was, silhouetted in the doorway. Over her shoulder the rehearsal was still in progress, but I had no time for the actors in that other drama. From the moment she appeared, she eclipsed everything else.

'There you are, Mark. Hullo, Vanessa.' She sounded her old cool self, but there was a slight vibrato underneath if you listened carefully. I froze, straining every muscle to match her calmness. Vanessa's presence suddenly became an unexpected bonus: I was glad she was with me, glad that our little tête-à-tête had the appearance of intimacy. How instinctively we read our own emotions into other people: I was always the jealous one, the one who needed to be told that he and he alone counted, yet I still used one woman to hurt another in the absurd expectation it would work. If I never learn, it must be because I don't want to learn, don't want to face a world in which other people hurt less easily than me.

Mechanically my eyes took in the differences between the new Helen and the old: the shorter, neater hair; the thickening around the hips; the subtler contours of a face no longer young. But the sense of change was quite overwhelmed by the sense of sameness. It didn't seem odd that I had once worshipped the woman: it seemed inevitable.

Only a few feet separated us, but it felt like a hundred yards: the space was charged with tension, between reticence and longing, between spontaneity and suspicion. I stood my ground, then Helen came over and kissed me on both cheeks. I responded warmly, but wished somehow there had been a single kiss: sometimes gestures which

28

seem to add something are really a diminishment. She said: 'It's been far too long,' and again I had a sense of distance, as if I were no more than a favourite uncle returning from Australia. She had always been more skilful than me at public displays of affection and I noticed how studiously she avoided catching my eye. I suppose she was afraid of the reproach she would see there, but there was none to see. In the excitement of rediscovery, all the smouldering recriminations just evaporated, as if time had stopped, as if we were still lovers, as if the last eight years hadn't happened.

And, in a sense, they hadn't happened. 1978, 1979, 1980, 1981, 1982, 1983, 1984: they were just numbers on a calendar, not a series of days and nights with a cumulative and transforming effect. Nothing in them was alive in the way the past had been alive and I was alive again now. Feelings I had thought dead reawakened as if from a long sleep and for a second I was back there again, in that innocent world where pain and regret and loss are not yet imaginable.

3

And yet I'm not normally a push-over in love. That was the absurd thing. I enter impetuously into relationships, but I don't bring my whole heart with me, not straight away. I hold back. I keep my distance. I'm slow with compliments, even slower with flowers. You see, I'm English.

With Helen, all those hang-ups went straight out of the window. After that party in Notting Hill in 1977, all doubt disappeared and I was left with only one heart, only one mind, only one hope. There was a linear certainty about my behaviour which now takes my breath away, and I've often thought since: if you only experience it once or twice in your life, that single-minded, demonic energy that sweeps all before it, shouldn't you channel it to some better use? Shouldn't you write a great symphony or found a religious movement or conquer a continent? Why be a zealot for love? Yet, in the whirlwind of the moment, love was all I wanted. When Geoffrey and not Helen answered the telephone the day after the party, I brushed him aside like a fly.

'I want to speak to Helen Danes.'

'I'll see if she's around.' With hindsight, the answer said a lot about their marriage. Unless she was actually in the same room, Geoffrey had the vaguest idea of his wife's whereabouts: he was so trusting and unvigilant he was almost an accessory before the fact, like a priest who refuses to lock his church at night.

Helen picked up the receiver. 'Who is it?'

'It's me. Mark Barham. We met last night.'

'I remember. You sound different on the phone.'

'Everyone sounds different on the phone: it's something to do with the upper glottis. Listen, we've got to meet.'

'You are funny.' She laughed lightly but without conviction. 'Why have we *got* to meet?'

'Because we'd be idiots not to. I'm free from five-thirty.'

'Then we'd better meet at six-thirty.'

'Couldn't you manage earlier? We need time to talk.'

'Six, if you insist, but that's final.'

'OK, I'll see you then. Don't be late.' I hung up, then realized I'd forgotten to fix a meeting place. When I redialled, Geoffrey again picked up the receiver first.

'I'll go and get her.' I suppose he was doing me a favour, but his lack of urgency infuriated me. Don't forget, I didn't yet know there was a Mr Danes, let alone that he was the biggest lunatic in London.

'That was my husband,' Helen said defensively when I suggested she hire someone younger to answer the telephone.

'Ah.' My hopes took a dip, then soared again. 'You didn't tell me you were married.'

'You didn't ask.'

'What does he do?'

'He's an accountant.'

'You're kidding.'

'What's so funny?'

'It's just rather incongruous. You don't seem the sort of woman to be married to an accountant.'

'How do you know what sort of woman I am?'

'Because I talked to you last night.'

'Only for five minutes.'

'Yes, but I'm a novelist, a sardonic observer of human nature with an acute eye for people's idiosyncrasies and foibles. They said so in the *Manchester Evening News*.'

31

'Crap. What are my foibles?'

'I'll tell you at six.' I hung up breathlessly and had to hold on to a chair to steady myself. In some flirtation there is a feverishness more frenzied than sex itself: a thrusting and a counter-thrusting so intense that the mind achieves a rapier-like precision it didn't know it had. That's how it was with Helen and me in those early encounters. Usually she fenced better than me because she cared less where her blade fell – but I had my days too, when my head was clear and my heart was racing and my adrenalin was high. It was certainly high that day. When we met at six, in a 'happy hour' bar next to the Park, I came straight out with it like a schoolboy.

'I'm in love.'

She smiled and said: 'That was quick,' as if I'd gone to buy a newspaper and returned quicker than expected. I should have seen a warning in that flinching from emotion, but I took it only as a challenge.

'No, I mean it. I've thought about nothing else since last night.'

Again she smiled. 'You are funny, Mark.' It was to become one of her favourite lines. I think she thought that if she could keep laughing at me, she wouldn't get involved, because laughter precluded seriousness. How wrong she was: laughter can be the most insidious, most dangerously intimate emotion in the world. We laughed at the cocktails with the silky names: Tequila Come-on, Misty Dreams, Anything Goes. We laughed at the tourists trudging down the Bayswater Road with rucksacks on their backs and maps of London blown inside out by the wind. We even laughed at my poor book and all the things in it that had seemed so serious and important twenty-four hours before that. We didn't stop laughing until we'd laughed ourselves into bed in a sleazy hotel in Paddington, with purple wallpaper and a gilt mirror suspended above the bed: the mirror was the biggest laugh yet . . .

Those memories now no longer make me laugh: I can hardly smile at them. They seem painfully distant, as if much more than eight years separated them from today's reality, and Rome and London were divided, not by a short aeroplane journey, but by unbridgeable cultural differences. They are not childhood memories: we were both around thirty and would have sworn, before we met, that we had known adult love before. But what we had known before must somehow have been insufficient. I can't think why else we should have thrown ourselves into that affair as if it were our first love and we were bringing nothing to it but ourselves. The laughter of that summer evening was the laughter of teenagers: gay, febrile, infectious. Helen didn't just catch the giggles from me, but my entire mood, my exhilaration, my abandonment, my freedom. And, though she qualified them later, she *did* say, in an unguarded moment of extraordinary sweetness, those words that were to haunt me later: '*I've never known anything like this.*' At such moments there is no danger of mishearing: the words resounded in my head like a roll of drums and I knew we were at one in more than laughter.

Even when the laughter stopped, we were still smiling: smiles of tenderness and forgiving, of excitement and repose, smiles of hullo and goodbye and why-can't-life-always-be-like-this? In those three dizzy months, we were the only people in London: everyone else evaporated, leaving the stage free for us. My friends became practically invisible: it was impossible to believe I had ever cared about any of them. As for the strangers we passed in the streets, they were just crude cardboard cut-outs, a back-cloth for us to play against. We revelled in that shared

33

egotism which pretends it is less egotistical for being shared; and out of the intensity of the sharing, the fierceness of the fusion, there came – or so it seemed then, and appears even more certainly now, so empty has been the intervening period – a great good. We eclipsed the world because we *were* the world, the sum of everything in it that mattered. We had so much to give each other, so much to say. With most people, conversation requires conscious effort, like riding a bicycle: one lapse of concentration and you're on the floor. With the very special few, there is no such fear: it's no longer a question of finding things to say, but of finding time to say them. You imagine that you could hold a conversation with them for ever, without exhausting your capacity to surprise and stimulate each other. I still remember the shock of discovering that, even with Helen, that was only a myth: the pain of the moment when we stood in a lift together and simultaneously looked at our watches – as if we were strangers terrified of being alone with each other in that confined space. I had never anticipated that howling vacuum.

Yet the vacuum was there. At the very heart of our love, something was missing. I yearned for a perfect union and didn't achieve one, not quite. At first I thought it was because of Geoffrey: the infuriating necessity of Helen's returning to him at the end of the evening. But there was more to it than that. For all her flashes of intense feeling, Helen wasn't absolute in her love in the way that I was. She was one of those people in whom the need to give was balanced almost equally by the need to withhold: not out of selfishness or frigidity, but because she wanted the act of giving to be special and personal and enduring. I remember asking her, when we had been lovers for more than a month and the question seemed reasonable to our state of intimacy, whether she believed in any sort of after-life; and

how she immediately said it was something she wasn't
ready to talk about. I have a more impulsive character, so
at first I resented her for being so guarded; but I later came
to value that quality highly, almost more than any she had.
She gave her body easily because she was an uninhibited
product of uninhibited times; but the rest of herself she
dished out in thimble-sized helpings, as if she was afraid I
would get sated if I gorged myself too quickly. I never did
find out if she believed in an after-life, and that hurts me
now. But I never got sated either.

Through Helen I got to know Geoffrey. I was wary of
meeting him at first – affairs with married women were
something my mother had warned me very sternly against
– but Helen thought it would be a good idea to get us
together and, naturally, I was curious. I should have
distrusted those chummy instincts in her, the easy embrac-
ing of hypocrisy, but it seemed ludicrous to feel guiltier
towards Geoffrey than she did, so I bit the bullet: an
informal dinner for three at their house in Fulham. I
brought a bottle of Beaujolais, because I was told he liked
Beaujolais, and wore a tie because I was told he would be
in a tie. For all the world it was like buttering up a
prospective father-in-law.

'So you're an author, Mark.'

'That's right.'

'What have you had published?' I made nothing of it
then, but the terminology was indicative. In Geoffreyspeak,
only Shakespeare 'wrote': everyone else, from Dante down-
wards, was an author who had things published. I don't
think there was any significance in the distinction, but some
distinction there had to be. He was a very precise man.

I told him the titles of my three novels, hoping he would
at least have heard of *The Positive Hour*, my big critical
success: it was said it would have been short-listed for the

35

Booker Prize if it hadn't been set in England. But he looked blank.

'Do you use a pseudonym?'

'No, my own name.'

'I'm sorry: I thought you had an alias.' Never had I been put down so quickly or economically. The unintentional insult cast a pall over the entire conversation, with Geoffrey's small-talk acting as a potent anaesthetic.

'We bought this place in 1973 when it was a buyer's market. Mortgage rates have almost doubled since then . . .'

'One of our neighbours used to have a job in publishing. Fascinating profession, I imagine . . .'

'Do you really type your own books? I don't think I'd have the necessary co-ordination in my fingers . . .'

'I'll just see how Helen's getting on in the kitchen . . .'

'How do you find Notting Hill Gate? My sister had digs in that part of the world in the sixties . . .'

'No, I think last summer was wetter. There were two whole weeks when it didn't seem to stop . . .'

'I wonder if Helen wants a hand with the salad . . .'

'Do you find that with the District Line too? I knew I wasn't imagining things . . .'

'Helen, I'm sure you need help with something. Helen!'

As he bolted into the kitchen for the third time, I suddenly felt angry with Helen for marrying the man. He was only two years my senior, but already he spoke in the thudding platitudes of middle age. How could he possibly win the affection of a high-spirited woman like Helen, let alone retain it? If I could have answered that question, I might have been able to forgive what happened later. But then, if I could have answered that question . . . There are things no thirty-year-old understands.

With his wife at his side, he did become recognizably

human and they kept up a tolerable husband-wife banter throughout the meal. It sounded like some of the conversations Helen and I had, but played at a third of the speed and without – dare I whisper it? – the same panache. The subtext was far more interesting than the text, for Helen smiled at each of us in turn and sent darting messages with her eyes, a practice of which she was fond. To me she said: 'Don't write him off: give him a chance'; and to Geoffrey: 'I only sleep with him: you're the one I married.' How I hated that 'only', yet how doggedly and patiently I did give him a chance, believing that if Helen wanted her threesome cosy, that was how it had to be.

From above the mantelpiece, Shakespeare watched the whole thing impassively. It was a cheap reproduction of a not very good portrait, in which the only features of note were the spaced-out eyes and an incongruous gold earring; but its prominent position made me more and more uncomfortable. English writers suffer from an inferiority complex about Shakespeare anyway, but this was like Casanova watching you make love: a wonderful inspiration, of course, but, well, a bit inhibiting, if you know what I mean. Finally, to break the spell, I made a joke about it, something to the effect that Geoffrey knew some better writers than the ones he had to dinner (ha ha, yawn yawn, have another glass of wine for being so modest); but all he said was 'Oh yes, I'm very fond of Shakespeare' and changed the subject. This was in the days before he came out of the closet, of course, when he was still quite shy about discussing his little deviation with strangers, and I had no idea of the magnitude of the understatement. I thought there was only one passion that mattered in that dining-room, and that everything else was bland and synthetic and moribund. I hope Shakespeare laughed.

4

Writer's cramp is a misunderstood complaint. It's usually likened to constipation, but the two conditions are quite different. A constipated man has something inside which he can't get out, but which he knows will one day have to come out, willy-nilly; a writer with cramp has nothing inside him at all. Or so he believes. Whatever normally flows through him and out of him suddenly dries up completely, and he has no certainty that the source will renew itself; there are no laxatives he can take, no stimulating drugs, no proven form of sustenance for that inner spring. It is a psychological problem with an all too painful physical aspect: the inability of the hand holding the pen to commit a single coherent word to paper. Some writers get attacks of cramp so regularly that it kills them off; others never experience it. Geoffrey's friend from Stratford had continuous diarrhoea for twenty years.

I used to know about the ailment only at second-hand, from anguished writer friends who moaned about their 'dry' periods and whose egos I had to massage back to health. '*Relax*, Frank,' I would say. 'You're still a marvellous craftsman with language. 'Don't be so *obsessive*, Tony: science fiction is a perfectly legitimate field.' 'I know it's a *roman à clef*, Muriel, but don't get so *involved* in it.' If I wasn't very sympathetic, it was because I found it hard to regard them as suffering from a disease I'd been lucky enough to escape. I just thought they were being self-indulgent and I wasn't. The issue seemed a simple one – until the disease attacked me.

It was the morning after the first rehearsal, the night I'd seen Helen again and all the hopes that had seemed dead had returned. You could say I'd had a bad night's sleep, but how inadequate an old cliché can be sometimes: the thoughts that filled my head as I lay awake made it the sweetest night's sleep of my life. In the morning, with my heart still singing, my body performed its daily rituals as if nothing had happened: opened its eyes at seven-fifteen and yawned; had a cigarette; shaved; had a pee; took a shower; had another cigarette; put on a pair of denims, a cheese-cloth shirt and sandals; consumed some strong black coffee and two slices of toast with jam; had a third cigarette; looked at itself in the mirror; double-locked the door of the flat; took the lift to the ground floor; shook hands with Giorgio, the porter; shouted 'Ciao, Francesca!' to the girl selling flowers at the corner of the piazza; bought the *International Herald Tribune* at a stand on the Corso Vittorio Emanuele; walked through the centre of Rome as if it owned it; reached the Piazza Navona at eight-fifteen precisely; sat down at the second table from the left in the first café on the south side of the square; shook hands with Giuseppe, the waiter; nodded at Bathurst in the next café (a rival novelist who works longer hours than me but has a less sure touch with character); sipped at a cup of black coffee; had a fourth cigarette; took a block of lined A4 paper and a green felt-tip pen from a leather shoulder-bag; reread the previous day's work and checked the running total of words; gave a deep sigh of artistic melancholy, rising ineluctably from the bowels; and wrote down the single word 'suddenly'.

This last ritual may need explaining. I always begin every day's work with 'suddenly', even if it means finishing the previous day's work in mid-sentence: it creates a feeling of urgency and gets me off to a fast start. None of my readers have ever complained. Prose style isn't what they're looking for in a Mark Barham pot-boiler and, if I keep the pot boiling by artifice rather than art, who's to notice? The critics left eight years ago and my bank manager says he prefers going to the movies, so I haven't yet been indicted for my crime. 'Suddenly' is there to stay.

But that morning *the second word didn't come*. Nine o'clock arrived, then nine-thirty, then ten, and still 'suddenly' sat there in magnificent isolation. At ten-fifteen, my pen hovered over it and I nearly struck it out in favour of something else. For once, however, the word was entirely apposite. A woman driven to despair by her husband's adultery had just slammed the door of their home and run out into the street; a hundred yards away, a masked man was waiting with a gun, not realizing the woman was his sister ... Sudden action of some kind seemed not just apt, but inescapable. It wasn't even a case of not knowing what should happen next: I had the plot all worked out and, as far as it went, I was happy with it. Given that neither my heart nor my mind any longer participates in my writing, the present story was an absolute cracker. Set in the second century of the nuclear winter, after the superpowers had obliterated ninety-eight per cent of the civilized world in their mad quest for ideological supremacy, it showed how human beings reduced to their primitive state could overcome the brutality in themselves and, through the healing power of love (epitomized by Laura, a social worker), build a society in which all weapons of destruction were obsolete. Cynically I could imagine the tears being shed in Milton Keynes as the *lire* rolled in in Rome – there's gold in them thar Cruise missiles. Yet cynicism is normally fluent because it is afraid to pause and take stock: on any other morning, my pen would have raced effortlessly across the page and I could have been home by twelve, my twelve hundred words completed. It's when the fluency stops . . . By eleven-thirty, I felt as if I could sit there all day and all the next day, with nothing to show for my time but 'suddenly' and that didn't count. In the next café, Bathurst was scribbling away like fury: it was humiliating.

I was not, repeat not, day-dreaming about Helen. She was there, of course, alive and well and kicking again in the deep sea-caves of the mind, but I wasn't consciously distracted by her. In London, she had been a distraction and I had to discipline myself hard not to think about her until my twelve hundred words were finished. Now, in the Piazza Navona, I applied the same self-discipline. However hard she pushed upwards in my mind, I kept her tightly battened down, so tightly that, during the whole three hours I sat looking at the piece of paper with 'suddenly' on it and wondering what followed, I had nothing you could call a 'thought' regarding her. She was just a throbbing pulse, safely under my control: my mind was free of her. And, if I could achieve *that*, I thought bitterly, if my will-power was that strong, why couldn't I produce a lousy twelve hundred words of action-packed melodrama in the nuclear winter? Why did my right hand, which moved the coffee cup to and from my lips with perfect freedom, find itself struggling to lift my pen off the table and, once it had lifted it, unable to put it to profitable use on the paper? The answer was childishly simple, but I was unwilling to face it.

At about twelve-thirty, the pulse burst. Without paying for my coffee, I shovelled my writing things into my bag and started running across the square in the direction of the Pantheon. Bathurst looked up from his notebook and blinked. A child on a bicycle swerved to avoid me. Tourists turned and stared, unused to sudden movement in this, the serenest of Rome's piazzas. But I took no notice. Only when I reached a telephone-booth did my legs stop pounding and my heart start to pound instead.

'Helen, it's Mark.' In my haste, I forgot the most elementary precaution. We used to have a strict code of safety on the telephone, something we developed instinctively without formally discussing it. I would say 'Is that Mrs Danes, please?' and she would give different answers according to the circumstances. If Geoffrey was in the same room, it was 'What number did you dial?'; if he was in the house but not within earshot, 'Helen Danes speaking'. Only if she was completely alone did she drop the formality. 'It's you,' she would say: a banal enough welcome, you might think, but not the way she said it and not when you realized the sentimental truth behind the unsentimental façade. When Geoffrey called, it was 'Hullo, Geoffrey'. 'It's you' was almost erotic in comparison.

Now, after eight years, it was 'Hullo, Mark'. I had fallen to the level of a husband, I thought sadly, with the lover's alertness to every nuance. At least she repeated my name, which probably meant she was alone. I surged ahead.

'When can we meet? Are you free this afternoon? I could pick you up in my car and we could take a drive out of town. The weather's perfect and it's been such a long time.'

'Yes, it has.' She sounded non-committal and I remembered how skilfully she'd kept me at a distance the night before, how she'd stuck doggedly by Geoffrey's side after the rehearsal, making any private conversation impossible. The greenest teenager would have read the signs correctly, but I was thirty-eight: a more desperate and irrational animal altogether.

'Well, how about it? You're not doing anything else, are you? It's a lovely day and we've got so much to talk about. When I saw you again last night – '

'Mark, it's over.' She spelled it out this time, not realizing that she was talking to a dyslexic: the words made no sense to me. I came straight back at her, finding all the fluency that had deserted me on paper.

'What do you mean, it's over? How do you know it's over? Unless we meet and talk, we won't know if it's over or not. We were younger then and we made silly mistakes, but we've still got a future together. I believe it, Helen, really I do. Whatever I did then, I'm sorry.'

How devious love is, even at its most intense. The world would have said she was the one who should be sorry: by apologizing first, I hoped to shame her into a reciprocation. But she proved as immune as ever to my tricks. There was just a long silence and I was left guessing what it meant. For all I knew, she could have been exasperated or speechless with fury. But I was fired by a lover's optimism: I imagined a sudden quickening in her eyes and her face softening in regret and I pushed at a door I thought was opening before me.

'It's no good hiding from each other, Helen, because it won't work. Rome's much smaller than London: you keep bumping into people whether you want to or not. Now that I'm acting in this bloody play, we can't avoid seeing each other. What's the point of pretending nothing ever happened between us? I'm here and I'm alive and I still love you. If we don't meet and talk, and talk *properly*, we're both going to suffer: yes, even you, Helen, whether you like it or not. Surely there's no harm in just talking . . .'

I left the words to hover innocently in the air, but I knew they were no more innocent than if I'd said: 'It's only an apple, darling.' Is there anything in the whole vocabulary of love more insidious than the suggestion that 'just talking' is harmless? Helen must have seen the danger, for she was wilier than me, yet the lie was so foolproof that she swallowed it. Yes, she admitted, rationally considered, there was no harm in just talking – provided that talking was all that was proposed and provided that a promise to talk once didn't mean having to talk more than once and provided . . . She hedged it round as many ways as she could and I shrugged and said, of course, that was fine: after all, I just wanted to talk. So we arranged to meet in Trastevere at four o'clock and I returned to the Piazza Navona to wait. Bathurst had gone home for lunch already, which meant he'd done a good morning's work, but I had no time for the old jealousies. I was fired by a deeper flame.

If I believed in a God, it could only be a God with a sharp sense of humour, much given to teasing and manipulating his creatures. I couldn't otherwise explain the sense I sometimes have that I am the victim of somebody else's practical joke, that someone out there is laughing at my discomfiture. If he really loved me, that unknown, unseen observer, surely he would want me to learn from my mistakes? Yet I don't find slipping on a banana-skin, for example, an uplifting experience: I feel only hurt and humiliation as my nose hits the floor. If there were a point to the banana-skin, if it was so positioned that, by treading on it, I avoided walking into a pot-hole a few yards further on, it might be a blessing in disguise. But it never is. It's the aimlessness of life's little practical jokes that I find so depressing. How many times have I heard the door-bell ring and hurried to answer it, hoping to find a friendly face on the doorstep, only to be greeted by a vacuum and the sound of scurrying feet! Whoever keeps ringing that bell has the strangest idea of a joke.

That afternoon especially, I felt myself the victim of a strange supernatural hoax. For there was no logic in

Vanessa appearing at the moment she did. On any other day I would have been safely back in my flat by two o'clock, typing up my twelve hundred words before taking a siesta. It was only my unproductive morning that made me linger in the Piazza Navona, vaguely hoping that, if I could keep Helen out of my thoughts, I might think of something to go after 'suddenly'. It was a forlorn hope, for by now no amount of will-power could keep my mind free of her and I looked forward to our four o'clock meeting with the intensity of a saint waiting to meet his God in heaven. I didn't even pretend to be writing by holding my pen poised in my hand, but sat there quiet and trembling, trying to prepare myself. Vanessa caught me totally on the hop. She appeared from nowhere, asked if she could join me and I had muttered 'Yes, of course' before I realized who she was. The words no more issued from my conscious self than a fart or an involuntary facial tic; but, by the time my conscious self arrived on the scene, we were sharing a carafe of wine and it was too late. From being the hunter, I was now the hunted, at the mercy of a younger and fitter predator.

'I do hope you don't mind, Mark. You seemed to be concentrating so fiercely that I was afraid I might be interrupting. It must take fantastic concentration, keeping the creative juices going day after day.' Her eye strayed to the unadorned 'suddenly' and a twitch of disappointment disfigured her face as she saw the poor return from my day's juices. I should have been professionally embarrassed, but I felt only triumph: it was gratifying to fall so far short of her ludicrous expectations. There are some people we hate to an irrational extent, people whose virtues we cannot emulate: we don't just hate them, we hate the intolerance in ourselves that makes us hate them so fiercely. In that sense – or so, no doubt, the practical joker masquerading as God would argue – we also need them: they are the purgatorial flames in which our hatred is cleansed. Vanessa certainly gave my hatred a roasting that afternoon.

'If I were a writer, I think I would live in Venice rather than Rome. Have you been to Venice? I first went there when I was fifteen, the year before Mummy died.'

'Yes, I've been to Venice.'

'I would sit at a window overlooking a canal and stare down into the water for inspiration. I find water so inspirational: it must be the way it swirls and eddies and gives an impression of transience. Have you ever found inspiration in water? I knew a violinist once who said . . .'

'No, I've never found water very inspiring.' Discovering there was no need to answer her questions, since she produced answers of her own before the most alert interlocutor could open his mouth, I let her monologue run its course. Only the lust of a thirty-eight-year-old man in the bright Mediterranean sun kept me focused on her at all. Her body was pleasantly curvaceous and, if she'd dressed with Italian flair instead of strait-jacketing herself in a tight T-shirt and jeans, you might have said she had sex appeal. Of her availability I had no doubt: I viewed our future relationship with the same certainty and cynicism as I expected to write twelve hundred words of pulp in a day. It was a bad morning for cynicism: in the same way as my writing dried up, Vanessa had a surprise in store for me.

'Listen, Mark, I've got a wonderful idea. Please don't say no.'

I shifted nervously in my chair. I'd been away from England for too long: was this how middle-class English-women made passes nowadays, or was she fishing for something else.

'I know we've only just met and all that, but I do have

46

three months to kill in Rome and I wondered – you'll probably find this awfully presumptuous.'

'Not at all, not at all.' I dug my fingernails hard into the palm of my hand.

'Well then, how would you feel about me writing a profile of you for a magazine? I'd really love to have a stab at it. I don't mean just a gossipy piece, but a serious, in-depth study of your career as a writer.'

Horrified, I stammered: 'You must be joking', a particularly feeble response in the circumstances. For it wasn't Vanessa's joke: she was too young, too earnest, too unsophisticated; she wouldn't have understood the absurdity of the proposal if I'd spent a hundred years explaining it. There was someone else – someone I couldn't see and didn't much care for, but whose presence I again sensed profoundly – who was laughing at my embarrassment. I'm at best an agnostic, but I found myself glowering at the church of Sant'Agnese as if it was my enemy's house.

'No, I'm perfectly serious, Mark.' And she was: she had no idea she was just the agent of a supernatural spoof. I should have realized He was too grand to go around pushing door-bells and running away: he had minions to do his dirty work for him. 'I know you're still very young and have got most of your writing days ahead of you, but isn't that an advantage? Most literary studies are written about people who are dead or nearly dead, and that's why they're so dull. You're only halfway through your life, so people will read the article and wonder what's going to happen to you in the second half. That's much more fun.'

I squirmed. 'Look, it's very sweet of you, Vanessa, but quite frankly no serious magazine would touch it.'

'Why not? You're somebody people have heard of.'

'Not enough people. I wrote three books which got good reviews and I've written another six which have sold well.

The only one which did both was plagiarized from a Spanish short story which none of the critics had read. People want to read about success stories, but I'm just one long failure: downhill all the way from age thirty. It would be too depressing for words.'

'Aren't you just being modest? Books *should* be read by lots of people. What you've done is to popularize the serious novel.'

The final cliché was too much. I banged my fist angrily on the table. 'Now let's get one thing straight, Vanessa. If you're going to write that sort of crap, it's not on. Forgive my asking such a personal question, but how many of my books have you actually read? Come on, how many?'

'Two.' From some hidden source, she found the grace to blush. 'It's not much, I know, but I do have a reasonable impression of your work: I'm not just a dilettante. There was *The Positive Hour*, of course – was that really plagiarized? I thought it was terribly individual – and that one set in the Caribbean.'

'*Hell Island* or *After the Triangle*?'

'*Hell Island*. I know it was only a thriller, but your hero was a wonderful study in the ambivalent values of espionage and I thought some bits really oozed class, particularly that scene in the High Commission. Daddy has friends just like that. You only *think* you're a failure, Mark: that's why you're such an interesting subject.'

Her hand inched towards mine across the table-top and I realized how much less hard-bitten I was than I thought. As the honey of her flattery seeped into my ears, the corners of my mouth defied all efforts to restrict them and curled upwards and upwards in pleasure. If she really wanted to write such wonderful things about me, was I man enough to say no? Of course I wasn't. The joker in the wings must have been laughing his head off, but I no longer heard him.

5

I chose Trastevere to meet Helen because it was relatively quiet. At four o'clock in the early spring, you can sit at a café and have a private conversation with a fair chance it will remain private. Trastevere is an old Roman word meaning 'across the Tiber', on the opposite side to the main *centro storico* where most of the tourists stay. It's been called the Roman Chelsea and, if you can imagine a Chelsea without the parking meters and the junk-food shops and the naff boutiques, without the endless crocodiles of punks and Sloanes and football hooligans and women pushing each other in the back with Peter Jones bags, a Chelsea moreover which is genuinely magical, in which exotic flowers seem to be cascading down from every window and the light falls so delicately on the ochre walls that you want to reach up and touch them . . . I suppose, if you could imagine that, you wouldn't be wasting time in Chelsea anyway, but if you *can* imagine that, you'll be halfway there.

I say 'relatively' quiet and there lies the key to my approach. If I'd wanted privacy, I would have suggested my flat or a remote suburban park; but I'd lost the instinct for secrecy. Whatever happened between us now, I didn't mind the world witnessing it, indeed I wanted the world to witness it so that it couldn't subsequently be denied. Wasn't that one of the things that had poisoned our first affair, the constant terror of Geoffrey finding out? I later wished he had found out and we'd fought a straight, clean fight over her. He held all the cards except one, but suppose he'd miscalculated and played his hand badly, suppose his concentration had faltered and he'd said the tiny word which would have given the game to me ... Dreams of what might have been are more dangerous than present fantasies: already I was rewriting history so desperately it was just a blur in my head.

She arrived at four o'clock exactly or, rather, she arrived just as the clock of Santa Maria was striking four, which, if you know Roman clocks, meant it was at least five past. How different she was from Vanessa. They were both new to Rome, yet Vanessa could live in Rome for the rest of her life and still be a misplaced Englishwoman; Helen knew instinctively which Roman ways it was important to adopt and which it wasn't. She was paler than Italian women, of course, and looked about her with the wonder of someone still discovering fresh beauties in her surroundings: in all other respects she could have been one of the natives. Her clothes had the true Italian *eleganza* and, when she asked the waiter for a *spremuta di limone*, the phrase slipped off her tongue as if she'd learnt it in the nursery. A foolish feeling of admiration choked me and all my prepared gambits went out of the window. Before I could mention the word 'love', she was talking about Geoffrey.

'I'm worried about him, Mark.' What a pack-horse love is, stumbling obediently wherever it's led. There was nothing I wanted to talk about less, but love told me that her worries should be my worries and, before I knew it, I was nodding in sympathy.

'What's wrong with him?'

'This play. It's destroying him, Mark. You saw him at that rehearsal last night: he was like a man possessed by demons.'

'Possessed certainly, but what makes you say by demons? He was a bit manic, but I also found him impressive in a way. I'd never seen him dominate a situation like that before.'

'Well, I never want to see him dominate a situation like that again. It was *sinister*, Mark: that's the only word for it.'

'I know what you mean, but that isn't the whole story, is it? He was doing what he likes doing best in the world. He was happy, Helen.'

'He may be happy, but the happiness is on a knife-edge and I can't bear the uncertainty of it. If the play doesn't come off, he'll kill himself.'

'A martyr for Shakespeare?'

'Yes.' There was no smile on her face, so I tried to keep the amusement from mine, but it was difficult. A perfect solution suddenly: Geoffrey sitting at the Bard's side on a heavenly cloud, asking him where he got all those wonderful ideas from: Helen and me disporting ourselves without guilt in the impure world below. Are there men so virtuous that they don't entertain such hopes? Ashamed of the darkness of my longings, I tried asking her about Geoffrey in a more disinterested way, but it was no good: my questions were blatantly loaded. When I asked whether she felt less close to Geoffrey as a result of the play, her eyes blazed with indignation.

'If you mean, is our marriage about to crack up, the answer's no, Mark. It isn't how close I feel to him that matters: it's how close I *want* to feel to him. Why can't you stop driving wedges between us?'

'I'm not driving anything, Helen. I just asked a simple question. As for the wedges, they've been there all along. *I* didn't put them there.'

'Oh yes you did.'

'How can you say that? You were the one . . .' I listened in dismay to my own recriminations. When you agree to 'just talk', you expect something more urbane than a lovers'

51

punch-up. Yet here we were, after only ten minutes, behaving as if eight years had healed nothing and the old wounds were still fresh. I started saying emollient things to take the heat out of the situation, then realized that concession would be fatal: we had to call a truce on equal terms or the struggle would be in vain. Love is nothing if not egalitarian: in my pain I could see Helen's pain, and our common misery was my only consolation. So we fought grimly on. There are people who claim it's therapeutic to argue, that differences need to be properly aired: they're generally good-natured noodles who can air differences in their sleep and haven't raised their voices since kindergarten. My rows with Helen were never therapeutic: they were like the writhings of a dying animal. And as we writhed now, and Trastevere's loveliest square ran with the blood, my mind flew back to an earlier bloodbath, to the day that love died.

It must have been the lousiest watercolour ever painted: a few insipid squiggles for the sea and a few even more insipid squiggles for the sky; in between a shapeless blob which, if you put two and two together, was meant to be a ship and, if you stared at it hard enough, had a blue sail. What a poverty of imagination, I always thought, to make that sail blue. The sea was already blue and so was the sky: the artist must have had monochrome vision or been a miser, parsimoniously eking out a few simple materials on the canvas. I'm biased, of course: when you've come to hate something as much as I hate that painting, you lose all objectivity, all detachment. Yet I remember, even before my hatred was engaged, looking at the painting in its niche over the bookshelf in the Danes' living-room and thinking what a sorry piece of work it was. When Helen said: 'Roger

52

and Jennifer gave us that as a wedding present', I didn't see the danger at all.

Geoffrey was out watching Shakespeare and we were alone. It was a typical Thursday in every way, except that, on this occasion, we did less love-making and more talking, serious talking. We confronted directly a question which we usually skirted round: could Helen ever bring herself to leave Geoffrey for me? That phrasing betrays me, because to my thirty-year-old mind the issue was simply one of nerve, of courage. I didn't see that maintaining the status quo might also require courage, but of a different kind. No wonder Helen had to spell out the significance of the watercolour so painstakingly.

'They gave it to *us*, Mark: don't you see? They didn't give it to me or Geoffrey, but to me *and* Geoffrey.'

'But that was five years ago. Are you sentimentally attached to the painting? Who are Roger and Jennifer?'

'Jennifer was at school with me. Roger farms.'

'Well, if they're your friends more than Geoffrey's, I'm sure he wouldn't mind you keeping it. Is it very valuable? Who painted it? Do you like it? Does *Geoffrey* like it?'

'Not particularly.'

'There you are then. Keep it for yourself and nobody will mind. Or, if you're really feeling guilty and screwed up, let Geoffrey have it: make a sacrifice. He'll probably never look at it again, but at least you'll have the satisfaction of being a martyr and knowing that you've done the decent thing. That's what you want, isn't it? Moral security.'

'No, that *isn't* what I want.' Her voice rose and I thought the argument was about to catch fire; but she was more sad than angry at my slowness. 'Forget the painting, Mark. Forget Roger and Jennifer. I only meant that as an example. There are dozens of objects all over the house – that corner-cupboard, those candlesticks, even that silly little ashtray – which people gave us as wedding presents because they wanted us to stay together, to remain one entity. Don't you understand? They were celebrating a *union*, not some temporary arrangement we could just tear up and throw away.'

I lashed out indiscriminately – when you're blind, what else can you do. 'What idiotic nonsense you talk sometimes, Helen. You sound Catholic or simple-minded or Victorian. Millions of people get divorced every year without their friends feeling upset that their wedding presents have to go with one or other partner. I've never met Roger and Jennifer and all I know is that their taste in art is excruciating; but I bet that thought never entered their heads when they were buying the painting, unless they're naïve and pretentious too. Why don't you face up to the reality? People give wedding presents for one reason and one reason only: because they're too bloody embarrassed to turn up at the reception empty-handed.'

'I hate you sometimes.' This time her voice didn't even rise: she just stared at me in shocked silence, as if a fairy tale had ended and I'd been turned back into a frog. We made it up quickly, of course, because lovers are escapists at heart and cannot look the death of love in the face; but, if ever a moment was prophetic, if ever there was a split second's truth more revealing than the half-truths before and after, that look provided it. Helen never did explain the significance of the painting: we drifted instinctively into less turbulent waters. Yet, as I now appreciate its significance – or should I say half appreciate it, like a man glimpsing a beautiful woman's face through a heavy veil – I know that Geoffrey had won and I had lost long before the final defeat.

That defeat came three weeks later. We were due to meet for lunch in the City and then see Helen's solicitor:

exploratory discussions about divorce were planned. I sat
for ten minutes in the restaurant, sipping a gin and tonic,
and made nothing of her lateness: the City was hot and
congested and the taxis crawled up Cheapside like overfed
dogs looking for shade. Then a self-important waiter in a
shiny black jacket – I remembered his officious, smirking
face as if it were yesterday – weaved his way towards me
with a telephone message. She didn't even have the guts to
tell me herself.

'I was frightened. Don't you see?' Eight years on, we picked
up exactly where we'd left off. We said in Trastevere what
we would have said in London if I'd rung her that afternoon
and asked why the hell she'd stood me up; if I hadn't been
too proud to show my pain; if I hadn't sat in my flat for
three long months and waited for *her* to ring me with an
apology. Even our language was unchanged. Still she said
'Don't you see?', not 'Do you see?', and still I chafed at
missing things she thought so obvious.

'No, I don't see, Helen. What were you so frightened of?
Was it me? Did you think I wouldn't understand if you
didn't come away with me?'

'No, it wasn't that.'

'If you'd come straight out and told me to my face, I
would have had to accept it whether I understood or not. I
couldn't have forced you and I wouldn't have wanted to
force you because I loved you too much. But just to leave
me guessing like that ... I felt so confused, Helen, so
humiliated, so *unloved*, Helen.'

'I know, Mark. I'm sorry.' As she said it, she suddenly
looked at me with some of the old tenderness, and I
thought: is eight years too long to wait for a moment like
this? Helen's love wasn't ubiquitous or unstinting: it didn't
keep you continuously warm like an electric blanket. When

it came, it came in waves, like the blasts of hot air from a furnace. The past tense rang clear as a bell in what she said next, but I scarcely heard it. After the dry years, the sweetness was overpowering.

'You weren't *un*loved, Mark. You silly, silly man, can't you see that I loved you too much? I was frightened. I knew I'd never be able to say goodbye forever in the middle of a restaurant, so I took the coward's way out. That's all.'

And, as far as she was concerned, that was all: a love affair brought to a clumsy end by the incompetence of one of its actors; a painful memory softened by a gracious apology in later life. There was no obvious regret in her voice, no suggestion that, if she had her time again, she would have managed things differently. She may have taken the coward's way out, was the implication, but she had wanted out then and didn't want in now. I can only explain my sudden sense of hope in terms of my own needs, for there was no evidence that she also looked forward as well as back. And yet I did experience that hope and I clung like a child to the thought which the hope inspired: that love of the kind she had described could never completely die. It was taking longer to resurface in her than in me, but in time it would resurface: she would never find the strength to keep it anchored to the bottom.

With the healing of the old wounds, the bitterness passed from the conversation and we parted on a light note half an hour later.

'*E finita la commedia, Marco?*' she said with a mischievous smile, adding a bit of local colour to her teasing.

'*Si, è finita la commedia, Helena.*'

Was it my fault if I gave the words a different meaning from her? If I didn't invest them with the same sense of finality? If, as far as I was concerned, only the comic part of the drama was finished, not the drama itself? If I envisaged a second, more serious act in which all would end happily? If, when I kissed her goodbye, I whispered '*arrivederci*' and not '*addio*'?

6

And I thought I was the one in love. Geoffrey's hymn to Shakespeare at the start of the next rehearsal was torrid beyond anything I had known.

'In this play and *The Tempest*, Shakespeare looked far beyond tragedy. He envisaged a love so pure that evil could not withstand it . . .'

These homilies were integral to his directorial method. You could say they were his directorial method, for he had no expertise in stagecraft and, when people asked what they should do with their hands or whether they should exit right or left, he was clueless: the sacred text didn't include those vital details. He could only pour his own passion into the empty imagination of his actors and hope that it would take. He reminded me of a fanatical football manager trying to galvanize a third-rate team. 'Don't do it for me, lads, do it for William. I want to see guts, I want to see commitment and, above all, I want to see *pride*. Now let's have good crisp diction in the second half.' Some football managers are so unforgiving that what chiefly motivates their players is fear, the terror of being crucified in the dressing-room post mortem. Geoffrey could be just like that: harsh, wilful, despotic. Behind his back we called him the Fuehrer.

I remember those pep-talks now more graphically than the play itself. I remember the extraordinary energy which emanated from Geoffrey's face as he talked; the way his glasses appeared to vibrate on the end of his nose; the odd contortions his body underwent when he used a gesture to emphasize a point; the cast sitting round in a circle, listening intently; and, above all, the silence. Nobody stirred, not even the chatterers like Vanessa or the incurable fidgets: Tony Barclay, who chain-smoked, and the man playing Leontes, a cretinous individual with red hair who kept massaging the top of his head as if he were shampooing himself. It's normally only audiences with a shared faith who are genuinely united, yet Geoffrey imposed a unity through the strength of his own convictions. Believers, agnostics and atheists: all listened with equal respect to what the high priest had to say. That was the true miracle. Only a few of the cast were real Shakespeare buffs: Peter Jansen, certainly; Joanie Shepherd, who thought playing Hermione was the most exciting thing that had ever happened to her; Walter, at a pinch; nobody else. The rest were just friends and acquaintances dragged in from the highways and the hedgerows to make up the numbers. Below decks philistinism was rampant: I heard Tony Barclay whisper that he wished it was Alan Ayckbourn. It was a motley crew all right, yet they all rowed together under the captain's lash.

Even I pulled my weight without complaining. I had thought I would be supremely detached, but part of me lingered on, like skin clinging to sticking-plaster. And the hidden adhesive, funnily enough, was not Helen, but Shakespeare. It was almost as if, through the voice of his disciple Geoffrey, I could hear the master calling. I've already admitted to feeling lukewarm about the man, but the thing about Shakespeare is that he's too big to reject out of hand: he lies in wait for you, like a God on whom you've temporarily turned your back. There wasn't a speech in the play which that cast didn't massacre, but from time to time there would filter through the stumbling delivery a phrase of such beauty that it commanded all my

59

attention, all my love. Eight years of cynicism would suddenly melt away and I remembered the days when I too wrote with hope; when words used in a certain way seemed to assume magical powers. Then, and then only, I forgot Helen.

She was there at that second rehearsal and did the things Geoffrey was too busy to do: offered everyone coffee and wine; answered the telephone; kept the small-talk going in the dining-room, where the actors who were 'off-stage' used to gather. Jealousy is usually caricatured as a sexual emotion, an obsession with not being in the right bed at the right time; yet I never felt more jealous of Geoffrey than when Helen was being supportive in this quiet domestic way. It's the peacefulness of marriage that glitters most when I press my nose against the window and peer inside.

That evening, and the immediately subsequent ones, developed with the flawed but compelling logic of a dream. When we weren't acting, we each reverted to our private obsessions and clung miserably on to them. Like a dog, I followed Helen from room to room and, like a dog, Vanessa followed me from room to room and, like a dog, Vanessa's father followed Vanessa from room to room, trying to stop anything hatching between us. Three dogs, each as mad as the others: for who could say whether my own craving was any further from sanity than the infatuation of a naïve young woman or a father's jealousy? After a while, I noticed that there was a fourth dog and that, whenever Vanessa's father appeared hard on Vanessa's heels, hard on his heels was Margaret. It didn't seem likely that anyone was hard on Margaret's heels, for she was painfully unattractive and had the nervous fulsomeness of someone who expects always to be single. She was playing Paulina, which was a particularly absurd piece of casting: Shakespeare's Paulina is a woman of iron resolve, while Margaret had the resolve of a plate of mushy gooseberries. In the chain of mad dogs, she seemed the least likely to get her teeth into her prey.

'Those two are well suited,' said Helen, at one of the moments when the chain was broken. Vanessa was on stage, so I was free of her attentions and her father's watching brief was redundant. I had followed Helen on to the balcony and, more to my liking than hers, we were alone. 'Margaret and Peter, I mean. A spinster of forty and a widower of fifty-five: it's pure Jane Austen.'

'And about as exciting.'

'Don't be bitchy. She writes a lot better than you.'

'I didn't mean she can't write.'

'I know what you meant and you're wrong.' Without love on both sides, the banter was as stale as last week's news. There was no affection, no inspiration, no instinctive reading of each other's minds: we might have been a pair of ageing cricket bores discussing prospects for the coming season. Helen said: 'Peter Jansen's lonely', as if loneliness were a physical ailment for which you took medicine.

'So's Margaret, I suppose?'

'Desperately. She came to Rome because nobody in England was interested.'

'Then why should Peter Jansen be interested?'

'He needs companionship. When you need it badly enough, you sometimes settle for second best.' I winced at the irony, but she hurried on before I could turn the comment on its head. 'I'm not saying Margaret's necessarily second best, because she's more interesting than she seems. She just needs to relax. As for Peter, at least some kind of romantic involvement would stop him being so obsessive about Vanessa.' She stopped and looked at me, coolly, calmly, but not without feeling. Her eyes were bright and alert, playing sensitively around the situation.

Was it only my hungry imagination or was there jealousy there? She muttered: 'I don't know what you see in her.'

'I don't see anything in her.'

'Then why don't you tell her so?'

I parroted: 'When you need it badly enough . . .' and she took a step back as if I'd slapped her. How can one account for the cruelty that finds such moments enjoyable? Yet I did enjoy it. I enjoyed seeing the detachment shaken and the mask slipping. When she put the mask on again, it was like a visor against an enemy.

'Please leave me alone, Mark.' How I hated that polite 'please'. 'Please' is for elderly aunts or strangers in a bus queue, but love isn't a polite emotion, or it isn't in me.

I said: 'Why the hell should I leave you alone?', then, before she could walk away from the argument: 'No, listen. You're right about Vanessa. I should tell her I see nothing in her. I should tell her she's stupid and naïve and mad to have anything to do with me. But what's the point? What could she learn from a prim little lecture about love that life itself – ugly, mean, complicated life – couldn't teach her a hundred times better? You've become such a purist you sound ridiculous. Yet here you are stuck with a man you don't love – '

'Don't say that.'

'I will say it. Here you are stuck with a man you don't love, reduced to pimping between Peter and Margaret, who are totally unsuited to each other and wouldn't recognize love if it walked into the room in a bright red loin-cloth. It's pathetic.'

'Is it?'

'Yes, it is. You used to be bolder, you used to have more spirit. What happened to all that?' I was about to beg, which love should never do, and I was about to whine, which is love at its ugliest, and I was about to bully, which isn't love at all. But I was saved, improbably, by Geoffrey.

'What the *hell's* going on out here?' We spun round and saw him glowering at us from the doorway. Helen flushed, but her fears were groundless: it wasn't the anger of an excluded husband, but a deeper passion. 'We're in the middle of the trial scene. If you two are going to talk so loudly, you'll have to do it somewhere else. I won't have my rehearsals disrupted like this.'

'Sorry, darling.'

'Sorry, Geoffrey.' I wanted to laugh aloud. Did he really think we'd just been talking? Was he oblivious to the implications of what he'd seen? But you can't laugh in a madman's face: it's like blowing raspberries at a lion. Chastened, we returned to the living-room and watched Shakespeare's great story of jealous love being travestied into extinction.

7

For two or three days nothing happened. I say 'two or three', not out of deliberate vagueness, but because I really can't remember which it was. I think Helen and I had our row on the balcony on Wednesday and I *think* Geoffrey telephoned on Friday or Saturday, but I could easily be wrong about both. Time flew past and yet time stood still: it was like being inside an aeroplane and having no impression of speed. A writer's life has few fixed points anyway, but a writer in love is a gipsy, a refugee from everything associated with the real world. I remember sitting in the Piazza Navona staring at the word 'suddenly' on scruffy bits of paper and I remember attending rehearsals at Geoffrey's flat at which Helen, significantly, was absent. But I didn't count the bits of paper or the rehearsals. I just waited for something to happen with the mounting desperation of a man who knew it wasn't going to happen.

When Geoffrey did telephone, he was peremptory to the point of rudeness. 'I need your help, Mark. We've got a crisis.'

'What's the trouble?' I asked, with a great show of concern. Geoffrey's idea of a crisis wasn't my idea of a crisis, but he was my only lifeline to Helen and I clung to him for dear life.

'Someone's buggering me about over the play. Could you meet me outside the Pantheon in twenty minutes.'

It wasn't a request: it was an order. Never mind that it was nearly midnight, never mind that I was running a bath. I said 'Yes, Geoffrey, of course, Geoffrey,' like a well-behaved schoolboy, and arrived at the Pantheon five minutes early. Geoffrey was already there, standing under one of the great pillars at the front of the building and looking impatiently at his watch. I expected at least a 'thank you', but there was only 'Come along, we don't have much time', and he set off down a side-street with me at his heels. Our conversation was dislocated and breathless, as if we were playing squash.

'You speak Italian, don't you, Mark?'

'Some. I'm not fluent.'

'I'm sure you're better than me. I want to get it across once and for all to that double-crossing bastard – '

'Who are you talking about?'

'Paparelli.'

'I thought he was your friend.'

'I thought he was my friend too. But I was wrong. Just watch this.'

We had come to rest outside a large house in a small piazza: Paparelli's house. Paparelli was the Italian businessman who had promised Geoffrey he could use his living-room for the performances of the play. Right then I was glad I wasn't Paparelli: Geoffrey pushed the door-bell so hard that his knuckles turned white. At the same time he muttered a dark, rambling soliloquy, like a Shakespearian villain lurking behind an arras.

'He's betrayed me, Mark, and that's not putting it too highly. He's had nothing but kindness from me, but he repays me with the sort of behaviour which just makes you despair of human nature. I can't bear the way people in this country are so untrustworthy. You'd think Shakespeare meant nothing to them. Bloody philistines.'

At this point, Paparelli's head appeared at the first-floor window, followed by the top half of Paparelli's body, bare and glowing in the moonlight, followed by the head and shoulders of a woman. The woman's shoulders were also bare: it didn't look a good moment to call on Paparelli. He recognized Geoffrey and shouted something insulting.

'What did he say, Mark?'

'He said your mother went to bed with a cart-horse. I didn't catch the rest.'

'Say something rude about his mother.'

Paparelli looked bigger than me. It wasn't the time for heroics, so I told him his mother was a nurse. He bristled suspiciously and asked, what did I mean, his mother was a nurse? If his mother was a nurse, then *my* mother . . . he suggested various professions. In *that* case, I retorted, his father must have been a *doctor*: that really threw him. He conferred anxiously with his woman, then banged the shutters of the windows closed. After about a minute, he appeared on the doorstep wearing only his trousers.

'*Chi sei?*' He *was* bigger than me, at least four inches. I flinched.

'*Mi chiamo* Barham. Mark Barham.'

'*Inglese?*'

'*Si.*'

He spat on the ground and said something indelicate about the Queen, followed by something even more indelicate about the Prime Minister, followed by some thoroughly offensive comments about the goal-scoring abilities of the English football team. I explained that I didn't follow football, that I'd been living in Rome for eight years and that I was only there to interpret for my friend Signor Danes.

'*Ah si*, Signor Danes.' He switched his attentions from me to Geoffrey and unleashed another volley of insults.

'What's he saying, Mark?'

'He's saying he hopes your play is an unmitigated

disaster. He hopes your leading lady catches venereal disease from the leading man. He hopes the scenery burns down. He hopes – '

'Tell him he can say what he bloody well likes, but we're going to put the play on whatever he bloody says. And ask the cretin why he's not going to let us use his house any more.'

I told Paparelli that his personal opinions were a matter for himself, but that my friend was very determined to stage the play. Was it true that he was no longer willing to provide a venue for this important production of a later masterpiece by England's greatest dramatist – and, if so, what lay behind that decision? I could so easily have stirred things up: instead I acted as the best friend Geoffrey had. Deep down, I must be less of a bad Samaritan than I think. How else does one explain these sudden flashes of kindness?

'*La costa.*' Paparelli made a *lire*-rustling gesture with his fingers which even Geoffrey understood.

'What's the trouble? Money?'

'Yes. I don't think you're paying him enough. What did you offer him to hire his room?'

'Two hundred thousand *lire* a night. Isn't that enough?'

Paparelli had better English than I thought. '*Cinquecento,*' he said firmly.

'*Five* hundred thousand? That's ridiculous. Tell him he's a greedy sod.'

I told Paparelli my friend thought five hundred thousand was probably excessive. He spat again. '*Cinquecento.*'

'Offer him threee and a half.'

'*Trecento cinquanta?*'

'*Cinquecento.*'

'*Quattrocento?*'

'*Cinquecento.*'

'He's not budging, Geoffrey.'

'Bugger this. I don't have time to haggle with the cross-eyed bastard. Tell him he can have his five hundred thousand, but there's nothing I'd love more than to shove a burning poker up his fat Italian arse.'

I told Paparelli he could have his five hundred thousand. He immediately burst into a grin and wanted to shake hands, but Geoffrey stormed off. He had gone three hundred yards before I caught up with him.

'You do realize,' I said, when I'd calmed him down and talked him into having a beer at a street-side café, 'that you're now paying that man more than two hundred pounds a night?'

'Yes, yes, yes.'

'It's too much, isn't it? I don't know what your other expenses are but, even if you sell every seat, you won't break even on the production. In fact, if you're not careful, you'll make a huge loss.'

'I don't care about making a loss.'

'I thought you were an accountant, Geoffrey.'

'Bugger accountancy.' Can contempt turn to respect with a single phrase? I had thought he was a small man, but there was something heroic in his disdain for the financial arithmetic of the venture. 'It's not the money I mind, Mark. If you want to do anything worthwhile in life, you have to be prepared to pay for it. Paparelli can charge what he wants: it's his house, after all. I just wish he wasn't so begrudging about it. Did you know he was a member of the Rome Shakespeare Society?'

'That clown? You're joking.'

'No, he is. Why do you think he agreed to let us use his house in the first place? When I decided to put the play on, I wrote to everyone on the society's list asking if they could provide a venue. Paparelli was the only person to say yes. But do you know what I found out then?'

'What?'

'The so-called Shakespeare Society in this God-forsaken city doesn't have anything to do with Shakespeare. It was founded by a group of scholars in the last century who were interested in putting on productions of the plays in the original English; since then it's just gone downhill. Only a few of the members are proper Shakespearians: the rest only join because the Society is also a wine club and offers its members a discount on imported French wines. Paparelli' – he spat the word out, but there was sadness behind the venom – 'is secretary of the wine club.'

'Then why on earth did he get involved with you?'

'Because he thought it would be a good chance to sell some wine. First he insisted on having wine advertisements all over the programme. Well, of course, I said that was OK because, as far as I was concerned, the programme was ancillary to the production and didn't impinge on its artistic merits. *Then* he wanted me to have a forty-five minute interval – forty-five minutes, Mark: can you imagine what that would do to the dramatic tension? – just so that he could hold a wine-tasting in the courtyard. When I said no and put my foot down, he wrote a letter saying he wanted to pull out altogether. That's what brought things to a head tonight. Do you know what I think, Mark? I don't think Paparelli's even *read The Winter's Tale.*'

'How many Italians have?'

'But why not, Mark, why not? It's a great masterpiece. Italians aren't barbarians: they're highly civilized. How can they be indifferent to a work of art which is so truly, inexpressibly, beautiful?

'How indeed?' I would have smiled if the pain behind the absurdity hadn't been so familiar. Yes, I thought, how can one accept without protest another person's refusal to love?

69

'Cheer up,' I said. 'It could have been worse. Paparelli could have wanted to sell hot dogs or insisted on having a stripper on at half-time. At least wine-tasting's perfectly respectable.' I offered the thought in consolation: I had underestimated Geoffrey's capacity to explode.

'It may be perfectly respectable,' he shouted, 'but it's got no bloody place in an evening like this. It's not a respectable night out for respectable people. It's Shakespeare. Shakespeare, Shakespeare, Shakespeare.' He started banging his fist on the table like a revivalist preacher and I had to grip his arm to stop him. His shouting had broken the stillness of the night as surely as a drunken brawl or a motorcycle roaring past in a cloud of dust. A light came on in one of the windows opposite and, further down the street, a young couple interrupted their kiss to see what was happening. The waiter looked on contemptuously: anyone who works in a Roman café has a master's degree in the study of eccentricity.

I said: 'You're insane, Geoffrey,' and meant it. I'd been diplomatic for too long: I didn't even bother with the apologetic laugh which would usually accompany such an allegation, casting doubt on its seriousness.

He looked at me quizzically. 'Am I? Yes, I suppose I am a bit.' When I go berserk it frightens me, yet Geoffrey contemplated his insanity with no more fear than a man looking at his face in the mirror. How could he look at that mirror without flinching? What did it mean, this serenity at the heart of his madness? He said: 'You probably think I'm a complete lunatic,' as if lunacy held no terrors.

I backtracked slowly. 'Not a complete lunatic, Geoffrey, but certainly a lunatic. As far as Shakespeare's concerned, you're absolutely bloody crazy. It isn't normal, is it, to love so obsessively?' The glib conventional wisdom must have wandered into the conversation by accident, for I rejected it as utterly as he did.

'I don't agree, Mark. Who's to say what's normal and what isn't normal? If love's a good thing, why ration it? I do know that Shakespeare's been the greatest love of my life, that he's given me more pleasure than anybody living ever could.'

'More than Helen?' I slid in with it like a snake.

'Oh yes.'

He checked himself, but the words were out before he could stop them. They should have given me hope – for what a golden opportunity they represented – but they sent only a sharp stab of pain through my whole being. That she should be so little valued *there*, in her own kingdom, in the place where she had set down her tabernacle and built fortifications around it . . . It all seemed so cruel, such a waste of human possibility, that I found myself hating Geoffrey the way you hate people who mistreat animals. He recanted quickly, of course: said that obviously he loved Helen too; that there wasn't a better wife anywhere; that they cared deeply for each other and, if she sometimes seemed to take second place to Shakespeare, it wasn't like being a golf widow and being relegated for trivial reasons. It was a decent enough attempt at uxoriousness but, when I got home, all I could think of was 'oh yes' and a woman on the other side of Rome in bed with someone who loved her less than a man who'd been dead over three hundred years.

In the morning I passed the news on, like a police informer. What ignominious roles love casts us in; yet hadn't Geoffrey said it shouldn't be rationed?

'I've known that for the last ten years.' At the other end of the telephone Helen sounded tired, as if she'd been sleeping badly. I didn't recognize the symptoms of a woman who'd been battered to exhaustion. How could I? I was too busy doing the battering.

'Well, don't you *care*? Doesn't it upset you that your husband is putting it about that Shakespeare means more to him than you?'

'You've no right to repeat what he said.'

'Oh I know that, Helen. I've got no *rights* in the matter at all. I'm a nobody, a has-been. I'm locked out in the cold while you and Geoffrey sit inside and pretend you're happy together. Except that you're *not* happy, either of you. I have Geoffrey's word for it that his one true love is William Shakespeare and I have *your* word for it, in a hotel bedroom in Bayswater in July 1977, after that film, when we spilt the wine and I had to ring for room service – '

'Eight *years*, Mark.'

'It may be eight years, Helen, but I still have your word for it, do I not, in Bayswater, on that lousy bed that creaked and rattled as soon as we moved, that you loved me more than you'd ever loved anybody in your life. Do you remember? Ever. Anybody. Ever. Anybody.'

The line went dead and I heard my own voice repeating the same words over and over again, as Geoffrey had repeated 'Shakespeare' in the café. Only this time there were no puzzled onlookers, no restraining hand to stop me making a fool of myself. I was alone, staring into the mirror of my madness.

8

The next night I slept with Vanessa for the first time. In one of my own novels I would have to give a grunt-by-grunt account of such a development, because that's what Mark Barham readers expect. I would have to remember what underwear she was wearing and pretend she was wildly turned on when I nibbled her ear-lobes. I would have to work in the names of perfumes and cigarettes and invent improbable positions for the human body. I would have to garnish the whole thing with sultry dialogue and put four-letter words into our mouths as we climaxed simultaneously, to show how wonderful it can be when you do it properly. I would have to tell lies to make people I've never met envious: what could be more distasteful? Yet I say it's only the way I earn my living in the superior tone of someone who thinks there are worse ways of earning a living. Sometimes I'm not so sure. There's only one thing more dispiriting than reading a really bad book and that's writing one. I slept with Vanessa and we woke up in the same bed in the morning. *Finita*.

Geoffrey wasn't amused. I don't know who told him – Vanessa's father probably, for I noticed him prowling around outside my house in the morning, like a dog who had lost his master – but he took me aside at the next rehearsal and confronted me with the fact as if I were his teenage son.

'I don't mind saying I'm annoyed, Mark. There's nothing disrupts a cast more than this sort of relationship. It's so damned unprofessional.'

'I thought we were amateurs.'

'Only in the sense that nobody's being paid. I'm doing my best to stamp out amateurishness and bring a proper sense of discipline to rehearsals, and you have to come along and behave like this. It's too bad.'

'Come on, Geoffrey. Do you think professional actors *don't* sleep together?'

'Of course they do. All I'm saying is that they should know better.'

'Even Shakespeare – '

'Keep him out of it, damn you.' Angry beads of perspiration formed on his brow. Did any saint guard his God's reputation more jealously? 'It's the principle that counts, Mark. I'm trying to get people to approach the play in a businesslike fashion and you're putting that in jeopardy by mixing love and business. It never works.'

'Who said anything about love?' I murmured, but he had already left to marshal his troops for the rehearsal. I went into the next room and heard him explain to an enthralled cast how love and sex intermingled in *The Winter's Tale*, as if he knew the first thing about either. The descent into farce was becoming inexorable.

Helen wasn't there, for the third evening running. My disappointment blended with hope, for surely this could be no coincidence? If I was really nobody, if those old feelings were dead and buried as she said, why was she so afraid of our eyes meeting across a crowded rehearsal-room? She was afraid, therefore the old feelings were not dead, therefore I wasn't nobody but somebody. How far apart those two poles are, being nobody and being somebody, and yet on what fragile grounds the distinction sometimes rests. Through the fog of rhetoric I could glimpse the flaw in my reasoning. Suppose Helen was only avoiding me because she was afraid of another scene? Or suppose she wasn't

but a man in my position prides himself on observing
[de]marcation lines scrupulously. A woman's attitude to
[domes]tic violence is rather a personal matter: it falls within
[hu]sband's domain. Perhaps the eight years that we
[had] been lovers had made me careless about such
[thing]s. Or perhaps I was just trying to attract Helen's
[attenti]on. I did notice she flushed slightly when I made my
[sugges]tion.

['But] it wasn't that sort of film at all,' she said quickly.
['There] was a lot of petty crime among the Polish com-
[munity] because everyone was struggling to survive, but
[there w]as no actual violence. It was more like a documen-
[tary th]an a drama: there were birthday parties and train
[rides] and funerals and a big wedding in a church. It was
[very m]oving really.'

['Yes,] darling.' Geoffrey patted her hand like a father and
[hot] hatred flared in me. If she'd married me, I would
[ha]ve patted her hand like that: I would have treated
[her as a]n equal because I cared for her as an equal and we
[would h]ave related like real human beings, not acted out a
[fak]an pantomime. How simple life seems when you're
[o]utside looking in. Angrily I left my coffee unfinished
[and ros]e to leave.

['Mark, there's one other thing.' Geoffrey sounded
[embarr]assed and I thought: Let him be embarrassed. If
[he's go]ing to harp on about my sleeping with Vanessa
[being u]nprofessional, I'll tell him to get lost; I'll tell him
[there a]re professional virgins all over Rome just *aching* to
[play Ca]millo in his crappy production and see if he believes
[me. I w]as spoiling for a fight but, when he finally came out
[with it,] it was too banal to fight over.

['It's a]bout Walter, Mark. He says he doesn't feel he can
[play the] Bear any more.'

['Why] on earth not?' Immediately I smelled a trap. The

avoiding me at all? Suppose she really did have alternative
engagements night after night? She had always enjoyed
socializing and, when women who enjoy socializing marry
madmen who fill the house with morons massacring Shakespeare, don't they have to do their socializing somewhere
else? Aren't they *entitled* to look for other entertainment?

And there, in a phrase, a different doubt loomed in my
mind. What kind of entertainment was she looking for?
Wouldn't a woman who'd been unfaithful once tend to be
unfaithful again? Suppose some new lover was filling the
vacuum which I had once filled? Where was she night after
night when she was avoiding me – if she was avoiding me?
Did I actually matter to her at all?

Within seconds, I was on fire with jealousy. What lover
escapes those flames? Jealousy is no more than the instinct
to hang on to what you've got. 'To have and to hold': even
the Christian marriage service acknowledges that the two
concepts are inseparable. I don't like knocking a fellow
professional and I mustn't criticize the dead because they
can't answer back, but for me Shakespeare got jealousy
arse about face in *The Winter's Tale*. He had this strange
wheeze – I remember Geoffrey calling it a 'dramatic
masterstroke', but then he would, wouldn't he? – of presenting jealousy as an *irrational* emotion. A man suddenly
gets it into his head that he is being cuckolded and, without
any evidence to support him, takes it out on his wife in a
hasty way. Violent rows, baby-battering, long speeches
about what happens when he realizes the glass of decent-
tasting wine he's just swallowed had a spider in the
bottom . . . It's all very sad (whoops, I mean tragic: sorry,
Geoffrey), but it's not true to *life*, not to life as I know it
anyway, here in Rome in 1985. Obviously jealousy can get
out of hand sometimes: William hit that nail squarely on
the head and all credit to him (he was an old man when he

wrote *The Winter's Tale* and going a bit gaga judging by some of the speeches). But I can't go along with his idea that jealousy is something rootless, an emotional aberration which attacks people out of the blue like a coronary. Jealousy isn't rootless. Its roots are all too obvious: need, longing, insecurity, all the old pains. And it isn't irrational. When I'm jealous, my mind examines different hypotheses with logical coldness; in the pain of my doubt I look everywhere for certainty. As soon as I'd postulated that Helen had another lover, what mattered wasn't revenge, but finding out if I was right. Did such a man exist? What was his name? Where did they meet? I didn't turn into a monster the minute the thought entered my head, as Shakespeare's hero does. I turned into a private detective, a more civilized animal altogether.

In one of my early novels, the ones that nobody but the critics read, I had a scene in which a husband realized his wife was being unfaithful just by looking at her face in the dressing-table mirror. I had toyed, I remember, with a car-key, an earring, a man's wristwatch: one of the physical devices writers use to show closely guarded secrets being betrayed by a moment's carelessness. But then I thought, no: it doesn't need a stage-prop to achieve that effect; if he'd known her that well for that long, he would be able to read her mind anyway. I must have been rather naïve, for I'd never been able to mind-read women that fluently myself, however well I knew them, and I can only suppose that I invested marriage with magical powers which I expected to understand better if I ever got married myself. It's that face peering into a shop window again: to an outsider, married couples operate with a certain confident smoothness which convinces you they must be telepathic. But I don't now think they are. You can tell some things from a human face, but not everything, not the things you most want to know. If I wrote that sce[ne] use a car-key like everyone else.

And yet the myth of the face persist[s] someone well enough, or badly enough (phrases should be interchangeable), yo[u] experience that what will be inscrutable world will be legible to you. When H[elen] quarter to twelve – I stayed on specially to wait for her and was engaged in a rat[her] sation with Geoffrey about Shakespeare's I stared at her face like a rattle-snake, exp[ecting] whether she had indeed been seeing L[uigi] Giuseppe. (In my mental picture it was a there are several well-known Roman st scppe.) But the sphinx guarded her secre[t] never met – I never expected they woul[d] down next to Geoffrey on the sofa with th[e] someone returning from the cinema. Perha[ps] reader after all: she *had* been to the cinema

'Good film?' Geoffrey asked, with supr I imagine he thought the cinema rather some people find one-day cricket vulgar.

'Not bad. It was that one about the Poli in New York after the War. *Strange Dawn.*

'I think I've just about heard of it. Wh Pasquino?'

'Yes.' The Pasquino is the only Roma[n] films in English. Everywhere else the because Italians don't like subtitles: fo[r] most civilized country in Europe is also

'No violence, I hope?' He turned to 'Helen hates violent films.' I said: ' immediately wished I hadn't. Geoffre[y] the cinema with Helen in the past, so i

Bear is the best part in *The Winter's Tale*. He just chases someone off the stage and eats him, without delivering a single iambic pentameter on the way. It was the only sort of acting Walter was up to: why throw away the chance of a lifetime?

Geoffrey explained. 'He tried the costume on yesterday and apparently it's too hot: he's got asthma, you see. I was wondering – '

Helen gave a great peal of laughter from the sofa. It was like a sound frozen in time, an echo of our great days together when the merriment never seemed to stop. 'Is Mark going to be Bear, darling? I do think that's a brilliant piece of casting. Please say yes, Mark. You'll be a wonderful Bear, I'm sure you will.'

'Oh all right. Count me in, Geoffrey.' Does anyone delude himself like a lover? I thought, because everyone loved furry animals, that the laughter was the laughter of affection; that the affection had risen to the surface from a deeper well of feeling; that it heralded a thawing, a turning of the tide, a new birth. By the time the mask slipped back into place, I had taken such comfort from that little moment of merriment that I left the house vibrant with joy. I was mad. I should have looked at the mask more closely.

Outside in the street, the private detective took over from the lover and I remembered a woman sitting on a sofa talking to her husband. 'It was more like a documentary than a drama: there were birthday parties and train strikes and funerals and a big wedding in a church.' Yet I had also watched *Strange Dawn* at the Pasquino cinema. There were birthday parties and there were train strikes and there were funerals. But I had sat through the film from start to finish and there had not, repeat not, been a big wedding in a church. All the way home the private detective whispered only one word in the lover's ear: 'Giuseppe! Giuseppe! Giuseppe!'

9

At home Vanessa was waiting for me in bed. I must be a very trusting man, because I always give women I've slept with the keys to my flat and never ask for them back. Sometimes I get them back anyway. One woman returned them all the way from America *recorded delivery*, I suspect because she had found our parting traumatically abrupt. I had to sign a receipt which, for all I know, she still keeps under her pillow in St Paul, Minnesota as a memento of Mark Barham, English novelist and shit – although, knowing the Italian postal services, it's more likely sitting under a pile of mailbags in Naples. But I never demand the keys back: such pettiness would only tarnish my adopted image, the insouciant open-all-hours bachelorhood that lures women into accepting the keys in the first place.

For Vanessa the keys must have been particularly useful. They meant she was able to leave the rehearsal with her father and not hang around obviously waiting for me. When Peter Jansen saw me taking no further interest in his daughter, but staying behind to talk to Geoffrey, the tension fell away from his shoulders like a silk dressing-gown and he wished me good night without hostility: perhaps he assumed that whatever Vanessa and I had got up to the previous night belonged to the past. After that I imagine he had a comfortable night's sleep, while Vanessa slipped out of the house and came round to my flat: fortunately, or unfortunately, we lived very close. It was a pretty enough piece of deception, within the tawdry codes by which such relationships operate. But there was a problem. I didn't *want* Vanessa waiting for me in my bed. When I got home and heard a silly voice say 'Surprise time, Mark', then saw that shock of red hair lying on my pillow, my heart sank to my shoes.

'What's the matter, Mark?'

'Nothing's the matter.'

'You look awful.'

'I'm all right.' As all right as a man feels when he's just realized the woman he loves has been lying to him; when she's told him she has to put her husband first and all the time been putting someone else first and her husband second and himself third, if that. As all right as a man dying of thirst in a desert.

'Do you want me to go?'

'Yes please. No, stay.' I thought I needed to be alone but, as soon as she offered to leave, she took away the need. That small gesture of renunciation glowed like a candle which I didn't want to snuff out: it was as if a woman I had thought insignificant had suddenly become a good woman, the sort a man turns to when he's in pain. Her young shoulders weren't broad enough to carry my pain, but they were all there was. I held her tight in my arms and then I think I must have cried, because I remember, not the tears themselves – there are some memories one throws straight in the bin – but Vanessa saying 'Oh please don't' and burrowing in her handbag for Kleenex. After that we talked. It was an odd conversation: for what could I tell you that wouldn't reveal her own cruelly small role in the drama?

'I've been let down by somebody,' I explained, as if I'd been gazumped on a house. What a clinging habit this English understatement is.

'A man? A woman?'

'It doesn't matter.' No, I thought, the sex of people who

let you down doesn't matter. It's when they rip your heart out and trample on it that their gender has a marginal significance.

'Have you lost some money?'

'Not a penny.'

'Then is it something to do with your writing?'

'Not really.' For eight years I'd written twelve hundred words a day: now there was only 'suddenly'. But how do you explain something like that to a stranger you only sleep with? I said: 'I'm upset and thank you for your sympathy because I need it. But let's not talk about the details.'

'Sure.' It was the voice of a disappointed child. I felt as if I'd slammed a door in her face, the same door Helen had slammed in my face, the door into the house where life is so much better than on the street. But she was streetwise beyond her years: she knew that such houses had back entrances, if you could only find them.

'Do you mind if I ask you something?' she said; then, when I said no: 'When things like this happen to you, you know, *bad* things' – how insufficient the word sounded, but wasn't it me who had introduced the false note of euphemism? – 'do you find yourself wanting to put your emotions into your books? Is that how writing works or is it just a silly misunderstanding which people have?'

'It depends on the writer. If I were a real writer – '

'You are a real writer.'

'No, I'm not. I keep saying this, Vanessa, but you won't believe me. I peaked three months before my thirtieth birthday. That's not real writing: it's adolescent promise – and you know what adolescents do with their promises.'

'All right, Mark, let's *pretend* that you're a real writer – I don't know why you're so touchy about it. If you *were* a real writer, wouldn't you feel like picking up your pen right now and expressing your feelings on paper?'

'I shouldn't think so for a minute. You see – '

'Do you mind?'

'Not at all.'

She fetched her portable tape-recorder from the next room and thrust the microphone into my face. This ritual was now a constant element in our relationship. If the sex was the jam, then the bread and butter was the series of recorded interviews on which her magazine profile of me was to be based. I suppose the exercise fed an area of my vanity – but I hope to God nobody I care for ever listens to those tapes. On this occasion, I held forth for five minutes about literature and feeling and how only idiots thought they were connected and what a nonsense it would be for a professional entertainer – for that's all any writer was – to drip pain on to a piece of paper and expect anyone to read it. The cynicism acted as a palliative, for my bitterness towards Helen weakened and other aspects of the situation came into perspective. I even paid some attention to Vanessa's feelings. Once I saw her wincing at my disdain and thought: is this a fair way to treat someone who's just mopped you up with Kleenex?

Eventually she said: 'Do you think all writers are as detached as you?'

'They are if they've got any sense.'

'Even great writers? Even – '

'Oh, not *him*.'

'Even Shakespeare?'

I growled like a dog disturbed in his sleep. You would think a non-enthusiast would be particularly unenthusiastic when his mind was preoccupied. But Shakespeare defeats ordinary logic. He isn't like a fruit or vegetable people don't happen to like, an option they reject without qualms because there are so many alternatives. For any English writer he is a constant presence: someone who can be spurned, overlooked, ignored, but never forgotten. Now, in my time of greatest despair, he didn't seem like a distraction. I may have protested mechanically at the mention of his name, but his presence in the room wasn't a real irritant. Our conversation gained a new freshness and, like the ash of an old cigarette, the cynicism I was pouring on to Vanessa's tape began to crumble.

'I don't know how detached Shakespeare was,' I said. 'Did he suffer? Was he unhappy? Did he write to come to terms with his grief or just because he enjoyed writing? I've no idea. You'd have to ask Geoffrey.'

'But do you think he was a passionate man?'

'Oh, I'm sure he was passionate. This contradicts everything I've just said, and don't apply it to me whatever you do, but, if he hadn't felt things so strongly, he couldn't have expressed them so bloody well, could he? A great writer isn't like a hack writer. He doesn't just do the same things better: he does different things, he's a different animal. There's a theory that genius is a God-given abstraction but, when it comes to expressing itself, it draws on very human roots. So there must have been events in Shakespeare's life which affected him profoundly, although I don't know what they were. From what I remember, all we know was that most of his love poetry was written to a man, not a woman, and that he was unhappily married.'

'How do you know?'

'Because, in his will, he left his wife his second-best bed, which was snide but predictable. I mean, you would leave your wife your second-best bed if you were the other way inclined, wouldn't you? They didn't invent bisexuals until Freud, so he must have had a rotten time making sense of his life. Perhaps he only wrote great plays because he was confused about his hormones.'

Vanessa giggled. 'I bet you'd never talk like this to Geoffrey.'

'Too right I wouldn't. He'd crucify me. He adores Shakespeare passionately, far more than I ever could, but he doesn't have what you have to have when you're that involved emotionally.'

'What's that?'

'A sense of humour. Without that you're lost.'

I condemned Geoffrey with an easy aphorism, yet wasn't that my problem too? I could crack jokes about Shakespeare, but not any longer about the woman with whom I'd spent the best, most laughter-filled, times of my life. Hard as I looked, I could see no ironic angle to the situation which would bring a smile back to my face. Helen had abandoned me, not for a principle, not for her husband, but for another man: you need to be remarkably serene to see the funny side of such a rebuff. I slept off some of the pain in Vanessa's arms but, when I woke in the morning, she had already slipped out of the flat and the pain was still there.

10

Do private detectives still follow people? Are there husbands and wives so jealous that they're prepared to pay hundreds of pounds to have their worst suspicions confirmed? You would have thought that, with modern divorce laws, the need to have evidence of adultery would have diminished and the market for private detectives contracted. But jealousy doesn't obey market forces. We pay surveyors to set our minds at rest about the houses we buy; we pay accountants to set our minds at rest that we're not paying taxes we can avoid paying. Isn't it worth a few quid to set our minds at rest about what *really* worries us? I bet there are small men in raincoats all over the world still sitting in their cars watching and waiting, waiting for a man to come out of a house straightening his tie or a woman to press a door-bell glancing furtively over her shoulder.

Even in Rome, the most relaxed capital city in Europe, I'm sure it still goes on. I imagine, if I'd made discreet enquiries among my Italian friends, I would have been directed to a little office above a shoe-shop on the Via Nazionale, where some unctuous man would have sat me down in an armchair, offered me a cigarette and said: 'What is your problem, Signor Barham?' I don't know what he would have charged to set one of his hounds on Helen's trail, but I could have found the money easily enough. *Hell Island*, my savage exposé of drug trafficking in the Caribbean, had made me richer than most of the pushers. *Nuclear Winter* would be just as lucrative if I ever

86

finished the damn thing. It wasn't lack of money that made me do the dirty work myself: I was just too involved to trust to someone else's snooping.

And aren't writers the best snoopers anyway? Looking for material, we call it, that rather unpleasant way we have of plundering everything we can from life and giving it back only in return for our royalties; of observing but not participating; of examining the make of people's clothes as we shake hands with them; of studying their faces and bodies as if they were biological specimens; of saying little to them, but meticulously noting the absurd things they say. I remember I once spent an entire week spying on one of my neighbours because I noticed that, whenever her husband crossed the road to buy a packet of cigarettes, she made a telephone call. At the end of the week she left her husband for her lover. Would anyone but a writer attempt to justify such behaviour? Yet I worked that detail into one of my books, the cigarettes and the telephone call, and congratulated myself on writing straight from life for a change. The right to privacy is a concept I barely comprehend. As I took up my position at a café about two hundred yards from the Danes' house and, by way of camouflage, propped a copy of *Il Tempo* against a carafe of water, I experienced none of the normal scruples.

It was half past one. Jealousy inflames the imagination, but I didn't suppose Helen would meet her lover before then. I knew she met him in the evenings because of the lie she'd told about the film, but it wasn't necessarily only the evenings. When it had been me, when it was my *turn* – and how bitterly that phrase revolved and twisted in my head – we had stolen time together at every opportunity. We avoided regular meeting times because regularity was a tyranny we dreaded: men returning from work on the 6.08 train, women playing whist on alternate Tuesday afternoons, all that complacent claptrap. Nobody seeks the illusion of freedom like a clandestine lover; nobody is so desperate to believe that time doesn't matter. Yes, I thought, Helen will want to see him in the afternoons as well as the evenings: if not this afternoon, then tomorrow afternoon; if not tomorrow afternoon, then soon. In Rome, as in all Mediterranean cities, the afternoon is siesta time. Shops close at one o'clock and open up again at four-thirty. Signs saying *Chiuso* are put up outside the museums and churches. The only people out on the streets are sweaty tourists scouring the city for a sign saying *Aperto*. Most Romans come home from work during the siesta, but I knew Geoffrey wouldn't be able to: his office was too far away, in the ugly EUR complex on the southern outskirts of the city which Mussolini built when he wasn't making the trains run on time. I didn't know what Giuseppe did during the siesta, but Helen couldn't have had things easier. I had ascertained that she was at home by dialling her number and ringing off when she picked up the receiver. Soon, surely, she would emerge from the house.

Half an hour passed and the Eternal City inched closer to eternity. A small boy played a few bars of Verdi on a mouth-organ while his mother collected money in a pocket handkerchief. Two motorcycles roared past, bringing up the dust from the street. A horse-drawn carriage took a party of American women to the Trevi Fountain. There was even the statutory idiot, the character you can't move an inch in Rome without meeting. This one had khaki shorts and a silly hat.

'It's Mark Barham, isn't it?'

'That's right.'

'Remember me?'

'I can't say – '

'McBride. Tim McBride.'

'Oh yes, that Christmas party. Engineering, wasn't it?'

'Near as a whistle, old man, near as a whistle. Want another guess? No. Marine insurance, since you ask. We're an odd bunch, always have been: neither fish nor bloody fowl. Do you mind if I – ?'

'Please do.'

'What's draught beer in this bloody language?'

'A *spina*.'

'Knew it was something like that. Waiter!'

He sat down beside me and started reading the sports page of the *Daily Telegraph*. He was a bulky man and the *Telegraph* is a bulky paper: I had to shift my chair twice to keep the Danes' front door in my sights. When he'd finished the sports page, he put down the paper and, for want of anything better to do, told me everything that had happened to him since 1954. There was high drama in four continents and nothing of any interest whatever: writers may have to scavenge for material, but they're not that desperate. When Helen finally appeared, I shot up from my chair and left him stranded in the Australian outback in 1967.

'Hang on, old man, you're missing the punch-line. What do you think she said after *that*? This will really crease you . . .' His story died in the sun and I set off after my prey without a crease to show for it.

Almost immediately, I wished I had hired a professional. Helen was a brisk walker and I couldn't follow her too closely for fear of detection. My only attempt at disguise was a tatty pair of dark glasses which probably made me more conspicuous rather than less. I nearly lost her crossing the Corso Vittorio Emanuele and I nearly lost her again in the Campo dei Fiori, where she turned left when I expected her to turn right, then stopped in a food-shop from which she emerged nibbling a bar of chocolate. It's those little things that hurt so much in love. I remembered being despatched to the shops at all hours of the day to satisfy that craving for chocolate, and how happily I would return with my booty. Who fetched her chocolate now, I wondered, as if the chocolate had anything to do with anything. In my pain I nearly ran up to her and offered to pay for the chocolate – what a pathetic, futile gesture it would have been – but she walked on quickly, negotiating the cobbled streets with ominous certainty. My heart sank further. It wasn't an afternoon wander: it was a well-trodden path between A and B.

I thought she might be heading towards Trastevere but, instead of turning right across the Tiber, she passed to the north of the Teatro Marcello and crossed the road towards the Tarpeian Rock, the famous precipice from which, when the lions in the Colosseum had had their fill, ancient Romans used to throw people to their death. The area beneath the Rock is now a favourite haunt of Rome's gay community who took far more interest in me than Helen. It's a quiet part of the city, with very little bustle to act as camouflage for a pursuer. I had to keep a full two hundred yards from Helen and again I nearly lost her. She went up a flight of steps and turned left and, when I got to the end of the street she'd taken, she wasn't immediately visible. Then I spotted her. She was no longer walking, but standing in the shadow of a house with her finger pressed against the door-bell. She had arrived at B.

I glanced around to get my bearings. Via Foraggi: I'd never heard of it. It was a quiet cobbled street not more than three hundred yards long and, when I got to the far end, having walked carefully along the side in shadow, I was overlooking the Forum, with the back of the Campidoglio on my left and the Colosseum away in the distance on the right. I walked back down the street and this time

paused long enough outside the house Helen had entered –
it was No. 76, double my own age – to take in the three
names on the door-bell. Giorgini, Tardelli, Coppo. Two
jokers and a knave, I thought darkly, the pain not eased by
this new sporting element in the mystery. But which was
the knave?

In a respectable country like England, this sort of riddle
takes a lot of unravelling. Suppose I had been in Richmond
or Wandsworth and the three names had been Brown,
Smith and Teddington-Millar. Direct enquiries of the
neighbours would have been impossible: they would have
asked 'Why do you want to know?' and not said a word
unless satisfied. I would have had to proceed by subterfuge:
consulted the telephone directory to find a Brown, a Smith
and a Teddington-Millar at the right address and, assuming all three were listed, rung each in turn asking to speak
to Helen Danes – some laborious ruse like that. Rome is
quite different. You will never be asked to mind your own
business because nobody minds their own business: vulgar
curiosity is understood and accommodated. On every resi-
dential street in Rome, however short, you will see an old
crone in black sitting outside her door watching the world
go by. She won't ask why you want to know about her
neighbours: she will answer your questions as comprehen-
sively as possible, to show how observant she is of life on
her patch. She's like those quiz programme bores who are
determined to show that they know everything and who,
damn them to hell, do know everything. It's tedious and
infuriating when you're not interested: when you're screaming with jealousy and confusion, their omniscience is a
godsend.

The senior crone in the Via Foraggi lived at No. 36. She
was sitting just inside her front door, peeling tomatoes on a
wooden board. At her feet a cat was stretched out in the

sun, which fell at an angle across the door, leaving the woman's face in shadow. She had stared at me as I walked past the first time and looked surprised to see me again. I imagine she thought I was a tourist who had lost his way.

'*Buon giorno.*'

' '*giorno.*' Her face relaxed. My accent was too good for a tourist. After a few pleasantries, I went straight for goal. How was Signor Giorgini in No. 76 these days?

'*Signor Giorgini è morto.*'

'Ah. *Scusi.*' One joker was eliminated immediately, but at a cost to the momentum of the conversation. The crone elaborated at length on Signor Giorgini's death. He had collapsed on his way to the tobacconist's: an omen, some people said. He was only fifty-three, but he hadn't looked after himself properly. Signora Giorgini had taken it very badly. She was having to sell some of her furniture to pay the bills and, according to Signor Coppo, who lived in the same house, she had become very religious. She was –

I interrupted quickly. Wasn't Signor Coppo that young man who worked as a tour-guide in the Vatican?

The crone looked disdainful. I suppose, when you're a first-class gossip, you look down on the second-raters. I had got it quite, quite wrong, she said. Signor Coppo wasn't young at all, unless you called fifty-eight young and that was five years older than Signor Giorgini had been when he collapsed on the way to the tobacconist's. And he didn't work in the Vatican as a tour-guide: he was an *avvocato in patrocinio*, a kind of lawyer. He and Signora Coppo were presently on holiday in Rimini where they had an apartment near the beach. There *was* a young man in No. 76 –

'*Chi è?*'

'*Signor Tardelli.*' Was it only my excitement as locating the knave so quickly or did her voice drop disapprovingly as she pronounced the name? Her knowledge of life in

No. 76 was encyclopaedic. She would have seen Helen coming and going and put two and two together; probably she had compared notes with Signora Benelli in No. 60 and Signorina Roncardi in No. 95. I was suddenly alarmed to have engaged such a thorough accomplice. If I asked if she knew a Mrs Danes, would she tell me Mrs Danes was married to an English eccentric with an obsession about his national poet? I was only skimming the surface. Where did her information end?

Signor Tardelli, she went on, didn't work in the Vatican either. She didn't know who I was thinking of. The only person on the street who worked in the Vatican was Signorina Manzoni at No. 12 and she wasn't a tour-guide, but a secretary for Vatican Radio. Signor Tardelli was far too grand to be a tour-guide. He was a very distinguished man, a journalist, and was said to speak five languages.

I winced. My jealousy had focused on sex: I hadn't prepared myself for intellectual competition. For no good reason – call it the hope which lies at the core of love – I had imagined a sweaty, inarticulate coupling, with pidgin Italian for pillow-talk: something transient I could expect to outlast. Tardelli's linguistic fluency was ominous: I'd rather have been told he was incredibly good-looking. Then the crone told me he *was* incredibly good-looking. I winced again. I was afraid of asking directly about Helen, so I enquired if Tardelli had an active social life – to which the crone said Signor Tardelli was a young man, *un giovane*, with a look so knowing that my heart fell still further. He was plainly a rival in a way poor Geoffrey had never been.

The fount of knowledge hadn't yet dried up. The crone wiped the knife with which she was peeling tomatoes on the hem of her skirt and put it down on the floor. Then she offered me a plum from a little wooden bowl. I took one and ate it, making sure to spit the stone out like an Italian, not do that embarrassed English trick of transferring the stone from the corner of the mouth to a handkerchief while nobody's looking. She nodded approvingly as the stone came to rest between the cobbles of the street, then asked what work I did. I tried to answer economically, but she was persistent with her supplementaries: I suppose, like all computers, she had to be properly programmed if she was to store information efficiently. Finally I got her back to Tardelli and pressed the necessary button to retrieve all known data on the subject: height and weight; number of previous lovers; employer's name and address; car registration number; amount of alcohol consumed in the last twenty-four hours. It would have been a fascinating print-out, but I had not time to read it. No sooner had the computer been set in motion than there was the sound of an opening door and Helen was outside in the street.

She shut the door quietly behind her, hitched her hand-bag over her shoulder and looked absent-mindedly around. A light breeze ruffled her hair and her white skirt shimmered in the heat. You wouldn't have thought a woman could be beautiful at a hundred yards, but Helen broke all the rules. She looked so shy, so natural, so innocent, as she took her place in the sun that my heart went out to her again: I thought, not of a woman who had caused me pain, but a small child looking for its mother. If she'd returned the way she came, she would probably have seen me. Instead she followed the street to the far end and turned left, from where a path zig-zagged up to the back of the Campidoglio. I followed for about fifty yards, but made no effort to catch her. After a few minutes she disappeared from sight, her stride seeming to lengthen all the time as she put distance between herself and the Via Foraggi. Perhaps she'd had a row with Tardelli, I thought hopefully; perhaps she'd said goodbye to him for the last time . . . But there's no mileage in hopes like that. If she'd been angry, she would have slammed the door behind her. Yet hadn't I seen her close it with an infinite gentleness, the way she used to close my door in Notting Hill Gate?

I lit a cigarette and leant against the wall overlooking the Forum, watching the tourists swarm like ants over the ruins. The sight inspired Gibbon to write *The Decline and Fall of the Roman Empire*, but I had no such exalted thoughts. I looked only for a way to make my pain more bearable.

11

I suppose if I'd been *really* mad – and how desperate the
state of mind that makes a man cling to that distinction – I
would have done something violent immediately. In my
anguish at Helen's infidelity – to me, you understand, not
to Geoffrey – I would have knocked on Tardelli's door and
beaten the hell out of him before he knew what was
happening.

But I didn't. I hung back. Perhaps I'm more English
than I like to think: even when my emotions were strongest,
I didn't lose my sense of fair play. I don't imagine a Latin
lover would have done what I did next, which was to give
Helen a second chance and then a third. Twice in the next
four days I followed her to the Via Foraggi and watched
her enter and leave No. 76 without challenging her. One
visit, even two visits, I told myself desperately, could be
perfectly innocent – for mightn't an Englishwoman simply
befriend an Italian journalist without any deeper involvement? But there were still those lies to Geoffrey. I caught
her out again when she claimed to have seen Claude Rains
acting in a film which, according to my fevered researches
later, was made two years after Claude Rains' death. She
was beginning to embroider her visits to the Pasquino
cinema with the nervous over-elaboration which comes
instinctively from guilt. In logic as well as emotion, everything pointed in the same direction.

By the time I met Tardelli face to face, doubt was no
longer possible. I had found out more about him during
my vigils in the Via Foraggi, for the crone continued to be

informative and had consulted fellow crones on points of detail. It was Signora Canto in No. 16 who told her that Tardelli had once been engaged to the daughter of a wealthy businessman and Signorina Battiani in the next street who confirmed that his first name was Pietro. On that most fruitful of grapevines, I learnt that Pietro Tardelli wss thirty-one years old and had come to Rome from Brescia when he was a student; that he had a piano in his apartment and liked fast cars; that he had tried to seduce two women in the street and succeeded with only one (I took comfort from this until his 'failure' was pointed out to me: a brigade of storm-troopers would have found her impregnable); that he kept irregular hours; that he never went to church; that his parents from Brescia had once visited him and smelt strongly of manure ... The crone passed it all on with meticulous relish, like a maiden aunt dispensing chocolates to her favourite nephew. I can't imagine why she thought I wanted to know so much about Tardelli: she probably assumed I was just a gossip like herself, only mobile rather than sedentary, prepared to travel halfway across Rome for some decent tittle-tattle. Or am I underestimating her? Was she a psychologist as well as a repository of information? Did she understand perfectly why I asked about Tardelli with such persistence? Could she see from the lines of pain on my face how I was taking her answers one by one and forging them into a hatred?

For, by any standards, Tardelli was an easy man to hate. When we first shook hands, he looked me up and down with something close to contempt: I might have been a beggar in the street, not a stranger making his acquaintance at a drinks party. The party was given by Brad Newton, an American friend of mine who added Tardelli to the guest-list at my suggestion. I told him Tardelli was a journalist with clout, an urbane, witty man highly regarded in Roman circles: Brad went for that type. Tardelli must have left his wit outside in his Alfa Romeo, or perhaps the crone had exaggerated his accomplishments, for he stood in the corner surveying the scene with an air of bored superiority, like a film star marooned at a party where he doesn't know anyone. He was certainly handsome, with clean, aquiline good looks and a great mane of hair. But it was also rather a cruel face and my first impression was that he wasn't Helen's type. It was wishful thinking at its most absurd – how could I know what her type was except by imagining a monstrous hybrid of Geoffrey and myself? – but the thought took root. How had her taste in men changed so dramatically? When you share something as significant as Tardelli and I had shared, you assume there will be other common denominators; you expect, even in your jealousy, to see qualities in the other person which you can like and identify with. But there was nothing. Tardelli might have arrived at that party from another planet.

'I believe you're a writer, Mr Barham.' The crone was right about his languages: his English was streets better than my Italian. 'Novels, isn't it?'

'That's right.'

'I haven't read any of them, I'm afraid. When you reach thirty, you don't always read as much as you should. Do you find the same thing?'

'Certainly.'

'There's also the question of time. I never seem to get enough.'

'I quite understand.'

Behind my back, my fists clenched. Was it then that my hatred burst the bounds of rationality? No man in his senses would read one of my books when he could be spending the time with a woman like Helen. Yet Tardelli's glib dismissal of my writing opened an unexpected wound, a sensitivity I thought I no longer had. Perhaps when you meet a genuine rival, you feel the need to pull out all the stops: in any event, I retaliated sharply.

'You're from Brescia, aren't you?' I asked.

He hesitated. 'Yes, I am. How did you know?'

'Something about your accent.' To be honest, I couldn't tell a Brescian accent from a doughnut, but metropolitan snobbery is the same the world over. Something told me a Brescian on the make in Rome wouldn't like to be reminded of his provincial origins. How right I was. Tardelli looked uncomfortable for the first time, his years of elocution practice shot to ribbons.

'You must know Italy very well,' he murmured, obviously wishing I didn't know it at all.

'Only quite well. I've been living here eight years.'

'What made you leave England?'

'The weather, basically.' It would have been punchier to say 'The woman you slept with yesterday afternoon,' but I funked it. There's something about taking bulls by the horns which is foreign to my nature: it must be that English reserve, still holding its own a thousand miles from home. I'm cautious. I like having my bulls anaesthetized before I administer the *coup de grâce*. Besides, I took a sick kind of pleasure in sticking pins in Pietro Tardelli.

'I imagine you're a journalist?' I asked smoothly.

'Yes, I am.'

'I thought so. You wear journalist's clothes. That shirt, for instance.'

'What do you mean?'

'No banker or lawyer would wear a shirt like that. It wouldn't look right somehow, don't ask me why. As soon as I saw you on the other side of the room, I thought: ah, a *journalist*, someone who knows what's going on in the world. You're not a sports reporter by any chance, are you?'

'No, no. I mainly cover the political scene.'

'Really? What paper do you write for?'

'I'm freelance.'

'How fascinating. You must be very successful to be freelance. You seem so young.'

'Well, there's a lot of luck involved: you know how it is.'

'Of course, of course.'

I flattered and toadied and Tardelli lapped it up like a dog, but still I could see the riddle of the shirt turning over and over in his head. It was just a plain white shirt, you see, probably the most inconspicuous article of clothing at the entire party. It was expensive, I'm sure: there was a designer's monogram on the cuff and the material was delicate enough to reveal the dark hairs underneath. Tardelli dressed with the easy polish of the Italian middle class, giving my inferiority complex another battering as I kept hitching up my badly fitting trousers and wishing I had ironed my shirt properly. Luckily, the insecurity of people who dress badly is far less acute than the insecurity of people who dress well. The latter may seem more confident, but the confidence is only skin-deep: at heart they are more afraid of failure than the naff dresser could ever be. How Tardelli chafed at the thought that his shirt had betrayed his profession from the other side of the room! And that he had been mistaken for a sports reporter!

Some teasing goes too far and becomes a form of cruelty: you learn that lesson on the school playground. But I never wondered if my baiting of Tardelli was excessive. In the jungle he and I inhabited, none of the normal rules applied. All I wanted was to undermine his complacency and repay the pain he had given me. He had Helen, didn't he? Who could blame me for using the knowledge I had gathered from the crone to cause him some slight twinges of discomfort?

100

I taunted him a bit more, then, when he left the party, followed him out to his car. The play-acting was over. The bull had to be confronted.

'Excuse me. I have to talk to you about something.' How ill suited I was for such a showdown. I sounded like a schoolmaster investigating an unsavoury incident in the showers. 'There's a woman you're seeing . . .'

He nodded, halfway to understanding. 'Are you her husband?'

'Yes.'

'I suppose that's why you've been pestering me all evening?' He tossed his head defiantly, making my hopes of putting him on the defensive seem faintly ridiculous. 'I want nothing to do with you: do you hear? I never argue with husbands about their wives. It's their fault every time, but they're too stupid to see it.'

His arrogance took my breath away and he had driven off into the night before I could think of a retort. Husbands, wives: there was something sickly and excessive about those plurals, like too much sugar in coffee. Yes, it was easy to hate Tardelli. He couldn't have angered me more if I had been Helen's husband.

12

The following night, on my way to the Via Foraggi, I saw a naked woman in a taxi in the Piazza Venezia. She looked about thirty-five and was sitting on the back seat strumming her fingers on her knee; on the seat beside her sat a small Dalmatian with a red collar round its neck. It was like a bold surrealist painting, for the woman didn't cringe from view, the way you or I do on the odd occasion when we find ourselves in a taxi with no clothes on, but sat bolt upright as if nothing was wrong. And apart from the lack of clothes, nothing *was* wrong. The woman's hair was immaculately arranged and she was wearing an obviously expensive pair of earrings; there was even a gold lamé handbag on the seat between her and the dog. You would have thought she was returning from the opera if Italian opera houses weren't so sniffy about nudity in the stalls. Only the impatient way she shouted at the driver to hurry when the lights turned green gave any indication that it wasn't a normal taxi ride.

When I thought about the incident later, I wondered if I'd been hallucinating. But there really was a naked woman in a taxi in the Piazza Venezia that night. It turned out that she *had* been to the opera, fully clothed, and had returned home to find her husband in bed with another woman. This made her (i) threaten to walk out on him, (ii) pick up the dog and say there, there, wasn't his master a wicked, wicked man and (iii) tear off all her clothes, screaming that she might be ten years older than the other woman but she had one hell of a sight better body. The husband, diplomatically (I believe he was a stockbroker), suggested that, as far as the two women's bodies were concerned, it was six of one and half a dozen of the other – but couldn't she at least put the dog down and behave like a grown-up human being? This left her with no option but to carry out her original threat: with dog but without clothes, she stormed out of the house. The dog's name was Rocco, by the way, and the opera was *I Vespri Siciliani*. It all appeared in black and white in the Italian equivalent of the *News of the World*. Oh yes, and the earrings came from Bulgari's.

Later I derived some comfort from that absurd story: from the knowledge that, on the very night when my own jealousy exploded, someone else had gone berserk and done something totally out of kilter with their normal character. The most terrible thing about jealousy is the way it excludes all other emotions, all awareness of that soothing everyday world in which life passes much more slowly. I did notice the woman in the taxi because it was hard to miss her; but I absorbed nothing else of my surroundings during that mile-long walk to the Via Foraggi. I moved like a zombie or a man walking in his sleep: it was eerie. Normally people who love Rome love her visible face more than all the treasures she hides away in museums and churches. They love the soaring architecture and the dancing fountains, the explosions of colour in the great squares and the light falling softly on old walls in the quiet backstreets. They love the sensation of walking where they've walked many times before and discovering fresh glories in a hidden courtyard or an unnoticed gargoyle. The roads leading to the Via Foraggi were the sort of streets I might have wandered down on a midnight stroll, seeking only a contemplative satisfaction, the sense of communion with a great city. But this wasn't that sort of walk. It was midnight, but there the comparison ends. I don't know that it makes any difference, but I didn't *enjoy* killing Pietro Tardelli.

My planning was haphazard, almost non-existent. I once wrote one of those thrillers in which a thriller-writer wanted to kill someone and, because he was a thriller-writer, tried to commit the perfect murder, without making any of the silly mistakes which gave his own villains away . . . except, of course, that he *did* make a silly mistake, because he was fallible and the only people allowed to be infallible in such books are the great British police – you know the sort of rubbish. Now the naïveté of those assumptions was plain: why *should* a writer be able to approach murder in that detached way, just because he happens to have written about other people's murders in his books? A writer's pain is as real as the next man's. His jealousy stems from the same roots, his hatred follows the same pattern, his madness, if he is mad, drives him screaming down the same dead-end alley. I chose midnight because it seemed sensible to do it when the crone was not at her post, but I took no other precautions. I bought a knife at a shop *where I was known by name* and I wore a pair of electric blue trousers which must have stood out in the dark like cat's eyes. I suppose you could say I was trusting in fate. Yes, I was mad all right.

Or was I? If what I was doing was wrong, an insane moral aberration, why did fate take my side so solicitously? The joker hidden in the shadows, the unseen figure who throws banana-skins in my path and laughs as I fall over them, was conspicuously absent. Did He hate Tardelli too? Did He share the view which in my jealous ravings I had crystallized: that Tardelli *deserved* death? They say – and they say it in Rome more than anywhere – that a God made us, a God who loved us so much that he gave his only son . . . Yet such a God would have loved Tardelli too, poor wretch that he was – and been with him in his hour of need. Why did all the luck that was going that night go solely and exclusively to *me*?

For I was lucky. Tardelli could easily have had visitors: not Helen, whom I had just watched returning home from another 'film', but someone else. He hadn't seemed the sort of man who lacked for company. Suppose he'd been sitting up chatting with a neighbour, something Italians do far more routinely than Englishmen: what excuse would I have given for my appearance at that late hour? Would I have been able to keep up a polite conversation with that cold knife pressed against the back of my leg and hatred blazing in my heart?

I was lucky he let me in at all. When he peered down from his second-floor window and, with a little grunt, identified who I was, it was all Rome to a hundred-*lire* note that he would slam the shutters and want nothing to do with me. Instead he did the unthinkable, the thing he said he never did with jealous husbands: he engaged me in conversation.

'What do you want?'

'I'd like to talk to you.'

'What about?'

'A private matter. I'm not going to shout.'

'You'd better come up.'

He pressed the entryphone button and I ascended to the second floor in one of those old-fashioned cage lifts with a cruising speed of one mile an hour. As I crawled past the first floor, a door opened and a white-haired old woman came out. She was only feet away but (luck, still luck, the Devil's luck), at the moment my face became visible, she was bending over to pick something up from the floor. By the time she raised her head, she would have seen only my feet.

I was lucky, too, that Tardelli was such a vain man. Often people you dislike intensely the first time improve on further acquaintance; or they become more relaxed, more amenable, in the security of their own home. As you look around and see the context of their lives more clearly – the chairs they sit in, the paintings they hang on the walls, the records they listen to, the books they leave open on the table – they become more rounded in their humanity and thus more acceptable. I was prepared, even at that late stage, to find Tardelli likeable. But he made it hard, God, he made it hard. He smiled contemptuously, as if he didn't know what my business was but looked forward to some amusement at my expense, then made me sit down in a chair while he leant against the mantelpiece preening himself on his nonchalance. The blood surged to my head and I thought: yes, it may be worse to kill a man than cuckold him, but at least I won't smile at my victim like that, at least I won't gloat . . . And the little tic of guilt that might, even then, have ambushed me and stopped me in my tracks, never came.

I suppose I was also lucky I was English. Tardelli didn't *expect* me to turn violent. From what he said, he'd faced this sort of situation before and survived it; he had the macho arrogance of a nineteenth-century rake with a score of successful duels under his belt. But with me his confidence wasn't rooted in physical strength. If he was confident, it was because he assumed I was a member of an anaemic race, someone who would whine and shout a bit but nothing more. I was bland, moribund, excessively polite. I wasn't *dangerous*, even at midnight. As we talked on – I don't remember a single word of that conversation, but I assume its theme was love and the betrayal of love – his security grew fatter and fatter on my Englishness. Do you think, if I'd come from Genoa or Palermo, he would ever have turned his back on me so confidently as he closed the shutters of the windows?

And, of course, I was lucky the windows *had* shutters. If there had only been curtains, I might have been visible from the other side of the street as I plunged my knife into his back. Someone might have heard his low grunt of pain or the crash as his body fell to the floor, rattling a glass ashtray on the table. I was lucky the knife did all its damage with one blow, for I plunged it in with more passion than science and wouldn't have had the nerve to pull it out and stab him again. And I was *incredibly* lucky that there was so little blood. He was a great bull of a man, but by the time I had checked his pulse, eased the knife out and stepped back from the body, only my hands were bloodied. I washed them in his kitchen sink, made a peremptory search for fingerprints and inspected myself in the mirror on the way out. It wasn't a murderer's face: in that brief moment of triumph it had the serenity of someone who had won a dead love back.

Luckily the old woman on the first floor was no longer to be seen. Luckily the street outside was deserted. Luckily there was a cloud passing over the moon as I retraced my steps to the Piazza Venezia. At the foot of the steps leading down from the Campidoglio, I ran straight into a police car: luckily, luckily for the last time, the policeman was slumped over the wheel asleep. Whatever avenging angel came with me the night I murdered Pietro Tardelli, he must have loved me with all his heart.

Part Two

1

Even then, Helen showed not a flicker of emotion. What a madman I must have been to think she would, for hadn't her self-control always been remarkable, even in the days when we were in love? She was, I think, the most aloof woman I ever knew: not in that ghastly, snotty English way, but with a dignity and grace that made you want to peer through the mask, not tear it off altogether.

I say our love was a special love and, when I say that, I embrace her feelings as well as mine. I believe that for a few short months I was *the* man in her life, the one she loved more than all the others, just as for me she eclipsed all other women, then and now, here and always. But my belief in my special place rested on quite fragile premises: the tiniest gestures, the simplest words, the briefest moments (and not just in bed) when she abandoned restraint and gave herself to me totally. A sudden generosity of feeling would surge through her, an impulse to give without counting the cost, an almost reckless surrender to the moment, and she would come alive as most people are never alive. It was because they were out of character that I trusted those moments so much. A woman who'd dealt in hyperbole and exaggerated gestures of affection could never have carried the same conviction.

She gave a clue in Trastevere when she said she was frightened of her emotions, frightened to break off the relationship in a face-to-face meeting because she wouldn't be able to go through with it. Perhaps if she hadn't fought emotion so determinedly, she would have gone mad herself, so there may have been a kind of wisdom in that dour, unrelenting struggle. But it certainly made life hard for me. Of all the people I've known well, she was the one I least understood. I was always several moves behind her. I never knew where I stood with her at a given moment. Long after the little trickle of signs of her love had dried up, I still imagined her repressing similar emotions, simply because the absence of outward emotion had meant so little in the past. In her enigmatic poise, she testified to the old axiom that you can't prove a negative: nothing was visible, but that didn't mean there was nothing underneath.

When I saw her next, two days after the murder, she was almost infuriatingly calm. I don't think I realized till then how much she, not Tardelli, had been the object of my hatred. I wanted her to suffer and she wasn't suffering, not visibly: I was cheated of that perverse excitement. And yet she knew of Tardelli's death, for she had been to the Via Foraggi that afternoon. I had followed her most of the way there, then retreated for fear of being noticed. What kind of woman could recover from such a shock so quickly? I thought I had loved her for her inner strength, that marvellous capacity she had for not succumbing to pressure, for being her own woman even when other people – and I was too often one of them – wanted her to be something different. But was this sangfroid really the same as strength? Perversely, I felt sorry for Tardelli for the first time. That he should be mourned so little . . .

'Is there nothing on at the cinema tonight?' I asked. We were with a small group of actors waiting in the dining-room, while Act Three was in rehearsal next door.

'No, I don't think so.'

'You seem to have been a lot lately: you never used to be so keen.'

'No, I suppose I wasn't.' She looked at me and I thought

112

for a moment I had rattled her. A flicker of confusion showed in her eyes, but it was only slight and the moment passed. I blame Shakespeare partly. If he'd found something for Perdita to do in Act Three of *The Winter's Tale*, Vanessa wouldn't have been at my elbow listening. She drew the obvious inference from our exchange.

'Have you two known each other a long time? I didn't realize.'

'London,' I murmured. 'Eight years ago.' I sounded like an old cricket buffer trying to remember when he first saw Bradman bat.

'How fascinating. Did you meet again in Rome just by chance? Isn't life strange the way it throws people together, then throws them apart, then throws them together again?'

Helen said: 'You can never escape the past,' and I said: 'The past belongs to the present.' Vanessa probably thought we were saying the same thing.

'That's right,' she said quickly. 'We try to divide our lives into separate compartments but the compartments aren't separate, are they? Everything belongs to the same indivisible whole. It's like one enormous – '

'Quietly, sweetie. Geoffrey doesn't want too much chatter.' Shakespeare hadn't put Polixenes in Act Three either. Vanessa's father was keeping his usual gloomy watch on proceedings.

'I'm *not* chattering, Daddy.'

'You're getting a little shrill, sweetie.'

'I'm *not* getting shrill!'

'Whatever you say, sweetie.'

Vanessa resumed her thesis and Helen and I exchanged glances. It was perhaps only a coincidence of timing, but there was a rapidity in the way our eyes met which, if not the same as tenderness, thrilled almost as much as tenderness. If we'd been alone – and how often that phrase has

113

come to my lips – we might have been able to build on the moment, for a perfectly shared thought is too intimate to be renounced. But we weren't alone. There wasn't just Vanessa and her father, but Walter, a young American called Al who was playing Florizel, and a ragged assortment of bit-part players. Shakespeare may have written some cracking stuff in Act Three but, if he was that hot shit, shouldn't he have spared a thought for the overcrowding in the dressing-room?

At this point Geoffrey thundered in. 'Where's that fucking French shit-shoveller?' This referred to Philippe, a neighbouring alcoholic whom he had bullied into playing Servant, a footling three-line part which severely taxed his abilities. 'Shit-shoveller' because he was an internationally distinguished archaeologist; 'French' because he was Belgian; 'fucking' because he was foreign and couldn't get his tongue round Elizabethan English. We looked at each other blankly.

'I want him on stage *now*. This is Shakespeare: it isn't a game of croquet. Have you seen him, Mark?'

'No, Geoffrey.'

'Helen?'

'Sorry, darling.'

'Bugger this. I've warned him, you know, I've warned him.' He stormed off down the corridor and rattled the bathroom door: when he found it locked, he kicked it in like a storm-trooper. Philippe was slumped over the bath, an empty wine-bottle clutched in his hand. Geoffrey yanked him to his feet and slapped him hard in the face.

'Wake up, you stupid pisshead, wake up!'

'I'm sho shorry, Geoffrey, I – '

'I'll give you sorry, you drunken French clown. Do you realize you've just fucked up one of the great moments in the play? This isn't bloody Molière or bloody Corneille or

114

bloody arty-farty Racine: the actors can't sit around scratching their arses for three hours because there's nothing happening. Shakespeare means drama which means action which means pace which means, if you're not on that stage in three seconds, you're a dead man. Come on, damn you!'

We watched hypnotized as Philippe was dragged on stage, propped against a chair and made to stumble through what he remembered of his lines; at the end of the scene Geoffrey flung him senseless into a corner and screamed that the next person he caught drinking while rehearsals were in progress would be flung in the Tiber. Nobody said anything, nobody even looked shocked. The boundaries of normal behaviour were being continuously redrawn.

After that Helen kept her distance meticulously: perhaps my enquiries about her visits to the cinema had scared her off, though she had been steering clear of me anyway after my bitter outbursts the previous week. I felt impotent and frustrated, then hope took root once again – what an opportunist love is. How is it, the demon in me asked, that she can take his death in her stride so easily? If it had really been love that took her to the Via Foraggi, she wouldn't be sitting there covered in smiles, playing the gracious hostess to Geoffrey's rotten actors: she would be avoiding everyone's eye, terrified to show the anguish within. The calmness that had seemed so chilling suddenly became a source of comfort. Tardelli hadn't mattered. He belonged to history, as I belonged to history – the only difference being I was still alive.

The next morning I went back to the Via Foraggi. A terrible thought had struck me in the night. Suppose Tardelli's body hadn't even been discovered? Suppose he had just been lying there rotting for three days? Helen would simply have rung the bell and gone away when he didn't answer. Wouldn't that explain her complete absence of shock?

The crone quickly set my fears at rest. Her eyes lit up when she saw me and she beckoned me into her house. Had I *heard*? No, I said, I hadn't heard. So she told me. It was as if all her life had been preparing her for that moment. Before she had fed me only crumbs of gossip: now she had a story worthy of her art.

It was Signor Tardelli, she said. Not, I said, Signor Tardelli in No. 76, the journalist with five languages? *Si*, she said, that Signor Tardelli, the one we had talked about so much. What had happened to Signor Tardelli? I asked. *Morto*, she said. What, I said, *morto*? *Si*, she said, *morto, finalmente morto*. That means two men *morto* in No. 76 in six months, Signor Tardelli and Signor Giorgini – did I remember him? – who had collapsed on his way to the tobacconist's. And Signor Tardelli, I said: was he also on his way to the tobacconist's? No, no, no, she said, something far worse, *molto più terribile*. Not cancer, I said. No, she said, not cancer: *assassinato*. *Scusi*, I said, had she said *assassinato*? *Si*, she repeated, in a macabre stage-whisper, *assassinato*. And she drew back her arm and made a stabbing gesture so vivid she might have been standing behind me when I did it. I blanched and had to lean against a chair. I felt revulsion for the first time.

She sat me down, poured me a glass of wine from a dusty, unlabelled bottle, then started making sympathetic clucking noises as if I were a bereaved relative. Tardelli was a good man, she said, a really good man: if she'd ever spoken ill of him, she didn't mean a word of it. At which she made a superstitious sign of the cross: an act of contrition, I suppose a Catholic would have called it. What a simple religion, I thought: you bad-mouth people when they're alive and say *ave Marias* when they're dead. Could I exorcize my own guilt that easily? I looked at all the religious bric-à-brac strewed around the room – the little crucifix over the mantelpiece, the candlelit icon in the corner, the porcelain Virgin standing on the radio, the rosary beads half hidden by an unironed skirt – and felt a stranger in a world to which I could never belong.

I asked who had killed Tardelli and she shrugged. Nobody knew, she said. Tuesday night he had been alive and Wednesday morning . . . she made another macabre gesture of death. Signora Giorgini, the woman on the floor below who had lost her husband six months before when he collapsed on the way to the tobacconist's and had now turned very religious, God help her, had noticed something wrong because Signor Tardelli's telephone kept ringing and ringing, even though he hadn't left for work because his car was still parked outside. There was also this awful smell . . . So she had fetched the police, who had broken down the door in the afternoon and there was poor Signor Tardelli, lying –

I nodded quickly. This Signora Giorgini, was she a short woman with white hair? Yes, I was told, Signora Giorgini was not very tall. Her husband was an enormous man, so they had made a strange-looking couple. As for her hair, it had turned white within six weeks of her husband's death, which went to show, didn't it? I nodded again. So it was Signora Giorgini who nearly saw me in the lift. I wondered if she'd registered that Tardelli had a visitor.

Talking of Signora Giorgini, the crone went on – I was used to her absurd *non sequiturs* by now – did I realize there was another English person who was often in the neighbourhood? Oh, I said, really? Yes, she said, her voice dropping in disapproval, there was a young woman of about thirty-five who had been a regular visitor at No. 76. She could tell me a *lot* about her if I was interested.

I shuddered, my whole body rocked with jealousy. Interested? I was riveted. But how could I show that interest to a stranger? How could I ask her this and ask her that and let her see my agony at her answers? Some pain is too personal, too private: you have to keep it buried like a secret treasure or it will explode. And hadn't I had my explosion already? So I just laughed and said they must be getting sick and tired of Englishmen in the Via Foraggi. Not at all, said the crone, not at all: I was welcome any time. And she pressed a plum into my hand to show that she meant it.

Outside No. 76, a team of removal men was lifting a piano into the back of a van while a young woman in black – Tardelli's sister, from the face – directed operations. I stopped to watch. Italian workmen never mind you watching them work, indeed they sometimes feel neglected if you don't. The piano was heaved into place, then a table was winched down from the window, followed by an enormous gilt mirror. I felt slightly disgusted. The man had only been dead three days and already his flat was being stripped and his possessions redistributed to his relatives. I winced as one of the men struck a match on the back of the mirror and the woman glanced in it to adjust her hair. In England the rites of passage are marked with greater respect, I thought. We may be hypocrites, but we're not vulgar . . .

Then at last, like an artery bursting in my head, the enormity of my position came home to me. I had spent the time since the murder in a strange, guilt-induced trance, not daring to look back at the Rubicon I had crossed. But even a lover's capacity for self-deception is limited. The truth suddenly ambushed me like a mugger in a darkened alley. I was not a foreign visitor observing a scene from

118

Italian street life. I was not an outsider, looking on while poor Signor Tardelli's piano was taken away. I was not above these events I found so distasteful. I was their cause, the only cause. Wasn't it my hand which had held the knife which had killed the man who had preened himself in that mirror? I felt exposed, like a naked child. Whatever my own pain, I had taken something which wasn't mine to take: now there was no retreat, no escape, nowhere to hide. Overcome with terror, the terror I hadn't experienced on the night of the murder, I fled breathlessly from the scene.

2

'Suddenly she tripped and fell to the ground. Her knee gashed and she let out a low grunt of pain. The rain streamed down relentlessly, soaking through her thin dress and sending cold shivers down her body. It was one in the morning, no time to be alone . . .'

In the Piazza Navona my pen raced across the page as if I was finishing an exam paper. The lethargy of the past week was gone. In its place came a feverish energy, an intellectual overdrive in which there was no time for pause or reflection. I don't know if I wrote well or badly: I just wrote as fast as a man can write, knowing that, if I stopped, I would be staring at a dead man's face.

Bathurst noted my activity with alarm.

'Publisher's deadline?' he asked as he sauntered home to lunch, his own morning's work completed.

'No.'

'Just feeling prolific?'

'Yes.'

'Good for you.' He pulled up a chair and asked the waiter for a Perrier water. There is something monumentally mean about Bathurst. It causes him such pain that I'm a third-rate writer, while he's only fourth-rate, that he goes out of his way to spite me. As for a third-rate writer feeling prolific, why, that might be almost as good as a second-rate writer, a far more dangerous animal. God knows how he would behave if I actually was a second-rate writer, let alone a second-rate writer feeling prolific, let alone . . . I wonder how the Bard dealt with the Bathursts in his life.

He watched mesmerized as I turned the page and carried on writing, line after line of tired similes and trite aphorisms. 'You know,' he began, the envy sticking in his throat, 'you know, it's good to see you beavering away like this. You've been looking a bit under the weather lately.'

'You're very observant,' I muttered, not looking up. '*It was a dark night, so dark Sheila could hardly see the outlines of the houses across the street.*'

'I'm sorry, perhaps you think I'm prying?'

'Not at all.' '*Alone, frightened, she remembered Nigel and wished she was holding on to his strong, tensile body.*'

'One does tend to notice these things. After all, here we are, you and I, carrying the flag for English literature in Rome. It engenders a certain comradeship, don't you think?'

'Absolutely.' '*What an incredible night's love-making that had been: like waves crashing on the sea shore.*'

My Biro ran out. Immediately I replaced it with another and swept on. I could sense Bathurst lapsing into a state of shock. Just for fun, I scribbled down 'The quick brown fox jumps over the lazy dog' ten times in succession, pausing for a milli-second before the fifth 'fox', then rushing on with a little grunt of triumph as the *mot juste* came to me. If people really want to hate me, I believe in making their job as easy as possible. What a pity it doesn't work with love.

Bathurst got the message, downed his Perrier and left. My writing slowed from a gallop to a canter, then from a canter to a trot. I even paused for a few seconds and looked around me. It was only ten-thirty, but the piazza was already crowded. Around the great central fountain people were milling two or three deep, trying to get a proper view of Bernini's extravagant stone figures. To the left, a crowd had gathered around a street artist who was sketching a red-headed girl in a T-shirt. On the other side I noticed a

121

tall man with a great mane of hair, staring in my direction. Tardelli, I thought. No, not Tardelli: someone looking like Tardelli. As I studied him more closely, the resemblance to Tardelli got slighter and slighter; but the slighter the resemblance, the deeper my sense of panic. If I was going to see Tardelli's face in faces as unlike Tardelli's as that, where was it going to end?

Hurriedly I resumed my writing, battling against a rising tide of emotion. It was like trying to write in the face of Helen, systematically suppressing the thoughts she inspired – except that I wanted to think about Helen and I never wanted to think about Tardelli again. But still he kept coming, his eyes boring through me like gimlets, his smug, arrogant face dancing in and out of my head – only it wasn't smug or arrogant any more. In death or, rather, in the ghostly half-life it now assumed, it was a gentle, rather wise face in which the smugness and arrogance were practically invisible, so much so that I wondered if they had existed at all. Had I killed, not just a man, but a good man? Or was that a retrospective adjustment, like the crone made when she tried to retract all the bad things she'd said about Tardelli with a sign of the cross? What sign of the cross could absolve me?

In my own books, murderers rarely experience guilt. They worry about being found out, of course, and they sometimes become introspective and melancholy for a few chapters so that the blood and violence can be spread evenly throughout the book. But I never let them feel anguish. If they felt anguish, then the hero would also have to feel anguish when he caught up with them and the heroine would have to feel extreme anguish that there was so much anguish going on around her: that's far too much anguish for a two-pound-fifty pot-boiler. It's not that I believe murderers don't go through inner torment: it's just simpler if they can gouge someone's eyes out, then knock back a gin and tonic without remorse. That way, the reader gets a general feel for which characters he's meant to like and which he isn't – and that's important. Mark Barham fans inhabit a very simple world, you see, which is why there are so few with an IQ in double figures. Good writers can project themselves into situations unprecedented in their own experience: bad writers keep finding themselves in situations without precedent in their books. I had come unprepared to the role of a guilt-stricken murderer.

Wrong-doing itself, of course, and the remorse associated with it, I was familiar with. My pursuit of Helen may seem ruthless in its exclusion of finer feelings and I sometimes wonder at my own callousness. But the callousness isn't impenetrable. I think myself tough-skinned and then meet people so much more tough-skinned that I start worrying I'm a haemophiliac. Through all that coldness and dispassion, shafts of normal human decency still manage to pierce.

Once, I remember, and only once, I hit Helen. Ironically, it was in the middle of the most trivial of our quarrels. She said Darlington was in Yorkshire and I said it was in Durham and, as we were on a boat on the Serpentine without access to a map, we were reduced to violent assertion and counter-assertion. Impotent to prove my case, I lost my temper and kicked her, not very hard, on the shin. Luck wasn't always on my side in those days, for her shin was already bruised from some other occasion and she let out a gasp of pain so sharp you would have thought I had stabbed her. But her pain was trivial to mine. I'm not a macho lover. I don't believe in the subjugation of the female by the male. I don't think physical dominance is the force that moves the sun and the stars. In the giving and receiving of pain, I found only a grotesque reversal of the ordinary exchanges of love. The hurtful things lovers say aren't so purely destructive because, when they are said, they have a strategic point: an intention, conscious or not, misguided or not, to restore the emotional balance on which love rests. Physical violence has no such justification, no such intent: it is the tip of an ugly iceberg, the instinct to destroy what one cannot possess. When I suddenly glimpsed the iceberg in myself, I recoiled in horror and my tears followed quickly on hers. Like a sick fool, I said 'It *is* in Yorkshire, it *is* in Yorkshire', over and over again until the pain went – even though my aunt had lived in Darlington for twenty years and I would have sworn then, and still would, that it was in Durham.

At other times too with Helen, there was remorse. How could there not be? Just because a man is demanding, just because he won't take no for an answer, it doesn't mean he believes he is worthy of what he demands or that the answer ought to be yes. At the moments of greatest fragility in our affair, when it seemed most obvious that it wasn't a love of unlimited scope but something which had a beginning, middle and end, my chafing at the impermanence of the relationship had a bitterness which it took all her sweetness to dilute. And then that very imbalance, between my bitterness and her sweetness, led inexorably to remorse, remorse which is at the very heart of an imperfect love. It undermines hope and elation and drains away confidence. It focuses the imagination on what might have been if X hadn't happened and Y hadn't been said and Z had been properly understood. It saps more positive emotions of their energy. In the end it destroys love. Yes, I knew about remorse. It was the emotional nursery in which I grew up – and in which I remained a child.

But this Tardelli thing was different. Its onset was slower, but it was more inexorable. There is a distinction, obvious even to lovers in an advanced state of madness, between a kick on the shin and a fatal blow to the heart. I couldn't placate Tardelli by swearing that Darlington was in Yorkshire: I couldn't placate him at all. But now that he was no longer a threat, I *wanted* to placate him. He had had his fling with Helen, just like me, and it was sad that that community of experience no longer existed. I even regretted – what sane man's mind performs these somersaults? – that such a vital source of intelligence about Helen had dried up. I knew what she wanted in 1977, what turned her on then; but it was Tardelli who knew what turned her on in 1985, who could have updated my information, who could have put me back on the right path. In my desperate bid to revive a dead love, I had thought of him as an obstacle. Had I got it all wrong? Should I have made him an ally?

On the other side of the piazza, I suddenly noticed a policeman standing with his hands in his pockets, smoking a cigarette. It couldn't happen in London, of course, but then neither could the Trevi Fountain or the ceiling of the Sistine Chapel or the pâtisseries on the Via Condotti. The policeman's casual stance probably meant he was off duty but, when you have something to hide, every policeman you see is on duty and out to get you. Instead of remorse, I felt apprehension. I buried myself in my writing and started to sweat. How much longer could my luck last?

The policeman finished his cigarette, took his hands out of his pockets and strolled off. After five minutes I did the same. *The Nuclear Winter* had run out of inspiration and, even excluding the ten quick brown foxes jumping over the ten lazy dogs, I had easily passed my twelve hundred words. On the way home I saw another policeman and then a third, only two hundred yards from my house. He wasn't smoking, his hands weren't in his pockets and there was a gun in the holster around his waist. I felt a great wave of nausea. In London, they say you know you're getting old when policemen look young: in Rome there are so few policemen that, if you notice three in one morning, it means you've committed a serious crime. Never mind that, in my case, it was also a perfect crime: no eyewitnesses and a motive so rooted in ancient history it would take a team of archaeologists to unearth. What mattered was this terrible remorse, sometimes just a nagging throb, at other times so strong it swamped all other emotions. I made my way shakily up the stairs to my flat and locked the door behind me. It was a shock, in the circumstances, to find Vanessa lying on the sofa reading one of my books.

3

'It's you,' she said, starting on an uncontroversial note. When I didn't take issue with the description, she tried to build on the feeling of consensus. 'It's me.'

I said: 'Hullo, Vanessa,' and thought: why couldn't Tardelli have killed *me*? It would have made things so much easier.

She kicked off her shoes in token of better things to come and brandished a battered paperback in the air. 'I've been reading *The Positive Hour* again. You know, it's really awfully good, Mark. That scene with the broken mirror, for example: I don't know how you think of things like that. How old were you when you wrote it?'

'Twenty-nine. No, twenty-eight. Twenty-nine when it was published.'

'That's amazing, just amazing. If I wrote something like this when I was twenty-eight, it would go to my head completely. Why didn't it go to your head?'

'It did go to my head. It just took a rather perverted form when it got there.'

'What do you mean?'

'I was so determined not to be a vulgar success that I rubbished everything I'd ever written, even the good stuff. Then I started writing rubbish. It served me right.'

'How fascinating. A sort of inverted snobbery?'

'If you like. Look, must we?' She was fishing in her bag for the dreaded tape-recorder. I wasn't in the mood, which is like saying that a man with two broken legs wasn't in the mood to run the marathon. I could no more have discussed the literary decline of Mark Barham than danced with a python.

'I'm sorry. You're not in the mood, are you?' There is something pitiless about insensitive people. When they finally grasp something which should have been obvious earlier, they state it with terrible baldness, as if accusing *you* of insensitivity in not making yourself clearer.

'Not really,' I said. 'No.' I lay down next to her on the sofa and she started running her hands gently through my hair, the way Helen had done. I'm not sure there's an art to running your hands through people's hair, or that it's something some people do well and others badly: in the repertory of physical affection it must be one of the most rudimentary skills. But I soon became so conscious that the hands running through my hair were the *wrong* hands, different from Helen's in a thousand indefinable ways, that I had to ask her to stop. She asked if she was hurting me and I said, no, she wasn't hurting me and then she said, with the same accusing clarity: 'You're not well, are you?'

'No, I'm not.'

'What's wrong, Mark?'

'I'm not sure.'

'Is your head aching?'

'Not particularly.'

'Have you eaten anything funny?'

'I don't think so.'

'Perhaps you're just tired.'

'Maybe.'

'Poor Mark.' She patted my hand vaguely, thwarted in her efforts at diagnosis. A sick dog could have described his symptoms better – but how do you describe the pain of loving a woman alive in all but her love of you? Or the anguish of killing a man in the hope of making things better, then realizing they're a hundred times worse? Or the misery of not knowing whether you're sick or mad or just very much in love – and what difference it makes?

After that, for want of anything better, we made love. Sex is more complicated than running your hands through someone's hair: it is an art, it is something you can do well or badly, and this time we did it so badly it hurt. Simultaneously we muttered: 'I'm sorry – that was awful', and the simultaneity was worse than the awfulness, for again it reminded me of Helen and the days when the simultaneous exclamations were not of disappointment, but joy. Before that moment, I had thought my dislike of Vanessa was only superficial, a reaction against her being second best. I had imagined a scale of being, with Helen at one end and Tardelli at the other and everyone else – Geoffrey, Bathurst, Vanessa, the news-vendor in the Piazza Venezia – clustered vaguely in the middle. Now I realized the truth was more sinister. *Everyone* who wasn't Helen I was destined, in some degree, to hate. Loving one person is supposed to be the key to loving everybody, but in me the love was still-born and had the reverse effect. Tardelli had got the knife, but it could easily have been someone else, could still be someone else. I lay on the bed next to Vanessa and wondered if she realized how closely she was consorting with evil.

Yet it had not always been so. Now that the clouds are massing above me, it seems a long time since I played, free and unconfined, in the sunlight. But I too was one of the innocent. As an infant I was so cherubic that my parents had to look very closely to see the taint of original sin.

Not that the sin was slow in coming. I said 'fuck' for the first time when I was two and I can only have been six when I was severely admonished after an incident in the school playground. Then came the little lies, then the medium lies, then the lies so big I've never dared tell anyone the truth. At the same time there developed a quick temper, a tendency to vanity, a suspicion of authority in any form. I won prizes at school for writing fey stories about small animals, but I wasn't one of those children who brought out the sentimentality in adults. Nor did I inspire great affection among my contemporaries: I was a solitary spirit, accepted rather than popular. It was Dave Moxon in 5B who had all the girls hanging round for him after school. I think he's in the BBC now.

But all this is small beer. Nothing in my childhood can explain the stabbing of Pietro Tardelli in the Via Foraggi. Until I met Helen, I was only a normally flawed human being: a little worse than average in some respects, a little better in others; not much in it either way. I suppose it was indicative that I was reduced to writing about life rather than living it, but that's a quibble. People who are really screwed up don't write: they act or go into politics. Until I met Helen – that phrase again, resounding through my history like a bell, for my life has a single watershed – there wasn't a wrinkle in my character which couldn't have been smoothed out by that great panacea, a good woman's love. We *were* innocent then – both of us, not just Helen.

And our love was innocent too. Some people reserve that word for children holding hands in the dark or teenagers trembling on the threshold of lost virginity: they would find it an odd way to dignify an affair between a married woman and a thirty-year-old bachelor about town. But I must insist on the terminology. When I say we loved innocently, I mean only that we were innocent of tomorrow and yesterday, innocent of other people's opinions, innocent of complexities, innocent of hatred, innocent of fear, innocent of everything which wasn't bound up with our love for each other. We scorned to live in the real world, but we created a world more real than the real world could ever be. And

130

to the little voice in me that whispers, 'It can't have been that good', I have to keep saying: 'Yes, it was that good. If it hadn't been that good, I wouldn't cling to those few sweet months as if they were all I had to savour for the rest of my life. If it hadn't been that good . . .' In my calmer moods I would dearly love to deconstruct the myth, to convince myself by the sour force of reason that none of it was as special as I remember. But it was special. Either that or I am psychologically incapable of destroying sacred things – and how could such a man contemplate murder? Unless he was mad, of course, which is where we came in.

There is a vice, much chastised by moralists of a certain type, known as 'living in the past'. Forward, they say, forward: look to the future, think positive. As someone who wasted eight of the best years of his life crying over spilt milk, I suppose I must plead guilty. But what the moralist doesn't understand – he never does, that's why he's a moralist, that's why nobody wants to talk to him at parties – is that the past is something far richer than a catalogue of precedents for the future. I can look out across Rome now and, instead of the familiar rooftops, see Helen's face as we sat in a restaurant in June 1977 and she told me what a lovely smile I had. Or I can feel the soft flesh between her shoulder-blades where I so often clutched her as we made love. I think I can even smell the white leather sandals she used to wear. What would a moralist understand of those memories? Yet they sometimes seem my only comfort in the gathering darkness. I almost think I could come to terms with the hatred in myself if I could remember even more clearly what love felt like.

4

It was no consolation, but Geoffrey's madness was also getting out of control. As the first night of *The Winter's Tale* approached, his impatience with his actors got steadily worse. There was no quarter given to late-comers, no pity for anyone who forgot their lines, nothing but rage for people treating the whole production as a joke. Not that anyone dared treat it as a joke: Geoffrey's earnestness was far too fierce to be argued with. But from time to time a natural human levity would burst through, an insistence that even bringing Shakespeare to the Romans – *particularly* bringing Shakespeare to the Romans, although you could never say that – had its funny side.

And how funny that funny side was. In that blackest week of my life, those rehearsals were the only thing that made me laugh. I wish someone could have explained the joke to Geoffrey, just as I wish someone could have explained to me why it was so laughable to treat Helen Danes like a goddess. We always see the best joke too late.

My Camillo came in for its fair share of stick. It wasn't a great Camillo: I can say that without fear of contradiction. It wasn't even a good Camillo or a middling Camillo or a Camillo which flattered to deceive. It was a bloody awful Camillo, its awfulness obscured by the fact that there was a bloody awful Leontes, a bloody awful Hermione, a bloody awful Polixenes and a Paulina so awful that blood imagery is inadequate. As Camillo, I supplemented lack of talent and experience with total lack of effort. At first I had exerted myself and poured about ten per cent of my emotional energy into the part: this gradually reduced to five per cent and, after Tardelli's murder, hovered between nought and one per cent like a dying man's pulse. I suppose Geoffrey's exasperation was understandable.

'Try to sound as if you *meant* it,' he would say. 'Shakespeare made Camillo a good man, a concerned man. You sound as if you don't give a damn.'

'I'm sorry, Geoffrey. I'm finding this speech a bit awkward.'

'What do you mean, awkward? It's you that's awkward. Are you saying Shakespeare didn't know how to write?'

'Of course not, Geoffrey.'

'Well, get on with it then. And more *feeling*.'

He bludgeoned and bludgeoned, but the feeling never came, not from me, not from anyone. His cast were afraid of him, so it was a well-drilled production, free of the worst incompetences of amateur drama, but he couldn't breathe his own love of Shakespeare into it or make the actors perform miracles because they loved him as director. I saw a man raging at his impotence to bring his love to fruition and I saw myself in a mirror. What an ugly face it was.

An extra strain had emerged by now in the person of Rupert. Rupert was eight years old and was playing Mamillius, the child prince who dies of a broken heart in Act Three – not a moment too soon in Rupert's case. The part is supposed to pluck at the audience's heart-strings: as Rupert played it, it was like having the back of your throat tickled with a feather. What is it about English children of that age that is so persistently vomit-making? Is it simply the embarrassed thought that we must once have been like that ourselves – too old to be truly innocent, too young to understand that other people matter? Rupert's plummy, self-satisfied voice fell on the ear like a nasty memory of childhood. It was hideously un-Shakespearean. If his poor doting mother hadn't been there, cooing every time he opened his mouth, I really think Geoffrey would have hit him.

'Less *wooden*,' he shouted eventually, his voice grating with impatience. 'Mamillius isn't an answering-machine: he's a human being.'

'Yes, Mr Danes.'

'Try to imagine what it *feels* like to have your father treat your mother like that.'

'Yes, Mr Danes.'

'This isn't a normal situation. It's a tragedy. The characters speak in verse, Rupert, because this is what we call heightened drama. Everything's bigger than in everyday life. You have to use your *imagination*.'

'Yes, Mr Danes.'

'Can we try the scene again, please? I want a really big effort this time, Rupert. Can you do that? Give it everything you've got.'

'Yes, Mr Danes.'

And he did. He gave it everything he'd got and it was still excruciating. Geoffrey's hands shot to his head, as if he wanted to tear his hair out in clumps. It was irresistible force meeting immovable object: something was going to have to give and it didn't look as if it would be Rupert.

When the storm finally broke, Joanie Shepherd took the brunt of it. Her Hermione, as I say, was bloody awful, which was a pity because Hermione is a good part, while Camillo, if Geoffrey will excuse me, is a bloody awful one, however it's played. The trouble was – and I'm not criticizing Joanie, because you could meet ten bloody awful Hermiones and nine of them would make the same mistake – she didn't *realize* she was bloody awful. It was something you assumed she knew, just as you assume that fat people realize they're overweight: she certainly joined in all the nervous self-deprecation in the dressing-room – doesn't it feel wicked, we poor amateurs playing Shakespeare, all that crap. But she had secret pretensions. Instead of keeping her awfulness simple, she embellished it with a hundred false refinements. During her great speeches she would impart a deliberate tremolo to every word with an 'o' in it – of which, Shakespeare being human and having only five vowels to play with like everyone else, there were rather a lot. At first everyone assumed it was a speech defect: what else could it be? Geoffrey did admonish her once but, with so much bad acting on view, he had to admonish selectively or we'd never have got past the first scene. So the tremulous 'o's slipped through his net. They became more pronounced, more tremulous, more emotive, until, by the time Geoffrey exploded, they had assumed an almost operatic splendour.

'Fo-or Po-olixenes,
With who-om I am accused, I do-o co-onfess
I lo-oved him as in ho-onour he required,
With such a kind of lo-o-ove as might beco-ome
A lady like me, with a lo-o-ove even such,
So-o and no-o o-other, as yo-ourself commanded:
Which . . .'
'STOP!'

To anyone unfamiliar with the type, Geoffrey's anger at that moment is quite impossible to describe. You need to imagine, not an averagely ratty director a week before opening night, but a man of primitive faith whose sacred temple had been vandalized. He dressed Joanie down with such a flurry of expletives that even the actors off-stage crept out to see what was going on. It was genuinely frightening. The biggest surprise was that Joanie was up to it.

'If that's the way you feel, I'm walking out,' she shouted. 'Come on, Dick.' And grabbing her husband by the arm (he was playing Antigonus – another bloody awful performance, incidentally), she swept out of the room before anyone could blink.

There was a tense silence. Geoffrey stood marooned in the middle of the room, making odd flailing gestures with his arms to try to calm himself. More to himself than anyone else, he muttered: 'Where have they gone? What does she mean, walking out?'

Tony Barclay took him gently by the arm. 'Resigned, old man, finished. You've lost your leading lady.'

Geoffrey was so numbed it still hadn't sunk in.

'Resigned? She can't resign. We're opening next week.'

'You tell her that.'

'I will tell her that. She's got no bloody right to resign. This isn't a Women's Institute bring-and-buy sale. It's Shakespeare.' For once it sounded flat, like the punch-line of a joke that's been told too often.

'It may be Shakespeare, old man, but Joanie's Joanie. You shouldn't have shouted at her like that.'

'I had to shout at her. She was terrible.' He looked appealingly round the room at the others, who huddled apprehensively in the corners. 'Wasn't she terrible? Tell me she was terrible.'

'She was terrible,' said Tony Barclay, biggest ham ever to wear doublet and hose.

'She was terrible,' said Walter, world-celebrated butcher of iambic pentameters.

'She was terrible,' said Vanessa, most over-*ingénue ingénue* of all time.

'She was terrible,' I muttered. The three-word statement of the truth felt as shameful as any lie.

Another tense silence followed. It was easy to agree that

Joanie was terrible, but how do you stage *The Winter's Tale* without a Hermione? I looked at Geoffrey and he looked at me and our eyes said it all. With only a week to go, it was Joanie or nothing.

'Mark, I think maybe – '

'I think so too, Geoffrey.'

'Probably I did go too far.'

'Probably you did.'

And so a small peace mission was set up, consisting of Tony, Walter and myself. Geoffrey wanted to come too and said he was ready to eat humble pie if that's what the bloody woman wanted, but we talked him out of it. Stay above it, Geoffrey, we said: you're the artistic director, not the personnel manager, let us handle this one. Blessed are the peace-makers ... The compulsion to do good can sometimes be as irrational as the compulsion to do evil, for there was no logic in my determination to keep that lousy show on the road. And yet I was determined. When we arrived at Joanie's house and got a belligerent reception on the doorstep, it was me who did the talking.

'Look at it this way, Joanie. It's not just a question of you and Geoffrey: there are a lot of other people involved.'

'It's no good, Mark. I'm fed up with the whole bloody circus. Did you hear the way that man shouted at me? It was disgraceful.'

'He's nervous. He gets over-excited.'

'It's no excuse.'

'He asked me to give you these.' From behind my back I produced a bunch of flowers which we'd picked up on the Via Condotti. Geoffrey would have had a fit if he'd seen how low we were stooping. Joanie accepted them and sniffed them suspiciously.

'He did, did he?'

'Yes. He felt really awful about the way he shouted at

137

you. He said he didn't know what had got into him. He told us to tell you how sorry he was.'

Joanie snorted. It wasn't a pretty sound, but at least it was progress. A light rain was beginning to fall, so she asked us inside and, with not very good grace, offered us a drink. Then she proceeded to grill us for our honest opinion of her as an actress. Tricky, very tricky. It wasn't that she couldn't take criticism, she announced, in the wounded tones of someone whose parents hadn't criticized her for anything till she was twenty-one. Obviously she had a lot to learn about acting Shakespeare and, if she didn't get a speech quite right the first time, she knew straightaway because acting was like that. Everybody made mistakes: that was only natural. She had always accepted Geoffrey's criticisms in good spirit, even when she didn't entirely agree with them, because he was the director and she trusted his judgement as an authority on Shakespeare. But *tonight's* outburst (she inserted a heavy pause, reminiscent of some of her clumsier moments as Hermione) had been pure spite. After all, she wasn't exactly a bad Hermione, was she?

It was one of those unfortunate things but, at the very moment she asked the question, she wasn't looking directly at any of us, but a point halfway up the right-hand wall, between the pink entryphone and the reproduction Monet. The question therefore had no obvious addressee: it just lay there uncertainly in the middle of the room and, as in a game of pass-the-parcel, nobody wanted to pick it up. I considered answering. After all, she had asked whether she wasn't *exactly* a bad Hermione, so there was room for equivocation: a bloody awful Hermione isn't exactly a bad one, if you choose to be literal enough. But then I thought, no, why risk it? Let Tony or Walter answer. Unfortunately their own minds had been through the same process. It was only when the fractional pause of embarrassment became a slightly longer pause of embarrassment, then a heavy silence of indictment, that we realized, again simultaneously, that an answer of some sort had to be given and fast. Our words of reassurance tumbled out with horrible lack of subtlety.

'You're a wonderful Hermione, Joanie. Nobody could do it better.'

'Your Hermione is first class, Joanie. You've got nothing to worry about.'

'Joanie, anyone who criticizes your Hermione doesn't know great acting when he sees it.'

This last was my own effort. I think it must be the writer in me but, when it comes to compliments, I don't believe in holding back. Of the three bouquets, Joanie certainly liked it best.

'You are sweet,' she purred. 'So Geoffrey was wrong to shout at me?'

'Absolutely.'

'And there was nothing wrong with the way I did that speech?'

'No, not exactly.'

'What do you mean, "not exactly"?'

'Well, there was perhaps one small blemish.'

'Ah.' Her face fell. Her hands trembled. Her whole body tensed. She had to take a gulp of gin before she was brave enough to whisper it. 'Come on, Mark, you'd better tell me. I can take criticism.'

I froze and looked to the others for help, but they turned their heads away. The cowards, I thought, the cowards. We had agreed our strategy beforehand. It was no good just wooing Joanie back into the cast: one of us would have to say something about those vibrating 'o's or Geoffrey would have another seizure. But why did it have to be me?

And how was I going to break it to her? She had an ego like an egg-shell: it would have been easier to tell her to change her deodorant. I crossed and uncrossed my legs, then took a deep breath.

'It's to do with your diction, Joanie.'

'My diction? Is something wrong with my diction?'

'No, of course not. It's good, Joanie, very good.'

'First class,' said Tony courageously.

'Excellent,' said Walter, fearless as ever.

'If I have a criticism, it's perhaps that you, well – ' my throat was so dry I could hardly get it out – 'you sometimes overdo the "o"s. Not much, just a little.'

'What do you mean, o-overdo-o my "o-o"s?'

'There, you've just done it.'

'Done what?'

'It's hard to explain. It's just a small idiosyncrasy of yours. How would you describe it, Tony?'

'Not quite sure what you're getting at, old man.'

'Walter?'

'Sounds all right to me.'

'Ah well, in that case I must be imagining it. Forget I even mentioned it, Joanie.'

'I'm trying to.' She gave me a withering look and turned to the others. What did *they* think of her Hermione? Quite frankly now, speaking as friends, no need to be polite, obviously all she wanted was the truth . . . Needless to say, she got no such thing. Tony flattered, Walter toadied and, after ten minutes, she agreed to come back, 'provided Geoffrey behaved'. Guaranteeing good behaviour from Geoffrey was like promising to make a bull-elephant clean his tusks with a tooth-brush, but we said we would do our best. Then we left. It was a fragile truce, however you looked at it. Geoffrey reacted sceptically.

'I'm not having her back if she's going to be a prima

140

donna, Mark. Hermione's far too important a part to be messed around with.'

'Well, if you're going to tell her how to act, do it tactfully this time.'

'Yes, yes, of course.'

'You're lucky to have her at all, so don't push it. We had to work really hard to calm her down.'

'Of course you did, of course you did. I'm more grateful than I can say, Mark. How much were the flowers?'

'That's all right.'

'No, please, I insist.'

He fumbled in his wallet and stuffed a wad of notes into my hand. It was far too much, but he overrode all my protests. I found it hard to believe sometimes that he was an accountant. Did he really spend his working days examining columns of figures in a precise, parsimonious, professional way? There was a side to him which didn't give a damn about balancing the books, which could be impulsive and generous in a quite disarming manner. I sometimes think, if it hadn't been for this and that, we would have been friends, even good friends. But this and that were much too strong.

Helen watched the pantomime over the money with a wry smile. I had been ignoring her all evening, trying to forget – as if I ever could – that she even existed. If she could take Tardelli's death so coolly in her stride, I thought, shouldn't I take a leaf from her book? Shouldn't I try to match her patience instead of battering her into submission?

And so I had changed my tactics. Instead of dogging her every move, I put on a little performance for her benefit. By doing all the right things, I hoped to accrue a little credit: so many bonus points for pacifying Joanie, so many bonus points for letting Geoffrey give me his *lire* when I could have been lofty and refused. It was me, not Geoffrey, who was the true accountant. I thought, if I did my sums right, it would somehow add up to love – never mind the little matter of Tardelli in the debit column. Is that what they mean when they say love is blind?

5

Above it all, Rome maintained a patrician indifference. One man was stabbed in his flat, another was madly trying to resuscitate a dead love, a third was going berserk for the sake of a long-dead writer. But the life of the great city went sweetly on. If this were a different story, Rome, not Helen, might have been the protagonist. For wasn't she the one passion we all shared? That and being English, which isn't so much a passion as a physical handicap you have to steel yourself to overcome.

Englishmen in Rome don't exactly fade into the background, but the background is so cosmopolitan it doesn't matter. All you have to do is develop a patina of Roman sophistication, the knack of giving the impression that you own the place. Some people will tell you Rome's very provincial compared with Milan: there's less night life, the opera's not as good, it's not such a serious city. Tell them to stick their seriousness up their *culo*. You don't have to be serious to be accepted in Rome. You don't have to do anything important or be someone distinguished. You don't have to wear a shiny black suit or have a business card with a string of initials after your name. You just have to look as if you're enjoying yourself. Or as if you're a Catholic. Or, better still, as if you're a Catholic enjoying yourself. There are still some about.

Rome must be one of the biggest refugee camps in Europe. Almost everyone who wasn't born a Roman has the air of having run away from somewhere else. From all corners of the world they come, people who've been square pegs in round holes in Zurich or round pegs in square holes in Michigan or oval pegs in rectangular holes in Sydney. And, by some miracle of geometry, Rome accommodates them all. I suppose you could say London's the same, only more so: there is certainly a greater spread of nationalities. But a lot of people end up in London more from necessity than love. They hang around and sulk, like people waiting at a station during a train strike. You don't see people sulking in Rome – just the occasional madman flipping his lid in the sun.

It would be heaven on earth if it wasn't for the other refugees. Nothing travels as badly as English reserve, English fair play, English etiquette, English irony: I sometimes wish I was the only one of my compatriots who knew Rome existed. That's unfair, of course. I'm sure Englishmen who meet me wince at my Englishness as instinctively as I wince at theirs. But why does theirs have to be so conspicuous? At least I make some attempt at camouflage. Half the expats in Rome decide it's hopeless to conceal their origins and make a great parade of them instead. They behave like walking caricatures of themselves, wearing absurdly unsuitable clothes and using expressions not heard since the Ealing comedies. Is there a nation on earth which slips as easily into bad self-parody as we do?

Or is the joke really on us? By us I mean those other, supposedly more sophisticated, Englishmen who are too ashamed to play the fool abroad; who delude themselves that it's better to be international than national; who spend their time looking for camouflage and finding there isn't any. We realize too late that nationality is like a mother or a father: you have to make the best of what you're born with because it's all you've got. I think I would have rebelled against whatever nationality I'd started with, because nationhood, patriotism, king and country mean so little to me. But it can be lonely not belonging to a club. I even wonder if I would have battened so desperately on to Helen if I hadn't been such a rootless man, an alien wherever I find myself. Rome eases the pain of that rootlessness better than anywhere I know, but it can't take it away. Even in my adopted home town, I'm an outsider, the face looking in through the window, too timid to force an entry by breaking the glass.

For I am timid. I can hold my own among the English *literati* but, when I meet men like Tardelli – arrogant, self-assured, supremely confident that the good things in life are theirs – I feel in need of a hormone injection. The difference between winning and losing no longer seems dependent on chance, but character; and I haven't got the character. A stronger man in my position would have taken on Geoffrey and won, not hung around waiting for victory to fall into his lap.

Yet it so nearly did fall into my lap, and in the most unexpected way. It was either the night after Geoffrey's row with Joanie or the night after that: I'm not sure which. Considering how well I remember the events themselves, it's strange that my sense of chronology should be so awry. I was too preoccupied with Tardelli – with the grim mental battle to convince myself that he hadn't existed or, if he had existed, didn't matter. I also think I must experience emotions quite separately from the passing of time, the way some dogs do: they will greet a master who's been absent ten minutes with the same enthusiasm as one who's been away for a week. If I had a better sense of time . . . but I don't. Let's just say it was *shortly* after Geoffrey's row with Joanie that Helen rang. How fertile a lover's imagination is. Before she could say a word, I had invested the call with overtones of high romance.

'Mark, I need help,' she said briskly. 'Geoffrey's collapsed.' And again my thoughts flooded into that tiny gap and filled it with an obscene hope. By the time I'd mumbled 'How terrible', Helen was a widow and I was chief mourner and the world was young again. It aged quickly enough.

'It's only exhaustion, Mark: nothing more serious.'

'You're sure it's not his heart?'

'Yes, yes. Dr Martin examined him an hour ago.'

'What did he say?'

'He said he'd be all right, but he needed complete rest for a week.'

'That will mean cancelling the play, of course. How did Geoffrey take it?'

'He didn't. I haven't told him yet.'

'I see.' The purpose of her call came home with painful clarity. I was to persuade the husband of the woman I loved not to work himself to death. What a fool's errand, I thought bitterly. But what was the alternative? No errand at all? I said: 'I'll come right round' and, when she said: 'Thank you, Mark', I wanted nothing more. That was Helen: she could fill simple words with a profound resonance because there was never any hype, never any mark-up. In the dignity of a precisely used language, she found a kind of eloquence. She knew she only had to whistle for me to come, but she had the knack of whistling softly, conveying intimacy through understatement. I was at Geoffrey's bedside in twenty minutes, as if I was passionately concerned for his well-being.

'You shouldn't have bothered, Mark,' he croaked, obviously embarrassed by my visit. For Englishmen of his type, there is no greater humiliation than being seen in bed at ten o'clock in the morning.

'It's no trouble, Geoffrey.'

'There's nothing the hell the matter with me.'

'No, Geoffrey.'

'I'll be right as rain tomorrow. You see.' Did he believe his bravado? It was hard to tell. Most people play elaborate games when they're ill, fishing for sympathy or admiration: in Geoffrey I saw an honest determination to be his own master again as quickly as possible. But he certainly wasn't going to be right as rain tomorrow or the next day. His cheeks were sunken and pale and the only colour in his face was the angry, bloodshot eyes: you would have thought he had been crying. He suddenly looked not just middle-aged but on the downward slope that leads to old age: a man whose fire has burned out too quickly. When I saw the heavy price he had paid for pursuing his favourite passion, I felt another of those moments of kinship: love had promised so much and now it was destroying us both. I began to plead with him, but he resisted stubbornly.

'Geoffrey, you need rest.'

'Who says?'

'Dr Martin.'

'Bugger Dr Martin. He's the worst quack in Rome.'

'Well, if you don't trust him, trust me. You look terrible, Geoffrey. I've never seen you like this before. If you don't take a few days in bed, you'll be in serious trouble.'

'How can I possibly take a few days in bed? The play's opening next week.'

'You'll have to postpone it.'

'I can't postpone it.'

'Then cancel it.'

'I can't bloody – ' A coughing fit stifled the rest of the sentence and he subsided weakly into his pillow. I looked to Helen for guidance, but she shook her head. 'Don't argue, don't force it': her shorthand was as vivid as ever. So we sat and dithered, not willing to concede defeat, not daring to press for victory. And, while we dithered, Geoffrey's iron will prevailed.

'I'll be right as rain tomorrow,' he repeated, the voice even feebler, the cliché even lamer. It carried no conviction, but neither of us had the strength to contradict him. We looked at each other with the resignation of losers, separated only by the bed, and by Geoffrey in the bed, and by the eight years that had passed for one of us and not the other.

The next day, to crown it all, Geoffrey *was* right as rain. His pre-rehearsal pep-talk was one of the most vigorous he had ever delivered. His cheeks glowed. His eyes shone with excitement. His hands weaved extravagant gestures in the air. His legs kept him not just upright, but soaringly, triumphantly erect. It was miraculous.

'What have you done?' I whispered to Helen. 'Given him steroids?'

'Don't be silly. It's all in the mind with him. He gets his strength from Shakespeare, nowhere else. Once the rehearsal's over, he'll probably collapse again.'

'Do you think he'll be all right?'

'I don't know.'

'Is there anything more I can do?'

'No, Mark. Thank you. You've been very sweet, but it's too late.'

'Too late for what?'

'Please don't start that again.'

6

And so the show went on. The first night was now frighteningly close and we dragged ourselves towards it like runners completing a race they no longer hoped to win. The atmosphere was tense, joyless. Anyone who wasn't there would find it hard to understand the claustrophobic nature of those rehearsals. It was like being locked in a church heavy with incense, and feeling, at best, an agnostic. People were gasping for air, but nobody dared say 'Open the window!': they were frightened to commit that terrible sacrilege. Then Tony Barclay did say 'Open the window!' and we held our breath. In a moment of sheer recklessness, he suggested to Geoffrey that it was time for a break. The play was due to open on Thursday. Why didn't we cancel Sunday's run-through and just try to *relax*?

At first Geoffrey looked shocked. What could possibly be more relaxing than Shakespeare? But then other foolhardy spirits leapt on the band-wagon. What a marvellous idea, just what was needed to restore everyone's zest, why hadn't anyone thought of it before, oh do let's. Geoffrey weakened slightly, then Helen took his arm and said: 'Darling, you do need a rest', and he caved in completely. With the air of a child conceding defeat – and how I shuddered at the intimacy of the moment – he put his head on her shoulder and muttered: 'All right then.' I think, underneath the iron will, his breakdown had frightened him and made him feel fragile and dependent. In any event, we now had a consensus. We would spend the Sunday before the final week of rehearsals having a cast party in the country.

I suppose for some people that phrase, 'cast party', has a glamorous ring: actors letting their hair down even further than usual; off-stage relationships developing in counterpoint to on-stage ones; shy Hamlets necking in the corner with nymphomaniac Ophelias. There must be cast parties like that going on somewhere, but our pathetic troupe never had what it took to get one together. There were too many non-actors posing as actors, which isn't the same as actors posing as people. I can't imagine that real actors would have treated the whole thing so self-consciously or invested a little excursion into the country with so much false emotion. Tony Barclay christened it the 'works outing' and everyone gleefully adopted the same middle-class affectation. People wore ludicrous T-shirts and carried a terrifying array of cameras. The omens were dreadful: no ancient Roman augur greeted three magpies on a Thursday with as much foreboding as I did the cricket bat in the boot of the Shepherds' car.

The stage for the farce was Lake Bracciano, an inland lake in the Sabatini hills, about forty kilometres north-east of the city. It was my suggestion: I was anxious to head off a stampede to the beach, which seemed the likely alternative. Lake Bracciano is one of those idyllic settings in which the ghastliest people become acceptable – or so I reasoned. In fact, if people are sufficiently ghastly, they will destroy any setting in the world. As our cavalcade of cars rolled into Anguillara, one of the small lakeside towns, and everyone piled noisily out, I wished it had been the beach: a very remote beach, with no other human life for five miles.

'This one has *calamari*,' said Vanessa, studying the menu outside one of the restaurants.

'This one has better pasta,' said Joanie, looking at another menu twenty yards further on.

150

'There's *zabaglione* over here,' Tony Barclay shouted from across the street.

'What's the general consensus?'

'I'm easy.'

'How much do people want to spend?'

'What's *fettucine al sugo*?'

'I say the view's the most important thing.'

'I really don't mind where we go.'

'Hurry up, everyone. Rupert has to go to the lav.'

'Hands up those for *calamari*.'

'I'm only having a salad anyway.'

'Let Geoffrey decide.'

'Look! There's a big table over here.'

'Why didn't someone book?'

'Do restaurants shut early on a Sunday?'

'I'm entirely happy with whatever people decide.'

'Can we sit down? My feet are killing me.'

'The *calamari* are much cheaper than in Rome.'

'Is everyone happy then?'

'Three cheers for common sense.'

Thirty-two and a half minutes after arriving in Anguillara, we sat down to lunch. I timed it from the start, cynically confident there would be chaos and determined to savour it. When I announced my findings, people got a bit indignant.

'You've been *observing* us, haven't you?'

'Trust a writer.'

'You naughty old pussy, Mark.'

'He'll put it in one of his books now.'

There is a numbing stupidity in the assumptions non-writers make about writers. I used to think I'd adopted a glamorous profession, but there's nothing glamorous in being a voyeur, which is the label you're given as soon as you make comments on the way other people behave. In rehearsals I'd just been Camillo, one of the crowd: now I was an outsider again, a slightly disreputable figure who didn't fit in. On the other side of the table, Helen laughed lightly.

'It's all right, everyone. Mark's not a serious writer.'

How the remark would have seared me eight years before! But I didn't take it as a snub. I saw she was just protecting me from the others' idiocy and I loved her for it. It was Vanessa who took offence – much to her father's embarrassment.

'Oh but he is, he is.'

'Gently, sweetie.'

'He's still a marvellous writer, whatever the critics say. You shouldn't underrate him, Helen. He's superb, quite superb.'

'Not now, sweetie.'

'His last book was brilliant from start to finish.'

'Sweetie, please.'

Her father's interventions were no good. The sheer passion of her outburst surprised us all and there was a suppressed buzz as twenty people put two and two together. Camillo scoring with Perdita wasn't in the text, but it made a damn good twist. Everyone stopped talking in mid-sentence and forkfuls of *calamari* were held suspended in the air. When Englishmen travel, the first thing they pack is their double standards. All the women looked disapprovingly at Vanessa and all the men looked enviously at me – apart from Vanessa's father, of course, and Geoffrey, who looked slightly ill. I should have been embarrassed, but my heart sang. At last, at last, the complacent, soporific calm had been broken. Then Helen and Vanessa really laid into each other. It was glorious.

'I'm sorry, Vanessa, but that's rubbish. Mark's a clever writer, but he's certainly not brilliant.'

'He *is* brilliant. You should read his early books.'

'I have read his early books. They're not bad, but they're also long-winded and pretentious.'

'Pretentious? What, even *The Positive Hour*?'

'Yes, even *The Positive Hour*.'

'But how can you say that, Helen? It's a marvellous – '

'Rubbish, absolute rubbish. You're too young to know what you're talking about.'

'Well, you're too *old* – '

'Sweetie, don't you think – '

'Shut *up*, Daddy. You haven't read any of Mark's books, so keep out of this.'

Geoffrey coughed. 'Can we talk about something else?' Outside the rehearsal-room he had no authority. He intervened as diffidently as Vanessa's father, in the weak voice of someone who wasn't going to fight. But his very weakness was eloquent. Helen saw the sad, tired look on his face and immediately simmered down. Vanessa followed suit. Tony Barclay told a funny story to break the tension and the meal got back on course. Some people glanced accusingly at me, as if I'd been responsible for the whole thing. But the more I realized I was responsible, the better I felt.

The whole episode was impossibly English, of course. I once saw two women in Naples literally scratch each other's faces because of a man. The crowd loved it and the man loved it and I think even the women loved it, at least the one who won. The fight was real, in a way that verbal fights are never real. It was fought with a passion which has generally been civilized out of us. And it was absolute. You knew it would have a winner and a loser and there would be no apologies afterwards. It was tragic, but also sublime. In comparison, Helen and Vanessa sniping about writing was a bit anaemic: it sounded like a minor scuffle at a publishers' party. But it still felt good being the man

153

in the middle. So what if the woman I wanted to win was the woman attacking my writing, not the one defending it? That was just one of those things: a perfectly normal irony in my crazy, upside-down life. At least Helen had committed herself, at least she had spoken with feeling, at least she had got angry – almost as if it hurt her that I wrote so badly. The very vehemence of her scorn seemed like a positive sign.

Looking at her across the table gave me all the old pleasures and frustrations. I tried to draw her into conversation but, after the flare-up with Vanessa, she was more guarded than ever, attending assiduously to Geoffrey and playing her role as director's consort to perfection. So I simply watched, an impotent spectator at the greatest show on earth. Her smiles warmed me, even when they were directed at someone else; her laughter sent a tingle of pleasure down my spine, as if I had caused it myself. There is something timeless in a lover's adoration: he has something fragile in his hand, but he doesn't know it is fragile. Yesterday, today and tomorrow form a seamless whole, as they are said to in the mind of God. The Helen of then and the Helen of now suddenly became quite indistinguishable: the same facial expressions, the same phrases in conversation, the same inner vitality. It was she, not me, who insisted the two women were different. What made me so certain they were the same?

7

After lunch we took to the water. There were paddle-boats for hire beside the lake and we squeezed into five of them like a party of schoolchildren. Cameras clicked. Wine-bottles were uncorked. Bunches of grapes were passed from hand to hand. We paddled the boats out into the middle of the lake and did what we'd come to do: let our hair down. Shrill English voices pierced the air with idiotic nothings and there were loud splashes as bodies entered the water, fully dressed or half-undressed, the white flesh gleaming like neon in the sun.

'It's freezing,' Dick Shepherd shouted, his arms flailing above his head as he gasped for air.

'No, it's lovely,' said Vanessa, swimming up beside me. She had taken off her jeans, revealing an absurdly brief bikini-bottom, and her breasts were visible through her damp T-shirt. 'Come on in, Mark.'

'No, thanks.'

'You should. It's gorgeous.'

'Later.'

'Coward!'

What is it about the most banal experiences that makes people invest them with romantic daring? I've been called a coward for not eating liver, a coward for not smoking pot, even a coward for not reading Tolstoy. The challenge was so laughable that I stayed dry almost as a protest. Vanessa swam off in a huff, her legs thrashing angrily through the water. Above us the sun blazed imperiously down.

'Heaven,' said Walter.

'Perfect,' said Margaret.

'Incredible,' said Tony.

'Brill,' said Rupert.

'Very satisfactory,' said Geoffrey.

Only I said nothing. Tardelli's face stared up at me from the water, forbidding peace. I could forget him when my mind was busy with other things, but not when I just wanted it to be empty of thought: I had lost that great gift. The mellowness of lunchtime gave way to melancholy, a sense that certain things were for ever impossible. Love seemed no more than a cruel mirage, a whirling merry-go-round from which I couldn't get off.

The logistics of the merry-go-round were more complicated than on land. Vanessa's father had to take to the water to keep an eye on her, then Margaret had to do the same to keep tabs on him. I think she wanted to show what a good sport she was, but she entered the water so gauchely and miserably, in a voluminous black swimming-costume straight off an Edwardian postcard, that she evoked only pity. My own prospects were even bleaker. Helen stayed close to Geoffrey, while I stagnated in another boat with Joanie and Walter. I watched wretchedly as Helen peeled off her dress and stretched out on the front of the boat in a black bikini. Geoffrey sat three feet away reading a book. As our two boats drifted together, I was able to make out the title. *Troilus and Cressida: An Essay in Ambiguity*. My eyes smarted with rage. What a wonderful fucking choice. What a *marvellous* way to relax.

'I do wish he'd give it a break,' Joanie whispered. I say whispered: you could have heard her fifty yards away. 'It's all right to be an enthusiast, but you do need some sort of balance.'

'I admire him,' said Walter earnestly. 'He has his great

156

passion and he sticks to his guns about it. Never mind what other people say.'

Joanie snorted. 'That's all very well, Walt, but what about his wife? She's entitled to some passion too, isn't she?' She turned to me with a bawdy glint in her eyes. It was such a horrible debasement of what I felt for Helen that I found myself wincing. 'What do you think, Mark? You know them better than the rest of us. How does that marriage of theirs work? What's the secret?'

'Well, it's rather hard to describe.'

'She seems such a lively, normal woman and he's so bound up in his books. I mean, I ask you. What do they have in common?'

'Yes, I've often wondered that.' I turned away to hide the pain on my face. Nobody parroted conventional wisdoms as unsubtly as Joanie: nobody was such a sure barometer of what the world was thinking. Listening to her, I suddenly realized that the world would have been on my side, not Geoffrey's: that the tide had turned so far against marriage that few people would have condemned Helen for walking out on a husband like that. She had told me I was asking too much and, deep down, I believed her. Was I wrong to capitulate to the old morality? Should I have fought even harder to free her from that awful tyranny?

Another half-hour passed. A few fleecy clouds drifted across the sky, but the sun streamed down regardless. It was very warm, above normal for early May. Joanie swam off to join her husband on another boat. Walter dived in after her and stroked his way lazily to the shore, where a man was selling ice-creams. Vanessa sunbathed topless next to her father. Even Geoffrey put down his book and nodded off to sleep. For everyone but me, relaxation was proving absurdly easy.

I don't know what made Helen swim over towards me. I was so used to being shunned that it came as a complete surprise. I was the pursuer, she the pursued: I assumed it would be that way till the end of time. But there she was suddenly, bobbing in the water beside my boat, her hair dripping down her shoulders, her bone-white body glistening in the sun. She smiled up like a mermaid in a dream.

'Cheer up, Mark. You look miserable.'

'I am mis-' I stopped myself just in time. Wasn't it her who had told me that self-pity was the ugliest face of love? And how could I be miserable any longer, now that she was there? I smiled back. 'I'm all right. I just find all this heartiness a bit hard to take.'

'I suppose you think we're all being very English?'

'Revoltingly English. Except you, of course. You're looking so lovely, Helen.'

'Oh don't start that. Please.'

'I'm sorry.'

She pulled herself out of the water and sat down next to me. Close to, her legs looked thin, as if she'd been dieting, but it was still a beautiful body – smooth, graceful, well used to relaxing. She swept the wet hair out of her face and we laughed in unison as the water splashed my trousers. The sweetness of the moment was intoxicating: we might have been on the Serpentine in 1977, before the darkness fell.

The boat drifted out into the middle of the lake, further and further from the others. Was He pushing it, I wondered, the mischievous, laughing God who had taken my side so shamelessly in the Via Foraggi? Helen said: 'Don't let's talk,' and, for a few minutes, we didn't. If the silence had lasted, it might have achieved more than words, but I lost patience. I had so many questions to ask, there was so little time. Greedily I reached for the stars.

'Are you happy, Helen?'

'What, now?'

'Yes, now, this very minute. Alone with me and everyone else too far away to matter. Wasn't this what we dreamt of all those years ago? And isn't it just as real now as it was then? Don't tell me it's dead, because I can see from your eyes it isn't dead.'

Her face creased in disappointment. 'Mark, you're doing it again.'

'Doing what again?'

'I don't know.' She twisted a lock of wet hair round her finger and looked back in the direction of the others. She sounded tired, drained. 'Pushing me. Forcing me. Bullying me. Trying to put words into my mouth. I hate it, Mark.'

'Then why did you want to be with me just now?'

She shrugged, as if the question didn't matter, and my eyes smarted again. Couldn't she see how crucial it was? 'I hoped it would be better this time, Mark. And anyway, you looked unhappy.'

'What's it to you if I'm unhappy?'

'I don't want you to be unhappy. Really, Mark.'

'Then do something about it.'

'I can't. You should know that by now.'

'I don't – ' I gripped her wrist angrily, but didn't finish the sentence. I wanted to explode. I wanted to tell her it was me who killed her rotten Italian lover, I wanted to tell her I knew too much to be fooled by that stale old line about sticking with Geoffrey. But something held me back. She knew nothing of this strain of violence in me: it would probably revolt her, the way all cruelty and brutality revolted her. So I said nothing and the moment passed. If I had spoken out then . . . But why delude myself: I let go of her wrist and dredged up a smile.

'I'm sorry. Don't let's argue.'

159

'No, let's not.'

'Friends?'

'Friends.'

We disengaged. Nothing further was said. The breeze quickened off the lake, the sun dipped down towards the hilltops. Soon the day would be over, or all that mattered of it. If we had just been friends, nothing could have spoiled the next half-hour: nothing could have disturbed that precious oasis of peace. But the demon in me wasn't yet at rest. My mind was in open revolt. It rebelled at the prospect which she seemed to accept so philosophically: that, when the half-hour was up, she must go back to Geoffrey and I to Vanessa. Two mismatches each as grotesque as the other; what did it matter that one had been consecrated in church? If a God had been in the church – and I doubted it – He must have laughed Himself silly at pairing off Geoffrey and Helen, the way He laughed Himself silly when Tardelli turned his back on me in the Via Foraggi. I looked at Helen's smooth, untroubled face – the eyes closed against the sun, the nose starting to redden – and felt an overpowering impulse to destroy that contentment. I said: 'Helen, listen!' like a man shouting 'Fire!'

She opened her eyes and stared at me. 'What is it, Mark? You're angry again.'

'Yes, I am angry. I'm fed up with all your lying and hypocrisy. You reject any serious involvement with me as if it was out of the question, but I can tell you feel something stronger than that. I can tell, Helen. At lunch you got really angry with Vanessa, and all because of my lousy writing: it *mattered* to you, I could see it mattered to you. Why can't you be more honest with me? Why do you have to pretend that all that motivates you now is pity – feeling sorry for me, coming to talk to me because I looked unhappy? Is that really all that's left?'

160

'No, it's not all.' She looked me sadly in the eyes – and how I would have loved that still, grave face if I hadn't hated it so much. 'You ask for everything and I can't give you everything, Mark. So I get nervous. I'm afraid of sending signals you might misunderstand. But that doesn't mean you don't matter any more. You're right about that. I haven't stopped – caring.'

'*Caring*? What's that supposed to mean? Now you sound like a social worker.'

'I don't mean to, Mark.'

'Well, you do. I wish you could hear yourself sometimes. You're not yet forty, but you sound as if you've forgotten what feelings are. You used to have such tenderness: now you block off at the slightest hint of emotion. Where's all your old passion? I don't know what went on in the Via Foraggi, but it must have been pretty tame stuff.'

'The Via Foraggi? What are you talking about?' The guilt lit up her face like a lantern. She could be a lousy actress sometimes. For a second I knew what it must feel like to hate her: not the momentary spite of a rejected lover, but the real thing.

'You *know* what I'm talking about,' I roared. 'Stop play-acting. Stop laughing at me. Give *me* some of that love, Helen, or you'll never be safe again. Never.'

She scrambled to her feet, white-faced with shock. I tried to seize hold of her, but the boat was rocking too much. She pleaded with me desperately.

'Please don't shout, Mark. You're being so unfair, so very unfair. I haven't been good to you, but I haven't been as bad as you think.' Before she turned away, she whispered a single word. It sounded like an afterthought, but her lips caressed it with deep feeling, as if she had loved me all her life. 'Patience.'

She dived overboard and started swimming back towards

Geoffrey's boat. I shouted at her to come back, then abandoned the struggle. I felt as if I had lost her for ever, as if nothing now could turn back the tide. To a normal man the word 'patience' must offer a wonderful palliative of hope: to a madman, it tolls the knell of final defeat.

I watched her swimming out of range, her head bobbing up and down like a cork in the water, then turned despairingly away. If I'd kept her in view, I might have saved her: I'm a strong swimmer and could have covered the distance in seconds. But I only woke to the tragedy when I heard Walter shouting to me for help. Together we dragged her body out of the water and laid it out on the shore. Walter tried to resuscitate her, but it was no good. The lake had already claimed her.

Part Three

1

I used to pity people who lived off memories. Old men reminiscing about the sporting heroes of their youth, middle-aged women looking at dog-eared photographs of themselves at twenty: that whole sad syndrome. When Helen was dead, I behaved no differently. What other nourishment was there? I fed off the memories and then they fed off me, wheeling above my head like a flock of vultures.

The smallest details lingered on – like the only time I saw Helen smoke a cigarette. We were at a Greek restaurant in Paddington in 1977 and it must have been after making love and not before, because we quarrelled violently. They say sex releases tension, but for me there is no more dangerous period than the half-hour afterwards, when the body is tired and the mind is free and the adrenalin comes trickling back looking for mischief. On my way to the bedroom, I never argue: I'll agree that my name's Othello or Donald Duck if it preserves the mood of harmony. It's when I'm dressed again that the venom returns.

I don't remember how it started, just the bitter concluding exchange. Helen said: 'That's typical of you.' I said: 'What's that supposed to mean?' She said: 'It's obvious, isn't it?' And I said: 'No, it's not bloody obvious.' It was one of *those* rows, in other words: sterile, circular, infuriating. I thought she was being obtuse and she thought I was being stupid. How much harder it is to communicate across a table than a pillow.

A waiter ducked in between us to remove our plates and

I fumbled in my pocket for cigarettes. 'Give me one,' she said sharply. I lit it for her and we smouldered away in silence for five minutes. You'd never have guessed she was a non-smoker: she held the cigarette with the same grace as she held her wine-glass and sent smoke billowing across the table as if she'd been doing it all her life. Her face was flushed and tense, but it hadn't lost its beauty. The spirit shone through it, irresistible to my eye. One's own anger can be frightening, but I wasn't afraid of Helen when she was angry – or I wasn't then. I think it was the certainty that it would pass that made it bearable: the thunderclouds rolling overhead with blue sky beyond. Later, when I couldn't see the blue sky, I panicked. In London I never knew that deeper terror.

Still angry, she stubbed out the cigarette. 'Do you really smoke forty of these a day? You must be mad.'

'I'd stop if I could, but I can't. I've tried.'

'Then you haven't tried hard enough. Do you ever think what you're doing to your body?'

'It's my body, Helen.'

'You'll be dead at fifty.'

'I don't care.'

'Then you should care. Life's for living, not dying.'

The clumsy aphorism fell across the table like a dead bird plummeting from the sky. It was a child's remark, banal by any standards. But children are so often right. The sudden affirmation of life was so true to what I loved in her that the truth mattered more than the clumsiness and I found myself clutching her hand across the table in complete submission.

'You're right, Helen, I can't argue with you. If I die at fifty and you're still alive, I'll never forgive myself.'

'Then give the damn things up.'

'I'll try.'

166

'You've said that before.'

'This time I mean it.'

'You always mean it. Oh, Mark.'

With the inflection of a word, sarcasm melted into affection and the sun blazed down on me from a cloudless sky. It wasn't Helen's way to labour a point, even a point she had fought hard to win. If she hoped to change me for the better, she tempered that hope with realism. Change was possible, but only gradual change, the sort other people had to marry to achieve. I was a stubborn pupil. I had strong prejudices and the intellectual armoury to defend them. I wasn't to be bought by platitudes or piety or sophistry posing as wisdom. It would take her more than a lunchtime to teach me that life wasn't for dying, but for living.

But she did teach me that. It seems a bit forlorn insisting on her capacity for life, when death claimed her so long before me and yet here I am, still smoking forty a day, untroubled by illness or remorse. One grows tired of upbraiding the universe that finds these anomalies tolerable; perhaps one also comes to understand their underlying logic. I could cheat lung cancer for fifty years and not have lived as full a life as she did. Would it really have been fairer if it had been me who drowned in Lake Bracciano?

As a matter of crude fact, she was thirty-three days older than me. That silly statistic emerged when we were still new to each other and hungry for the most trivial information. We swopped our exact ages as we swopped our birth-signs and our schools and how many lovers we had had before. I can't remember why we took the trouble to count the days so meticulously but, once the fact stuck, it became the subject of regular teasing. 'Let's face it, Mark: you're thirty-three days less grown up than me.' 'Am I going to say boring things like that in thirty-three days' time?' We both saw the irony of the situation: it was I who had done the ageing, not her. She belonged to youth for life, as some people belong to the National Trust for life. She could have lived thirty years longer and still died young.

Where did she get it from, that intense, overwhelming vitality? I often wondered that, at those moments of high excitement when some strange power seemed to course through her and leave me trailing far behind. It had nothing to do with physical stamina, for she wasn't what you would call an energetic person. She got out of bed late, tired easily and had no compulsion towards activity for activity's sake. She dressed her age and dressed well: she never chased fashions or became obsessed with the outward forms of youth. It was the spirit that stayed young, that kept its resilience against all the odds. Even a dull marriage couldn't quench it – and wasn't that the greatest paradox of all? She had done what to most liberated women of her generation was unthinkable: settled down in her early twenties with the sort of man guaranteed to bring middle age closer. What could be more suicidal? It was me who guarded my freedoms and my independence so jealously, who followed the fashion of the time and played the field for all it was worth. By rights, the dead weight of habit and security should have crushed the individuality out of her, while I grew stronger and wiser with each passing adventure. But it didn't work out like that. As I moved past thirty and then some, not thinking it mattered very much, not feeling inwardly different, something gradually calcified in me which in her remained fresh and undiminished. I couldn't give a name to it and, if I could, it might never have happened. But it was there all right. It was in her eyes, her lips, the movements of her hands. It lurked behind her every smile like an accusation. Why can't you live life to the full like me? Why is it you that's dying?

Or was it all an illusion? Perhaps she only had more life in her than me because I gave her that life, just as I give life to the characters in my novels. Was all that precious vitality just a product of what I arrogantly call my imagination?

There was certainly no general consensus that she was an extraordinary woman. That struck me with chilling force as we huddled together on the shore of Lake Bracciano, waiting for an ambulance to come and take away the body, waiting to go home, waiting to get away from each other now that the party was over. People looked at the ground or the sky or out into the lake, anything to avoid catching someone else's eye and remembering the unbridled laughter of an hour before. There is a terrible injustice about such moments. Someone can spoil a party by dying, just as they can spoil it talking too loudly or throwing wine in the hostess's face; and the opprobrium of being a killjoy attaches to them whether they've deserved it or not. People resented Helen for drowning – and underneath the shock and the mute obituaries you could hear the resentment rumbling. A voice said: 'I thought she could swim', as if swimming was one of the accomplishments all good Englishwomen learnt.

'She was such a nice woman,' said someone else, too mean to use a larger epithet.

'I don't know how Geoffrey will manage without her.'

'Did she have any family?'

'I was sitting next to her at lunch. She was really enjoying herself.'

'Why didn't she shout out earlier?'

'Was she really thirty-eight? She didn't look it.'

'She loved cats, someone said.'

'What a wretched thing to happen.'

'They should have lifeguards at these places.'

Don't think I expected hyperbole or eloquent tributes: it wasn't the moment for oratory. But complete silence would have been preferable to the trite nothings people mumbled to fill that terrible vacuum. My sense of isolation was unbearable. I wished I wasn't so alone in feeling that something had gone which couldn't be replaced. I wish there had been a more general anguish. I wish there had been some sharing of my conviction – deeply felt, sincerely held – that Helen was special. It was like being a solitary believer in a crowd of atheists. Was I mad or were they blind?

And yet many people subscribe to this myth which haunts me, the myth of the Great Love: the idea that, in everybody's life, there is one person whom they love more than everyone else and whom, on their death-bed, they will remember as eclipsing all the others. It could be their childhood sweetheart, the person they married or someone they had an affair with in middle age. Or it could be somebody far more fleeting. I knew a woman once who talked about a man with whom she shared a two-hour train journey as if she'd never known true love before or since. Her eyes danced as she described him and she quoted more interesting remarks of his than most of us make in a lifetime. I don't think she would have referred to him as the great love of her life because she had a fine sense of the ridiculous: the forlornness of the statement would have hurt her pride too much. Her husband was a decent, hard-working man who hadn't shouted at her in twenty years: how could she tell him how quickly and effortlessly another man had hit all the notes he'd missed? But I know which of the two men she loved more; and I could recognize in her hero-worship of a stranger the symptoms of my own disease. We had erected false idols and couldn't bear to admit it.

And there it is again, that instinctive religious imagery. It took Helen to bring that out of me, for I'm not a believer in the conventional sense and I don't interpret other events in my life in spiritual terms. Yet how else can one understand the significance of a Great Love? If one didn't want and need a hierarchy of being, in which one person not only surpassed all the rest but transcended them, what would it matter that I loved Helen three times more than X and ten times more than Y? That would just be a natural consequence of a world rich in inequalities. Out of twenty women, one will always be prettiest, one cleverest and one sweetest. Occasionally (I believe the odds are 399–1 against, which, if true, means the English education system isn't quite as bad as I remember it), the same woman will be prettiest, cleverest and sweetest. But I'm not interested in statistics of that sort. Helen wasn't an arithmetical fluke, but a spiritual pointer. In leaving the other women in my life so far behind, she attained a different plane of being: human in the fullest sense, but close enough to perfection to make perfection itself seem possible. I needed someone to put on that pedestal and she was the best there was.

How much harder the death of hope is than the death of love. The first is absolute, the second only relative. So long as Helen was alive, I could tell myself that the love in her had not died: that somewhere, somehow, some time it would return. There was comfort to be taken from the inflection of her voice, the ambiguity of her manner, the varying expressions on her face. I could imagine events taking a sudden miraculous turn in my favour. I could still dream . . . With her death even that flimsy crutch was removed. I was alone.

Driving back into Rome on the night of the drowning, I felt as if it was me who had died and not Helen. My hands stuck rigidly to the steering-wheel as if they had been set in cement. My eyes stared fixedly at the number-plate of the car in front. My lips pursed tightly together, stopping the great howl I felt in my guts from finding the air. In the passenger seat, Vanessa sobbed quietly away. She had hijacked my tears, but I felt too numb to be irritated.

Two stupid lines of Tennyson (I *hate* Tennyson) began to revolve in my head. "'Tis better to have loved and lost/ Than never to have loved at all.' Even self-confessed purveyors of pulp have their standards: for me the twee use of "'tis' for 'it's' is the literary equivalent of greasy chips. But the lines got under my skin, the way a silly musical jingle sometimes does. I kept thinking, yes, that's true: it *is* better to have loved and lost. Would I really be happier now if I'd never met Helen? How would I have known what life was if she hadn't taught me?

Then we ran into a big traffic jam on the outskirts of Rome. Cars ground to a halt, horns blared, drivers rolled down their windows and shouted at each other. The cacophony was pure Italy. On a normal day I would have tolerated it, even enjoyed it. Now that all hope had died, my system was too frail to withstand the pressure. I felt crushed and isolated by the frenetic activity around me. And then, as my mood changed, I thought, sod you, Tennyson, what do you know about anything? You're a boring Victorian fart, with ridiculously sentimental ideas. 'Tis not right to pay any price for love. 'Tis not worth all that joy if only an empty husk is left. 'Tis better to sit at home and pick one's nose than take that absurd risk. It was lucky the car was stationary: I couldn't have trusted myself to drive with due care and attention in the five minutes that followed.

172

Vanessa, farcically, started combing her hair. The tears dry, the grief overcome, the proprieties observed, she pulled down the sun-flap and studied herself in the mirror. I can't excuse the violence of my reaction, for when had I grieved for more than ten minutes over someone who hadn't mattered to me? But the violence was genuine: it came from the gut. I thought of a dead woman who could never have combed her hair in those circumstances, who could never have committed such an obscenity; and I shouted 'Don't do that!' as if she were holding a lighted match to a petrol tank. God knows what she made of my behaviour. It must have sounded like the raving of a madman. But she put her comb back in her handbag with the guilty start of someone caught shop-lifting – and the guilt redeemed her. She could have looked open-eyed and said 'Don't do what?'; but the childlike acceptance that she was doing something wrong, without quite knowing what it was and why it was wrong, wasn't the stuff on which hatred can feed. I buried my head in her shoulder and mumbled an apology. The driver of the car behind gave a mocking hoot of his horn, but I took no notice.

'You're cut up badly, aren't you, Mark?'

'Yes.'

'You were close, weren't you, you and Helen?'

'Pretty close.'

'Poor Mark. You'll be all right. I'll look after you.'

'Thank you.'

How delicately she trod that tightrope, between saying too much and saying too little. A great abyss was yawning beneath her, but she didn't see it and, because she didn't, kept her balance. Choosing simple words, and the right simple words, wasn't normally one of her gifts. She either over-elaborated or used limp platitudes which hung like soggy washing on a line. This time she discovered the gift.

Call it accident or call it inspiration: she struck the ight note with the same grace and certainty I associated with Helen. And, as I heard the note, the guilt passed from h~ to me like an electric current. How long could I go on scorning her for not being Helen, for inhabiting a lower plane of existence? Did they not, in the end, share the same universal root?

The traffic crawled back into motion. The horn-blaring stopped. The shouting subsided. The sun set over the Aventine hill, gilding the highest domes with light long after it had passed from view. The city woke up for the night and the streets began to fill up with couples window-shopping or strolling arm in arm with *gelati* in their hands. I dropped Vanessa off at her father's and drove back to my flat alone. I had thought I had died with Helen, that she had left a vacuum that could never be refilled. But already a little voice was whispering: it need not be so. Already I could see ways of making the vacuum howl less painfully. Already Helen's great genius for life was finding the means to revive me.

2

When I got upstairs, the telephone was ringing. Its sudden raucousness unnerved me, reverberating round my small flat like a tinny alarm-clock, but I made no effort to pick up the receiver. It was probably Julian or Giles or Philippe, one of the coterie of fellow bachelors who like to drink with me in the early hours of the morning and talk about their emotional problems. I seem to act as a magnet for that type of person. It must be something to do with being a writer, though, if they really think writers know more about life than other people, that's the biggest problem they've got. Would it have gratified them to know I had a gigantic emotional problem of my own? I ignored the telephone and started getting undressed.

But the ringing persisted. It droned on relentlessly, like a bad-mannered guest outstaying his welcome. A casual caller would have given up sooner: the persistence suggested urgency. Reluctantly I surrendered to my curiosity.

At the other end of the line, a man was crying. He made no effort to say anything, just sobbed quietly into the phone: it was like a macabre variation on the anonymous heavy-breather. Tears have an individual signature, like the spoken voice; but until you've heard someone crying, you don't know what their crying sounds like. It was pure intuition that guided me to the right answer.

'Geoffrey?'

There was no answer at first, then, through the sobbing, I heard a stifled 'Yes'.

'I'll come right round.'

I drove the mile and a half to his house in not very good grace. My role promised to be an awkward one. If his grief was extravagant, I would feel a perverse temptation to outdo him; if it was muted, I would rage at his easy self-control. There seemed to be no feelings we could honestly and openly share.

To compound the awkwardness, Geoffrey was wearing the most ridiculous dressing-gown I have ever seen. The mottled green pattern was painful to the eye and it was several sizes too big for him. The bottom came down to his ankles and the sleeves were so long he had to keep flicking them back to maintain the use of his hands. It was probably just a Christmas present he had never bothered to exchange, but the indelible impression was of a stunted child who hadn't grown up. I hadn't come to pity him, but it was impossible not to.

'Oh my dear Mark, my dear Mark.' He clung forlornly on to my arm, too shy to embrace me properly, too feeble to let me go. I had only previously seen him get emotional about Shakespeare: Helen had never engaged his feelings to the same extent. At the lake, when her body was brought ashore, he had stayed reasonably calm. People muttered how brave he was and one didn't need to be fanatically British to admire that tight-lipped dignity. But now all those pent-up feelings were being released, they came sprawling out in a hectic, uncontrolled rush. The sense of disintegration was terrible: it was only a week since he'd broken down before. I sat him down in a chair as if he were an invalid, incapable of doing it himself.

'You must think I've completely cracked,' he croaked, holding his head in his hands as if it were throbbing with pain.

'Not at all, Geoffrey. I understand.'

'She meant so much to me.'

176

'Of course she did.'

'I feel so alone now.'

'You'll be all right.'

'I've got to let my feelings out somehow. It's so good of you to listen.'

'It's the least I could do, Geoffrey.'

We carried on like this for nearly five minutes, the bereaved husband and the concerned friend, the one who had suffered a tragic loss and the one who wasn't supposed to have suffered so much. I acted as his loyal sponge, absorbing his pain, soaking up his grief, drying his tears – and I acted well. He stole all my lines, but I didn't report the theft. It was as if, with Helen, there had died the part of me which hated Geoffrey for being her gaoler. I was living in a world beyond emotion, in which all feelings seemed an insufficient reflection of what had caused them. I had thought of madness as a circuit overheating: now I realized what a cold condition it could be.

I had forgotten Geoffrey's madness. It had appeared to be submerged under a natural human grief, but it suddenly resurfaced, as jagged as a rock rearing out of the sea. In a weak voice, he mumbled: 'I don't know how I'll be able to face people tomorrow night.'

I stared at him.

'What are you talking about, Geoffrey?'

'The play. We've got a full dress rehearsal.'

'You're surely not – '

'Mark, we're opening on Thursday. There's no way we can cancel now. Every hour of rehearsal is vital. Act Four's still a shambles and I'm terrified about Joanie's big speech in the trial scene. We've got to work right up to the last minute. We can't let – '

'Geoffrey, stop. This is lunacy. Helen's dead, your wife's dead. There's a funeral to arrange, relatives to contact, your own emotions to cope with. You can't go on play-acting at a time like this.'

'I'm *not* play-acting. This is Shakespeare.'

'Fuck Shakespeare.'

'What did you say?'

'You heard. Listen, Geoffrey: stop thinking about yourself for a minute and think about Helen. Do you think she would have wanted you to go ahead with this play? Do you think she would have been pleased to see how little she meant to you?'

'She didn't mean little to me.'

'Then prove it. Mourn her properly. Cancel the play. Where's your self-respect?'

He didn't answer. He didn't have an answer. Cringing in the chair, pitifully shrunken inside the outlandish dressing-gown, he had no self-respect left, no inner strength to marshal in his defence. It was hard to believe that this was the Geoffrey we had nicknamed the Fuehrer, so masterfully had he held sway over us. When he did speak, it was like the babbling of an old man.

'You're right, Mark, you're absolutely right. I should cancel the play. Common decency and all that. Helen's parents would be very put out if they thought I didn't care, and they would think I didn't care because neither of them knows the first thing about Shakespeare and why he's important. I know it's not the ideal time to put on a play, even a great play, a very great play, Mark. But dammit, Mark, it's not as if it's *The Importance of Being Earnest* or something silly like that. People will say I'm a monster, but I'm not a monster, you know I'm not a monster. I'm just someone consoling himself the best way he knows. Shakespeare's all I've got left, Mark – can't you see that? If I lost him too, where would I be? Where would I be without Him? *Where would I be?*'

I put my hand on his arm. It was throbbing as if an electric current were going through it, a life-giving current I didn't dare switch off. And all the anger I felt at his mad, blind egotism froze on my lips.

'You'd be lost, Geoffrey,' I said gently, 'quite lost. I know that. But don't forget, whatever happens to this production, you won't be losing Shakespeare. You can put on other productions, you can read the plays. Shakespeare's always there in some form. Isn't that what matters?'

'You're so right, you're so right.' He gazed at me with new respect, as if I were a foreigner who had demonstrated an unexpected fluency in English. 'Shakespeare's always there,' he repeated, like an advertising man sampling a new slogan. 'Shakespeare's always there. How true, how very true. He knew that himself, you know. He knew he'd last for ever. "Not marble nor the gilded monuments of princes – "'

' " – shall outlive this powerful rhyme." '

Again he gazed at me respectfully. 'That's it, that's the line. I didn't think you – '

'Oh come on, Geoffrey. It's a well-known poem. I'm not completely illiterate just because I write novels.'

'No, of course you're not. I'm sorry. Do forgive me.'

His eyes misted over and he got up and walked out on to the balcony. I followed him and together we looked out across the city. The night air was fresh and clear and there was something massive and reassuring in the familiar skyline. Every dome, every turret, every rooftop seemed solid and permanent, as Shakespeare was permanent and Helen wasn't. For a short moment, what we had lost didn't seem irreplaceable: there were untapped riches in what remained. But then I stole a glance at Geoffrey and saw the poverty of my position compared to his. He wasn't thinking about Helen, but Shakespeare; and the serenity in his face made clear which was the greater love. I had known that for years, of course: there was no shock in rediscovering it. But the facts of life don't always hurt most when they're new: sometimes an old familiar truth can pierce as deeply as the most shocking revelation. No, Geoffrey, I thought, no. You can't take refuge in Shakespeare that easily because I won't let you. I comforted you five minutes ago, but now I will take away that comfort. You have given me pain, so I will give you pain. I will bring you down to my level. There must be a natural limit on how long people can behave well, just as there is a limit on how long they can go without sleep. After half an hour's kindness or generosity, the worm turns. Some people can manage an hour and the real goody-goodies do it for two hours or more. But I'm a thirty-minute saint, always have been. Having given Geoffrey my best for so long, I now gave him a little of my worst.

'I take it the production's off, then?'

'What do you mean?'

'Well, if Shakespeare's always there, whether he's being performed or not, what's the point in carrying on? It will only upset the people who are less fanatical than you. Why can't you simply cancel and keep Shakespeare to yourself, so to speak, as a source of comfort. That's what you want, isn't it?'

'Yes, of course. It's not one production that matters: it's Shakespeare as a whole. You're right about that, Mark, you're quite right.' He nodded vigorously, acknowledging the force of my logic. But it was a bitter pill to swallow and soon he was begging again, his eyes bulging in their sockets like a dog's.

'Mark, I do just wonder – '

'No, Geoffrey.'

'Surely if – '

'No, Geoffrey. You're backtracking, Geoffrey.'

'Maybe I am, but look at it this way, Mark. If Shakespeare has any value at all, it must be in reminding us that life is superior to death and that tragedy can be overcome. *The Winter's Tale* is one of his most positive and life-enhancing plays. What better way to commemorate Helen than to perform it?'

I shuddered. 'Do you think she would have thought that?'

'I'm not sure. I hadn't really thought about it. She wasn't as keen on Shakespeare as me, but she still – '

'Geoffrey, she *despised* Shakespeare.'

'That's a lie. That's not true. She never said that.'

'Not to you maybe.'

'What are you saying?' He stared at me in confusion. I could have retreated and said Helen's views on Shakespeare had come my way by chance, that he should read nothing into my comment. But I didn't want to retreat. I wanted him to know the pain I knew. I wanted to taunt him with his inadequacies as a husband. I wanted, even at that late hour, to confront him man to man and win. He looked me straight in the eyes and I nodded at the question he didn't dare ask.

'When, Mark? Here in Rome?'

'In London.'

'But that's nearly ten years – '

'Eight. Nine in August.'

'And yet you still care so much: I can see it in your eyes. Did she give up on you?'

'You could say that.'

'Extraordinary, quite extraordinary. I had no idea.'

He looked at me without recrimination, without malice. It was as if he realized instinctively that my pain was greater than his: that, if one of us deserved the other's pity, it was me and not him. How I hated that magnanimity –

and how I laboured to convince myself that it wasn't magnanimity, but weakness. I had wanted to make him angry because Helen was worth getting angry about. Even in death, her love was a prize I would burst every sinew to win. Geoffrey's gentlemanly restraint mortified me, flooded my mind with feelings of loss and regret. If we had grasped the nettle then, Helen and I, if we had told him we wanted each other and not him, would he just have furrowed his brows in that mild way and said 'Extraordinary, quite extraordinary'? I honestly think he would. He could no more have got angry then than now: he would have caved in without a fight because he wouldn't have thought the fight worthwhile, wouldn't have thought any fight worthwhile unless Shakespeare was the prize. Wasn't that his tragedy? And my tragedy? And Helen's?

I would like to say we exchanged forgiveness, the way Shakespearian characters do in the fifth act, all generosity and goodness and sublime sentiment. But there was no forgiveness to exchange. I hated him for not hating me more and he probably hated me for saying he was mad to carry on with the play. Only a great effort of will saved me from an overwhelming bitterness. I tried to think of Geoffrey, not as someone who hadn't loved Helen, but as someone Helen had loved. That way it was easy to see where my duty lay, what I had to do if I was to keep faith with the woman I had lost. Yes, I thought, wincing at the prospect but at the same time relishing it: I would humour Geoffrey's madness for Helen's sake; I would cushion his grief to do her honour; I would move heaven and earth to get the bloody play produced, just so she could see what a good man I was. I trailed forlornly after my mirage and Geoffrey trailed just as forlornly after his.

3

'But I won't be in the right mood,' moaned Joanie the next morning, when I told her the play was still on. 'I can't act when I'm not in the right mood.'

'None of us will be in the right mood.'

'How can I do my part properly if I'm feeling all flat inside?'

'How indeed, Joanie? But it's what Geoffrey wants.'

'I do think he's being silly. Why can't he just drop the whole thing?'

'He says it's all he's got left. You can see what he means.'

'Oh very well. I suppose we'll all have to play along. Hey-ho. Just so long as he's not expecting a sparkling performance from me.'

No, I said, I didn't think Geoffrey was expecting that: he would quite understand if her Hermione lacked its normal zest. But it was important that everyone should give of their best for Helen's sake and for the sake of the production. No false heroism was needed. And could she, by the way, bring a bunch of rosemary to that evening's rehearsal? Geoffrey wanted it as a prop in Act Four . . .

The others greeted the news with the same astonishment.

'He's crazy,' said Tony.

'He's taken leave of his senses,' said Walter.

'Can't you get him to a doctor?' said Vanessa's father.

Yes, I said, he was crazy. Yes, he had taken leave of his senses. No, I couldn't get him to a doctor. He had warned me categorically not to waste time fussing about his health. The play was his health. We owed him our support whether we thought he was mad or not. I knew it was hard, but could people please try to treat that night's rehearsal as normally as possible? Costumes were to be worn, but there would be no make-up till the dress rehearsal.

All morning I acted as Geoffrey's aide-de-camp, rallying the troops, reviving confidence, quelling the chorus of dismay and disbelief which greeted the news that we were to carry on. It was uphill work, but I enjoyed it. It may stretch credibility to call a production of *The Winter's Tale* by expatriate Englishmen the real world; but to a writer any world is more real than the world of his books, particularly if they are bad books. The flurry of telephone calls gave me an exhilarating sense of importance, of doing useful admin work in the service of someone else. I had a brief taste of what it must be like to be a civil servant or an accountant or a lawyer – one of those nine-to-five jobs I had turned my back on so contemptuously. And I rather liked the taste. In three weeks I had moved from the outer fringes of the production, sardonically observing the excesses of those taking it more seriously than me, to its very epicentre. If Geoffrey remained the artistic driving force, I was now administrator-in-chief, the man keeping the nuts and bolts in place. You could say it had happened by accident, but it wasn't only an accident. I needed *The Winter's Tale*, just as much as Geoffrey did. All that urgent diplomatic activity freed my mind from a far less pleasant chore: the contemplation of a world inhabited by two unappeasable ghosts, Helen and Tardelli.

For he had not drowned in the lake with Helen. The guilt of his murder wasn't expunged by the second death, indeed its complete futility was now clear. I hadn't got my pound of flesh from Helen – the perverse satisfaction of knowing that I had got through to her somehow – and I never would. Now that I had to carry a deeper pain, I could have done without that cross.

It was still less than a fortnight since the murder: long enough to hope that I had got away with it, not long enough to shake off the fear that I hadn't. That Monday morning was a particular nightmare. Every tall man I passed seemed to have Tardelli's face. Every policeman in every car seemed to be staring at me. Then I remembered about plain clothes policemen and, as soon as I saw the same face more than once, assumed I was being watched. A city in which I could lose myself had become a city in which there was no possibility of privacy. Even the newspaper vendors had eyes that followed me everywhere, like those old portraits which so fascinate children that they spend hours crawling behind furniture trying to look at the face without being seen.

Then suspicion turned to certainty. From a thousand hostile faces, one suddenly emerged with special menace: a little po-faced man with a moustache and a rather flamboyant way of lighting cigarettes. He was everywhere: in the street outside my house, in the Campo dei Fiori, in the *tavola calda* where I had lunch. To confirm my suspicions, I caught a bus from the Piazza Venezia to the Stazione Termini and then another bus back to the Piazza Venezia. He was in both buses, staring listlessly out of the window as if these were journeys he made very day: I never caught him looking at me. Heaven knows what kind of selection process Italian plain clothes policemen go through, but it must be far more rigorous than their English counterparts, with their lantern jaws and badly fitting suits. In his own small way, the man was an artist, someone who had laboured to perfect his craft. I turned round to see if he was still following me and he glided in and out of a shop like a ballet dancer.

Too lazy to shrug him off, I decided to put his acting to the test. We sat down at adjacent cafés, ordered beers and propped open our newspapers. Then, just as he was looking forward to ten minutes without having to concentrate, I crossed over and shook him by the hand.

'Pietro?'

That threw him all right. He looked blank, so I asked after his wife and family, complimented him on losing weight and told him he was an old rogue drinking beer when he should be at his desk working. When he finally said *scusi*, but his name wasn't Pietro but Paolo, I recoiled in amazement and said, *molti scusi*, but he had an uncanny resemblance to my old friend Pietro Arconi, the well-known businessman. Wasn't life *straordinario*? Yes, he agreed, it was *straordinario*, so I fetched my beer and started up a conversation. My own name was Mark or Marco, I quipped, which, considering his name was Paolo, was only one letter away from being another extraordinarily funny coincidence. At which I gave a merry little laugh, thinking that he wouldn't be able to join in the mirth and would be at a disadvantage. But he promptly responded with an even merrier and, in histrionic terms, *better* laugh, and I was suddenly afraid.

I had underestimated him, you see. In acknowledging the artistry with which he followed me, I assumed it was a skill he had developed because he had no other. He tailed the people he was told to tail, just as sniffer dogs sniff where they are told to sniff. He did it well, but it was still a rather animalistic function, relying more on the senses than the intellect. His reports would be sent in and filed, then analysed by the intellectual heavyweights: no cost-effective police force would send its heavyweights out on to the street.

But this man was a heavyweight. When he'd recovered

from the shock of my Pietro gambit, he was quite at ease in conversation, sketching in a character for himself with convincing fluency, as if he'd been doing it all his life. He was a Neapolitan, he said, who had come to Rome twenty years before to find work. His business was importing and exporting cheese and he had a small warehouse out on the road to Ostia. He had a wife and three children, but his friends called him *il lupo*, the wolf, because he was a ladies' man. He couldn't help it: some men were like that and which of us was really strong enough to say no if the right woman came along? Oh, and by the way, he *hated* dogs. They were bringing Rome to its knees faster than the Red Brigades. Only the other day, on the Via Babuino, he had seen a Great Dane, in full view of everyone . . .

It was a superb performance. If I hadn't seen him take that bus from the Piazza Venezia to the Stazione Termini and a bus back to the Piazza Venezia two minutes later, I would have been completely taken in. He was just a jumped-up cop, of course, grabbing some camouflage out of thin air. But if I ever wanted to put that character in a novel, the dog-hating, lady-killing, cheese-selling slicker from out of town, I'd take him as my model. The performance struck the note of superior truth, the achieved reality more real than the natural reality, which only artists can attain. If the cast of *The Winter's Tale* had had a quarter of his acting ability, we'd have sold every ticket three times over.

Upstaged, I took my leave of him ten minutes later. I had to meet some people at the airport, I said, perfectly truthfully: there was no point in concealing the fact. Ah, he said, his curiosity as casual as cocktail party banter, relatives from England perhaps?

'Not my relatives. Someone else's.'

'A friend?'

'Yes.'

'It's kind to do such things for a friend. Doesn't your friend have a car?'

'Unfortunately not. She's dead.'

'Ah, *scusi*.' He looked more perplexed than sympathetic. A second corpse wasn't part of the script: he had thought he was tracking a single killer, not someone whom death followed round like a swarm of bees. For the first time he came in with a clumsy line. 'An accident?'

I nodded. 'She drowned.' Would he have kept up his guard if I'd said: 'No, I killed her too'? The tension was electric. Then, as I left, he made a second mistake. I glanced over my shoulder to see if he would follow and caught him nodding to a man in glasses loitering outside a bar on the other side of the street. The man in glasses threw down his cigarette and, by an extraordinary coincidence, arrived at the airport within two minutes of me.

4

I hadn't met Helen's parents before: she had never introduced us. Geoffrey was all right because he was Geoffrey: naïve, trusting, unworldly. It wouldn't occur to him that his wife was being unfaithful, so there was no danger in our meeting: it even helped legitimize the affair. A mother's eyes are sharper: she will look very closely at any man her daughter tries to pass off as 'just a friend'.

At the same time, I felt I already knew Bill and Martha Tobin. A lover isn't just a gourmet: he is an archaeologist. The thirty years in which I hadn't known Helen had a fascination equal to the eight years in which I had. One doesn't need to have definite views about genetics or education or social conditioning to feel that kind of curiosity. Helen's past was the seedbed of her present enigma; and I would rummage eagerly through it for clues to the things which most puzzled me about her. I knew a lot about her family, warts and all – and there were some big warts. One of her grandfathers had fought on the wrong side in the Spanish Civil War; the other had spent six months in prison for a misdemeanour in St James's Park. Her parents lived in Croydon. They had five cats and bought the *Radio Times*. Yes, I knew the Tobins all right. The elderly couple coming out of the customs hall at Leonardo da Vinci airport were no strangers: I picked them out of the crowd with perfect confidence.

'You must be Mark. It's so kind of you to meet us.'

'How do you do, Mr Barham.'

I felt the immediate thrill of a successful prognosis. In

189

my mental picture, Helen's mother was the sort of woman to greet a stranger by his Christian name; her husband would be more formal. Exactly so. It was like splitting the atom: Helen's warmth and Helen's restraint, so puzzling in conjunction, became far more explicable when separated.

I said: 'This must have come as a terrible shock.' The busy activity around us devalued all sense of tragedy, but the nettle still had to be grasped.

Mrs Tobin took me by the arm. It might have been Helen herself: the instinctive physical intimacy was just the same. 'Oh it was, it was. She was our only child, you know.'

'We caught the first flight,' her husband added laconically.

'Were you there, Mark – when it happened?'

'Yes, I was. There was a great party of us out on the lake. It all happened very quickly, if that's any comfort.'

'Did she say anything before she went?'

'It wasn't like that, I'm afraid, Mrs Tobin. I'll tell you more in the car, if I may.'

'Yes, of course.'

I carried their cases out to the car, fighting a passage through the crowds waiting at the entrance to the terminal. The Tobins looked uncomfortable amid the hurly-burly: I had the impression they weren't used to international airports. Outside in the sunlight, they blinked and looked around them like visitors from another planet. Their clumsy attempts at mourning – his a black tie so shiny it must have been bought that morning, hers a dowdy woollen dress, too heavy for the Mediterranean spring – only heightened the effect of pathos. When I saw how much more than Geoffrey they shared my feelings, I felt a great upsurge of sympathy. I helped them gently into the car and drove off at a reverential pace, as if they were my own flesh and blood.

On the *autostrada*, high-rise blocks of flats drifted past.

190

'Are we far from the centre?' Mr Tobin asked, a bit perplexed. It wasn't the Italy of the picture postcards.

'Forty minutes or so. I told Geoffrey five o'clock. We'll be early.'

'Is the traffic bad?'

'We'll be all right on a Monday.'

Mrs Tobin was more direct. 'Couldn't Geoffrey come himself?' She was clutching a handkerchief in her hand, ready to dab the tears which threatened every time she spoke, but there was still room for the suspicions of a mother-in-law. I remembered something Helen had told me years before. It was her mother who told her she'd be mad to marry Geoffrey, her father who said she'd be mad not to. I picked my way carefully. Geoffrey had *wanted* to come to the airport, I explained, but been prevented by unforeseen circumstances: that was my diplomatic term for a lighting rehearsal, which is how he was really spending the afternoon. I half hoped she would probe the euphemism and arrive at the truth by a gentle parabola of disappointment. It would all come out anyway and hurt whenever it did. But her curiosity took her no further: perhaps she already knew Geoffrey too well.

In the mirror, I could see the plain clothes policeman who had followed me to the airport sitting in the passenger seat of a taxi. He must have been half-expecting me to catch a plane out of the country: I wondered if I would have been arrested if I'd tried. What would he report to his superiors about the elderly couple I had met off flight BA252 from London? Their names could be culled from the official passenger-list, but would mean nothing. They would seem utterly irrelevant to the enquiry into Tardelli's murder. Yet weren't they, in one sense, its true origin? If they had never met, if their genes hadn't fused in that extraordinary act of creation . . .

'She was never a strong swimmer,' Mrs Tobin announced, interrupting my train of thought. She said it to herself and she said it to the world: there is a level of grief at which the two become quite indistinguishable. 'Do you remember that time at St Ives when you had to swim out to rescue her?'

'I think it was Penzance, darling.'

'Penzance, St Ives, wherever. She got caught by the tide and swept right out, poor thing. She was only eight or nine. I stood on the beach waiting for you to get back with her and I thought I was going to die. I'm so sorry.' The apology referred to her tears, which suddenly streamed down her cheeks faster than her handkerchief could dry them. Her husband said: 'Please don't cry', and I said: 'Please don't apologize.' It was me she heard.

'You're right: I shouldn't say sorry. What's there to be sorry for? If I don't cry now, when will I cry? I've got to get it out of me somehow. If she'd had a brother or sister, it wouldn't be so bad now, but she was all we had, there wasn't anyone else. What have we got to look forward to back in England?'

The stream of tears became a cascade. I pulled over on to the hard shoulder and turned off the engine. The taxi behind, rather conspicuously, did the same. Again Mr Tobin managed to hit the wrong note.

'Do drive on,' he said quickly, unable to conceal his embarrassment. 'She'll be all right in a few minutes. There's no need to stop.' The tightness angered me, the way Geoffrey sometimes angered me, and I thought: why do English women have to marry English men?

'It's all right,' I said. 'We've got plenty of time. You have a good cry, Mrs Tobin. I cried too, you know.'

'Did you?' She looked at me, understanding perfectly. 'Yes, you would have, I suppose you would have.' So she did know: I wondered how much Helen had told her. Two days before I would have been embarrassed: now I wasn't afraid of a mother's wrath. How much less divisive the love of the dead is than the love of the living. I put my arm round her and made vague comforting noises in her ear. In the back seat, Mr Tobin looked at his watch.

'She was so alive, Mark: that's what's so terrible. She wasn't meant to die young.' Again she went straight to the heart of the tragedy. My own thoughts, my own feelings, my own sense of loss: it was like talking to Helen and communicating so fluently that words were superfluous. Psychiatrists named the Oedipus complex long ago, an excess of love for one's mother. Perhaps they should also invent a term for the love of a mother-in-law or a mother-in-law *manquée*. In the intimacy of that moment, the thirty years between us mightn't have been there. I murmured: 'People like Helen never really die', and she said: 'Exactly, exactly, exactly' again and again until her tears were dry. After that we drove on to Geoffrey's in silence.

Thank God, the lighting rehearsal was over. Geoffrey welcomed the Tobins as if their arrival had been the only thing on his mind all afternoon. He offered profuse apologies for not coming to the airport, said all the right things about Helen and ushered them into the spare bedroom. No son-in-law could have done more. As soon as the door was shut behind them, his tune changed.

'Have you told them?' he hissed.

'About the play? Not yet.'

'Why the hell not?'

'Geoffrey, the mood wasn't right. They didn't want to hear about *The Winter's Tale*, they wanted to hear about Helen. Do try and keep a sense of perspective. You'll have to tell them yourself.'

193

'Oh all right. I do wish you'd help me. Martha's very touchy, you know.'

The blood surged to my head. 'Touchy' meant slow to appreciate what a good time it was for Shakespeare. 'Touchy' meant vulnerable to normal human emotion, not driven by mad obsessions. 'Touchy' meant decent and sensitive and gentle and humane – everything Helen and her mother were and Geoffrey could never be. I looked at him with hate in my heart and wondered how long I could go on loving him for Helen's sake. If he could have understood, I would have tried to explain; but there was a glaze of uncomprehending egotism over his whole face, like a film of oil. Wearily I said: 'Let me handle it, Geoffrey,' and he gripped my arm with the craven gratitude of a beggar.

Handling it proved easier than I expected. Again Helen helped me. I remembered a little fragment of conversation we'd once had about art: art with a small 'a', I hasten to add, for she loathed pomposity on the subject and did much to cure me of mine. 'Mummy and Geoffrey live on different planets,' she said. 'She thinks his obsession with Shakespeare is like one of those wasting diseases that small children get.' I hadn't seen the extent of the obsession at that stage, so I thought the comparison fanciful. But now that I had to break the news about *The Winter's Tale*, it steered me in the right direction.

'Geoffrey's in a bad way,' I began. Mrs Tobin was sitting on the side of the bed, still very teary; her husband was hanging up a suit in the wardrobe. 'He looks as if he's managing all right, but underneath he's taken it very badly. I don't think he's ever had to cope with this sort of thing before. We all have our way of getting over grief, but you may find his rather strange.'

Mrs Tobin looked at me anxiously. 'What do you mean?'

'Sometimes activity for activity's sake can be the best

194

solution. If you leave your mind free to wander, you can get dragged right under. Geoffrey's not a very strong person. Don't think of him as a man: think of him as an ailing child. I know that's a terrible thing to say, but it may help you understand how – how he's reacted. He needs to find strength from somewhere.'

I stopped, hoping I had said enough, but the Tobins looked at each other blankly. Damn Geoffrey, I thought, damn that sick monstrous ego. I wondered how long I could ramble on without using the word 'Shakespeare'. People turn so readily to religion in times of crisis: no bereaved husband is condemned as insane if he goes to church for the first time in twenty years. But a poet? A writer of stories which people dress up in doublet and hose and silly hats to perform? How does one explain to the uninitiated the charisma of a secular saint? But I had underestimated my audience. The Tobins mulled over my riddle and got halfway there.

'He's still got Shakespeare,' Mrs Tobin said, looking at the print of the balcony scene from *Romeo and Juliet* which hung above the bedstead. 'That will be a comfort.'

'Wasn't he going to put on one of the plays here in Rome?' her husband asked. 'Helen said something in a letter. I suppose that's all out of the window now.'

'Well, as a matter of fact . . .' I told them in a few short words. They were shocked, not outraged. Mr Tobin muttered: 'I think it's a bit much.' His wife dripped a little harder into her handkerchief. But there were no histrionics. I said Geoffrey wasn't a callous man, just an eccentric with eccentric needs, and they believed it more than I meant it. I suppose men who marry better women than they deserve are also likely to get better parents-in-law than they deserve. It's so unfair. No sooner had I patched things up for Geoffrey than I felt a sharp moment of bitterness. What had he done to be a winner while I struggled so hard to lose gallantly?

5

'The ending of *The Winter's Tale* isn't a happy ending in the conventional sense. The mood is one of transcendent joy. The protagonists aren't just miraculously reunited with each other, but changed for ever by the experience. The moral of the play couldn't be simpler: love is stronger than death, love will triumph over death . . .'

It was hard to be unmoved and none of us was unmoved. Geoffrey's five-minute speech before the dress rehearsal was truly extraordinary: I can remember it almost word for word. He didn't mention Helen by name and that seemed at first unbearably false, an unnecessary, self-destructive stoicism. But somehow he made a virtue out of the hypocrisy. Everyone knew what was going on underneath, everyone understood the mad English heroism of his performance. He may not have loved Helen enough, but he had still loved her: he still needed steel in his soul to put her death behind him. And what steel! It may have been escapism, but it was escapism of a peculiarly splendid kind. For Geoffrey, Shakespeare wasn't a retreat from reality, but a journey into reality. As his eyes danced and his cheeks glowed and his hands performed their spidery gestures of emphasis, the most hard-bitten philistine would have had to re-examine his prejudices.

'Wasn't he marvellous?' Vanessa whispered, as the cast trooped from the living-room into the bedroom to put on their costumes. It was the first of two dress rehearsals: the second was to be in Paparelli's house the following night.

'Marvellous.'

'Where does he find the courage to do something like that? I couldn't: could you? I'd just go to bed and cry for a week.'

'You're different, Vanessa.'

'You don't mind that, do you?'

'Of course not. It's the human thing to do.'

Reassured, she kissed me quickly on the cheek. I looked round to see if her father still had us under surveillance, but he was too busy helping Margaret arrange her head-dress. The quiet domesticity of the scene seduced the eye like a Vermeer masterpiece. I watched fascinated as, with infinite gentleness, he slid a hair-pin in behind her ear and patted the hair back into place. It was like being upstaged by an older and better actor: how much more subtly and tenderly that relationship was blossoming than my fling with his daughter . . .

Then farce undershot the solemnity of the occasion. I knew it would happen: somewhere, somehow that practical joker in the wings would find a way to disrupt the proceedings. The actors were on their best behaviour, but I had reckoned without Signora Bonnetti, the wardrobe mistress. Heaven knows where Geoffrey had got her from or what daft altruistic notions made her volunteer to make the costumes. She belonged to a section of Roman society that outsiders rarely penetrate, the *nouveaux pauvres*: down-at-heel aristocrats of modest means, fading gentlefolk still dining out on the fact that they had a Pope in the family in the thirteenth century. Her face wouldn't have looked out of place on an old Roman coin and she had the manner to go with it. Being measured by her at her rambling old house in Trastevere had been an intimidating experience: one felt incontrovertibly her subordinate. Now that her big scene had come, she moved imperiously into the centre stage.

'No, no, no. That does not go like that. What do you think you are doing? You are supposed to be a queen and you look like a gipsy. *Basta!*'

The first object of her scorn was Joanie. Joanie has a full bust: I think one can say that. Joanie also knows she has a full bust: I suppose that's inevitable. Now Shakespeare makes no reference to the size of Hermione's bust and, as the part was played by a boy, one wouldn't expect him to. A full-busted Hermione is therefore just as appropriate as a flat-chested Hermione, provided she can act or, in Joanie's case, provided she's the only person available to play the part. So let's get one thing straight. I'm not making any criticism at all of the size of Joanie's bust. A lot of perfectly decent, ordinary people with no perversions of any sort go for that look – and particularly, as it happens, in stage queens, who look far better statuesque than willowy. There was a Tosca at the Opera the other year who couldn't kiss the Mario because she couldn't reach him. The audience *loved* her.

On the other hand, there are full busts and full busts. It's nothing to do with size: it's to do with carriage. I'm a man, so I have no personal experience, but I suspect that breasts are like second-hand cars: if you have no confidence in what you're selling, you won't sell. Not over-confidence, mind you, just confidence. There are thousands of women all over Rome with a forty-two-inch bust who could have worn the low-cut silk dress Signora Bonnetti had made for Joanie and looked like Shakespeare's Hermione: Queen of Sicily, daughter of the Russian Emperor and utterer of the serenest lines in the play. It was a stunning dress. Signora Bonnetti was mistress of her craft and had a right to be disappointed. When she said Joanie looked like a gipsy, she was understating the problem. A gipsy Hermione would have been quite all right: a little bold, but well within the accepted codes of Shakespearian interpretation. But Joanie didn't look like a gipsy. She looked as if she'd spent twenty years pulling pints at the Red Lion in Hackney, leaning against the bar chatting to customers with a vodka and tonic in her hand. She murdered that dress, no question. Aesthetically I was on Signora Bonnetti's side, one hundred per cent. It was her tactics that were wrong. The word 'gipsy' was a mistake: correction, it was dynamite.

I don't know what part of England Joanie comes from. Chorleywood? Reigate? Maidenhead? Near enough to London to think the world owes her a living, not near enough to know what living is like. But I know exactly the stratum of English society she belongs to. One could define it in a hundred ways, but why spend hours fishing for the right words when the right words are there? In that particular stratum, where one enjoys a certain position but lacks the confidence to be scornful of other people's attacks on one's position, one is very sensitive to being called a gipsy by a foreigner. One does not take being called a gipsy lying down. At the word 'gipsy', in short, one hits the roof.

'Look here, you arrogant bitch, I'm not going to be spoken to like that.'

'Are you telling me my business?'

'Yes, I am telling you your business. You don't know what the hell you're talking about.'

'How dare you say that?'

'I'll say what I bloody well want. Fucking cow!'

Signora Bonnetti was an educated woman. She spoke good, rather literal English, with a reasonable vocabulary. But I don't think she'd heard any of the words Joanie used in the next thirty seconds. And the torrent of Italian invective with which she retorted was equally meaningless to Joanie. I edged towards them, ready to provide simultaneous translation, but it was too late for diplomacy. The

199

fight was for real. I wish Joanie had put a tenth of the feeling into Hermione that she showed in that slanging match.

Geoffrey appeared in the doorway, looking tense and confused. 'What's going on, Mark?'

'Your costume lady's upset Joanie.'

'What about?'

'Her bust.'

'Her what?'

'Her *bust*. Breasts, cleavage, you know. There are some questions of presentation involved. Aesthetic considerations.'

'It won't affect her speech in the trial scene?'

'I shouldn't think so.'

'Then I don't have time to worry about it. Sort it out, would you?'

I sorted it out. This involved telling Joanie, in English, that she would be a stunning Hermione and telling Signora Bonnetti, in Italian, that Joanie mightn't be a stunning Hermione, but she was all we had, the director's wife had died the day before and feelings were a little tense. Vanessa also mediated by suggesting that Joanie would look better if she held her shoulders back. She duly did so and, lo, the bust problem disappeared. Well, not disappeared: redefined itself. Instead of looking like a barmaid, she looked like a World War Two battle-tank, her bust preceding her like a gun-barrel. It wasn't pretty, it wasn't Shakespearian, but at least it had a stiff sort of regality. Signora Bonnetti clucked approvingly and Joanie gave a huge smile and said: 'I knew we were arguing about nothing.' For a few seconds normal diplomatic relations were restored. Then it was Rupert's turn. I saw him whispering with his mother in the corner and overheard enough to smell trouble. You would have thought that conceited little monster would have enjoyed looking like a Renaissance prince in a Titian painting, which was the effect of the highly ornate doublet and hose Signora Bonnetti had made for him. But Rupert's egotism had many refinements.

'Mummy?'

'What is it, sugar?'

'I can't wear this. I *can't*.'

'But, angel, it's a *lovely* costume. Mrs Bonnetti's gone to so much trouble.'

'It's sissy.'

'Of course it isn't sissy, lambkins. That's what little princes wore in those days. You look so handsome, handsome, handsome I want to kiss you, kiss you, kiss you.'

'No, Mummy, I shan't, I shan't.'

Geoffrey poked his head round the door. 'Act One in ten minutes, everyone. No more smoking please, Tony. You won't get into the character in time. Is everything all right, Mark?'

I sidled up to him, trying to keep things low-key. 'Not exactly. We've got another problem.'

'What's wrong?'

'I think Rupert's feeling a bit self-conscious.'

'Self-*conscious*? What about? He's eight years old, for Christ's sake.'

'He feels sissy in that costume.'

'Oh sod that. What does he expect to wear? Jeans and a T-shirt? A tracksuit? Tell him, if he doesn't wear it, there'll be big trouble.'

'What did you have in mind?'

'*I* don't know. Think of something. Don't boys like that get pocket money? Hit him if you have to. I'm not having him bugger us about. Yes, Walter, what is it?'

'Geoffrey, I've been thinking about one of my lines in Act Three.'

'What's the problem?'

'I'm not quite sure what Shakespeare's getting at. You see . . .'

Geoffrey threw himself heart and soul into the new problem. Never mind that it wouldn't make the slightest difference, whereas a Mamillius in jeans would make a travesty of the whole production. It had to do with Shakespeare and was therefore a question of Art, not admin. I braced myself to sort out Rupert alone, not encouraged by seeing Signora Bonnetti already in conversation with his mother.

'What is this word, "sissy"? I haven't heard it before. Does the costume not fit properly?'

'No, it isn't that, Signora. It's a lovely costume and *I* think he looks simply wonderful. The trouble is, well, he thinks he looks like a girl.'

'A girl? *Una ragazza*? Is he mad? That's how boys dressed in those days.'

'I've told him that, Signora, but he just won't listen. Is there nothing you can do to make him look a bit more like a boy and less like a girl? Perhaps if his tights were black rather than purple . . .'

'I think what Barbara's trying to say, Signora . . .' I slithered in desperately, seeing the veins on Signora Bonnetti's forehead turning purple, but it was too late. If her set-to with Joanie was like rival flower-sellers quarrelling in the marketplace, this outburst belonged to grand opera. There was a positive cadenza of insults: about the English, about people with no aesthetic taste, about women who couldn't keep their children under control. It was in Italian, but I had no time to translate: she had slammed the door behind her before the most seasoned diplomat could have done a thing. Even Geoffrey heard. He interrupted his little textual seminar with Walter and asked me

202

what the hell was going on. When I explained, he told me to sort it out and sort it out fast. The rehearsal was starting in five minutes, he was too busy, he didn't have time . . . Grimly I said a prayer to the patron saint of suckers, men who are nice to men they've cuckolded out of a misplaced sense of guilt. Let Helen see this, I thought, let her know who really loves her. Then I clouted Rupert round the ear.

'Put that costume on now or there'll be trouble.'

'What kind of trouble?'

Damn children. Damn people who have children. Damn people who tell you how adorable they are. I clouted him again, harder, and he ran to his mother. Damn mothers.

'Mr Barham hit me, Mummy.'

'You poor lamb. I'm sure he didn't mean to.'

'He did, he did, he did.'

'You didn't mean to, did you, Mark?'

'Yes, I did, Barbara. I'm sorry. It's called discipline.'

'You brute. What right have you got to discipline Rupert? Wait till I tell his father.'

'Barbara, by the time you tell his father the rehearsal will be over and it will be too late. I want Rupert in his costume in two minutes. Right, Rupert? Two minutes.'

'Shan't.'

I clouted him again: third time lucky. He started scrambling into his costume while his mother whimpered: 'Poor lambkin.' Joanie muttered: 'You bastard.' Vanessa winked. When Geoffrey came back into the room, the entire cast was ready. I'd learnt not to expect thanks from him, but he found time to pat me on the back and say: 'Well done, Mark: I'm awfully grateful.' I was getting used to small mercies.

The rehearsal itself went badly. No, not badly: excruciatingly. We plumbed depths of histrionic awfulness I hadn't known existed. Not a speech was left standing, not a phrase was unbloodied. What mad arrogance made Shakespeare boast that his words would last for all time, 'so long as men shall breathe or eyes can see'? If he'd known what we would do to *The Winter's Tale* in 1985, he would have had his entire works destroyed twenty-four hours after his death.

Despite the awfulness, people were still gung-ho: their blasé confidence was worse than what they did to the lines. Those who'd acted before told me it was perfectly normal. Dress rehearsals always went badly, it was the perform-ances that counted, everything would be all right on the night. Excuses flew around like confetti: there was no general sense of failure. Are real actors quite so complacent about their performances? Or is blinkered optimism univer-sal to people who dress up in silly costumes and declaim iambic pentameters into the night air? Mr and Mrs Tobin perched bravely on a sofa and watched the whole thing through. I had told them the play would make Helen's death easier to cope with, that it would be an act of renewal. As we took a ragged curtain-call and they clapped politely, I could hardly look them in the face.

Geoffrey's post-mortem was surprisingly stoical. 'I think Act One was a little lacking in pace,' he began, trying to decipher the notes he had been furiously jotting down while the rehearsal was in progress. Lacking in *pace*? It was funereal. Fluffed lines, crashing furniture, costumes split-ting at the seams, props not there when needed: each calamity capped the last one, like a well-rehearsed farce.

'More feeling, Rupert. Not quite so stiff, Joanie. Less flapping of your arms, please, Tony.' Geoffrey delivered earnest, precise notes and we all looked at the floor in embarrassment. Something had inexplicably snapped in him while the rehearsal was in progress. There was none of the inspirational fervour we had come to expect, none of those savage, intolerant outbursts we had learnt to fear. His points were apposite, but lacked conviction. He didn't sound as if he cared whether the actors took any notice. And he was blind, wilfully blind, to the underlying causes.

Rupert's lack of feeling, for example. Yes. Rupert's performance did lack feeling. He made damn sure it lacked feeling. Having been bullied into wearing the costume, he stood stiff as a ramrod and delivered every line like a Japanese computer. Mamillius is such a beguiling part that its main danger is an excess of sweetness. Drained of sweetness, it became a travesty: one had an overpowering urge to kick him in the arse. I got so incensed that I hissed at him to stop buggering about, but he just stuck out his tongue and went his own sweet way. His mother told him he was adorable.

And Joanie's stiffness. Yes, Joanie was stiff all right. She carried herself as if she'd just had major surgery to her spinal column. The comments on her gipsy's bust had wounded her deeply and she had to show she was superior to them. Showing she was superior to them meant assuming a massive air of dignity and holding her bust motionless in front of her like a church lectern. The sonorous pomposity of the performance defied description.

As for Tony's arm-flapping, what can I say? He did flap his arms and it did give a ludicrous aspect to his performance. But it would have been ten times worse if he hadn't flapped his arms. You see, the poor man's costume caught fire. He threw away his cigarette just before going on stage and let a bit of smouldering ash fall into the crease of his doublet. When smoke appeared, he identified the problem and, with some violent heaving movements, snuffed out the fire – all within the space of two lines of verse. He deserved a medal, not criticism.

I think the evening's only redeeming feature was the old-fashioned courtesy with which people behaved. Signora Bonnetti had no time for it, Rupert was too young to understand it. But it somehow kept the rest of us afloat. People knew Geoffrey had suffered a tragic loss. They knew, even if they didn't understand, that this play was to be his way of purging that suffering. And they played along. The rules had changed, but they respected the new rules as much as the old ones. They were English.

And me? The ex-English cynic, the one who'd hoped to leave all those hypocrisies behind? Inwardly, I still doubted if it was wise, this blind tribal loyalty, everyone clinging desperately to a madman's coat-tails. But my hand was forced. I wasn't going to rebel. I wasn't going to rock the boat. I wasn't going to be the one to say: no, we must stop acting like this. So I played along too. 'A feather for each wind that blows,' says the hero of *The Winter's Tale*. Not for the first time, Shakespeare got there nearly four hundred years before me.

6

'Are you Mr Barham?'

'Yes, that's right.'

'Can I talk to you, please?'

The white-haired old woman on my doorstep the next morning had a strange air of self-confidence. Her English was excellent and she looked me straight in the eyes like a well-trained policeman. I'd never seen her before, but she didn't treat me like a stranger. There was something welcoming in her manner, an appeal to common experience – as if we shared the same doctor or had known each other years before. She wore a plain black dress, very common among Italian women of her generation, and was holding a brown envelope in her hand. I squinted to see if it had an address or stamp, but it was unmarked. The mystery deepened. On another day I would have kept my distance, afraid she was a crank after my money. But with Helen's death I'd moved on: I'd left that frightened insularity behind me. At times of crisis, it's the cranks you want to talk to.

I helped her upstairs, holding on to her elbow as she negotiated the creaky wooden steps. She wasn't strong and her joints were stiff: arthritis, probably. When she sat down, she gave a little sigh as if sitting was painful. Then she looked around the room and again I had a sense of dislocation, of something not quite right. When people visit strangers' houses, they inspect them with an open mind: they don't measure them against their preconceptions because they don't have preconceptions. This woman was all preconception. She seemed anxious to see if things were as she expected, to confirm that I was the sort of person who someone else . . .

I didn't have to wait long. When she'd stopped studying the furniture, she looked at me and said: 'Helen sent me.' My throat dried and I gave an involuntary shiver, as if the window had burst open and an icy blast of air swept through the flat.

'Helen? When? How?'

'Yesterday.'

'But she died two days ago. She was dead yesterday.'

'I know.'

'Then what are you telling me? What is this? The dead don't talk to the living; they don't send people on errands like that. How did you find my address?'

She dipped into the brown envelope and pulled out a photograph. I snatched it angrily from her and looked at it. Hyde Park, 1977. Helen and me arm in arm next to a tree. The Serpentine behind us, glistening in the sunlight. In the sweetness of the memory, all my anger evaporated. We asked a passing American woman to take the picture, because we were bored of photographing each other and wanted to pose together. Helen said: 'Now we can be blackmailed', and we laughed about the picture falling into the wrong hands and tried to look naughty and intimate as if we were taking a wildly silly risk. I remembered the moment vividly, but had never seen the picture itself: we split up before the film was developed. I turned it over. 'Mark Barham, 23A Piazzetta Cortoni'. It was Helen's handwriting: the elaborate 'a's were unmistakable. The last word was smudged, as if she'd written in a hurry and not let the ink dry. I felt frightened.

'Where did you get this? Did you know Helen?'

'I was a friend.'

'An old friend?'

'A new friend. We met at Christmas.'

'Why have you come to me? What does it mean?'

She said it again. 'Helen sent me.' And again my throat dried and, in a second of wild imagination, the old woman's features dissolved into Helen's. I stared at her.

'Yes, yes, you said that. How did she send you? Are you a medium or something? I don't understand.'

'Not a medium, no.'

'Then what?'

'It would take too long to explain.' She bowed her head shyly, like a coy girl. I had thought she was well into her sixties, but perhaps she was younger. Her eyes were full of life and her neck was that of a fifty-year-old. I poured her a glass of water and put my hand on her arm.

'Don't worry about time. I have all the time in the world. Tell me about this photograph. Did Helen give it to you?'

'Yes.'

'When? Recently?'

'Last month.'

'Why did she give it to you? Why did she write my name on the back?'

'Because she wanted me to pray for you.'

'To *pray* for me?' I looked at her open-mouthed, pole-axed by a four-letter word not in my vocabulary. All sorts of religious images started to swirl around in my head – crucifixes, statues of the Virgin, bald priests in flowing white robes – but nothing I could associate with Helen, my Helen, a woman of flesh and blood who drew her mystery from the earth and nowhere else. I shook my head in confusion. 'I don't understand. Helen didn't – I'm sorry, I don't mean that, I don't know whether she did or not, we hadn't talked about such things for years. It's possible that . . . Go on, anyway. Why were you going to pray for me? Couldn't she pray for me herself?'

'Of course she could. But she wanted me to pray too. We prayed for each other.'

'A sort of pooling of resources? I don't mean to be facetious.'

'Yes, that's it.'

'I see. And she prayed for your friends?'

'Not my friends. My husband.' She indicated her black dress. 'My dead husband.'

'Ah yes. I'm sorry. And she kept a photo of him, did she?'

'Yes.'

'How odd. I don't mean odd. I mean, how touching. Did you – did she give you a picture of anyone else? Apart from me? Her husband or – '

'No. There was only you.'

'How interesting.' I smiled. I couldn't help smiling. The smile stretched the corners of my mouth until they hurt. So it was only me, only me who – who what, though? Are those we pray for necessarily those we love most? Don't people sometimes pray for their enemies, or for friends they think need help? It was thirty years since I'd prayed on a systematic basis. 'God bless Mummy, God bless Daddy, God bless Susie, God bless Auntie Rachel and Uncle Frank, God bless Lucky . . .' I ran my fingers nervously over the photo and wondered if I really wanted this unique distinction.

Then, in a blinding flash, it came to me. The hair, the eyes, the black dress, the strange spiritual assurance. In my head, a dead man and a dead woman started to scream their innocence.

I said: 'I know you now. You are Signora Giorgini. Your husband collapsed and died on the way to the tobacconist's.

210

You live at No. 76 Via Foraggi, in the flat below Signor Tardelli who was murdered. It was you Helen came to visit.'

'Yes,' she said, staring at me in amazement. It was her turn to look frightened.

I'm not a callous man. I have most of the ordinary qualms, the ordinary scruples. I could never cause an animal pain and, until Rupert, who deserved it, I'd never whacked anyone smaller than myself. Six days out of seven, I'm reasonable, considerate, even sensitive. It was Helen who disturbed the balance in me, who blotted out – sometimes for quite long periods – those normal human feelings.

For, in that blinding moment of truth, Tardelli should have consumed all my remorse: my whole body should have been racked by the tragedy of that farce. Whatever his faults, whatever he had done in his life, he was no more than an innocent bystander in my struggle for Helen. He deserved better of me.

But my thoughts weren't of Tardelli. My remorse swelled to a crescendo only later, only when I'd made my peace with Helen. Her innocence of what I'd suspected her, and my joy in that innocence, obliterated everything else. I questioned my visitor with feverish curiosity, not understanding all she said, but burning to know the facts: the real facts, not the mish-mash of fantasy my jealous imagination had concocted.

She had met Helen by accident, she said, on one of the bridges crossing the Tiber. They were travelling in opposite directions, but found themselves standing together in the middle of a pedestrian crossing, waiting for the light to go green. Something about Helen had seemed special and welcoming: she looked like a person who didn't shy away from strangers but embraced them generously. It was only a week after her own husband had died: she was looking for friends.

'What did you say?'

'I just said: "Do you mind if I talk to you?" She was very kind. We had coffee together.'

'And then?'

'We started meeting more often. We found we had a lot in common.'

'Did she talk about me at all?'

'Not then, no. We talked about more general things.'

'Like what?'

'It's hard to explain.' Again she bowed her head coyly. I don't think I've ever seen religious faith worn so lightly: she whispered the sort of credos Geoffrey trumpeted. 'The need to love people, the difficulty of loving them properly, the importance of looking beyond this life to the next life.'

'Heaven and Hell, you mean?'

'No, not Heaven and Hell. We didn't use words like that. We were very suspicious of the old religions: they made so little sense. We wanted to make our own religion. Perhaps that was arrogant.'

'Not at all. You were only looking for answers that made sense to you. We all do that, don't we? It all sounds so natural, so – innocent. I don't understand, I just don't understand.'

She looked at me anxiously. 'What don't you understand?'

'If it was like that, if that was all – why was Helen so secretive about it? She told lies, you know, Signora.'

'Helen did? Helen told lies about me?'

'Yes, definitely. More than once. When she was meeting you, she told her husband she was going to the cinema or made some other excuse. Don't ask me how I know, but I do know. Why did she have to do that? Why, Signora?'

There was a long silence. The question lingered forlornly and we were each as miserable as the other that there was no easy answer. My mind chafed at the sheer irrationality of what had happened, Helen's failure to conform to a pattern of behaviour I was able to understand. Signora Giorgini held her head in her hands, bewildered by what I had said.

'I think perhaps she was embarrassed,' she said at last. 'Her husband disapproved of me, you know.'

'Geoffrey?'

'Yes, I think he was called Geoffrey. He didn't like me. He thought I was bad for Helen.'

'How do you know? Did you meet him?'

'Helen told me. She said they had argued about me. I told her not to worry and that people with strong beliefs always had trouble being accepted. I told her she should be patient and try to get him to see her point of view. Perhaps she just gave up trying. Do you think that was it?'

'Yes, maybe.' My eyes smarted with pain. How typical of Helen to do it that way – for wouldn't a woman who took a lover on the side do other things on the side too? Her little bird, she called it, the free spirit imprisoned within her which she sometimes had to release for her own sanity; the independent corner of her being which she kept jealously to herself. She used to say she could never give herself one hundred per cent to another person, not to Geoffrey, not to me, not even, it seemed, to Signora Giorgini or to that other who used Signora Giorgini as His mouthpiece. If she had told me everything, I might somehow have understood, for there was nothing unlovable in what she had done, quite the reverse. Tardelli's worldly affectations could only have diminished her: instead she had reached for something higher than herself. She had moved on, while I had stayed complacently where I was. Yes, it was easy to admire that evolution, to see it as part and parcel of the Helen I had looked up to so religiously. But now her secretiveness had found her out, just as my jealousy had found me out. It was hard not to feel we were all being laughed at.

'Tell me something,' I said urgently. A great hatred towards Geoffrey was rising in me, but I kept it in check. 'You said Helen wanted you to pray for me. What did she say exactly?'

'She said you were in pain and she couldn't help you herself.'

I nodded sadly. 'She was right about the pain. Can you see it in my face, Signora? You looked so pitying just now.'

'Yes, I can see it.'

'And did Helen tell you everything about me?'

'Everything.'

'You seem very certain. Everything's more than she told me, you know, and yet she and I were close, very close once. If she told you everything, then she told you what she felt about me. Did she love me, do you think?'

'Oh yes.'

'And did she still love me?'

'Oh yes.'

'Right to the end?'

'Oh yes. Her love changed, but it was still love. If you hadn't asked so much of her, you would have seen that. There was her husband . . .'

'Yes, I know. Geoffrey. Mad, tyrannical Geoffrey. Dull, stupid, blind, self-centred Geoffrey. He got between me and Helen and then he got between you and Helen. There's only one sort of love that man understands: necrophilia for a dead writer. Everything else he crushes and tramples on. How can you forgive that, Signora?'

'Because there's no other way. If we can't love people like that, we can't love at all. Love is – '

'I know, Signora, I know.' I cut her off in mid-sentence, but I wasn't being rude. The additional words were superfluous: however that sentence was going to end, I knew it was heading for the truth. I'd been a sucker for one sort of love and now I was becoming a sucker for another. Those three 'oh yes's were still ringing in my ear like a fanfare: they couldn't have sounded sweeter on Helen's lips. What a fool, I thought, what a fool. How totally I had misread the situation. It was Helen who had kept faith with our love, not me; who had seen that the nature of the love had to change if it was to survive. I clutched the sides of my chair, not wanting the conversation to end. Beyond the sweetness of consolation, I could sense a deeper excitement. Perhaps the dead could talk to the living, perhaps Helen could belong to the future as well as the past. I had thought I would have only memories: the prospect of something better suddenly seemed tantalizingly real. I'm not a religious man: I haven't the temperament to make those great leaps in the dark. Most of Signora Giorgini's claims I'd greeted sceptically, not willing to give them a literal application. But suppose I was wrong about that too?

'"Helen sent me",' I said in great excitement. 'That was what you said. "Helen sent me." What did you mean exactly? She was dead when she sent you. Did you have a dream about her?'

'No.'

'Or hear her voice?'

'No, no. It wasn't as simple as that. I just knew it was what Helen wanted. I can't explain. I just *knew*.' She must have seen my disappointment, because she gave a gentle sigh of sympathy. 'I'm sorry. I wish it had been something more dramatic, for your sake. People used to have visions in their sleep or a heavenly angel would appear to them. It's not like that any more. You're looking for a miracle and I can't give you a miracle – only that I'm here and that Helen wanted me to be here. Don't ask for more. Don't expect more.'

I nodded. 'I'll try not to, but there's still so much . . . Please tell me something, Signora. Do you feel as close to Helen as you did before? Can you communicate with her as you say she's communicated with you?'

'Yes, I think so.'

'Then could you tell her something – for me?'

'Of course.'

'Tell her I'm sorry. Tell her I didn't love her well enough, but there's still a long way to go. Tell her not to give up on me. Tell her to be patient and wait for me – wherever she is.'

She smiled at my copiousness. 'That's a lot to tell a dead woman. I'll try to remember it all. When she asked me to pray for you, she told me the prayers wouldn't be wasted. I can see what she meant now. I even think you'll be talking to her yourself soon.'

'Maybe. Maybe.' My voice weakened, my excitement cooled. Moments of religious fervour can be as short-lived as other climaxes of passion: something can seem intensely real one minute and an embarrassment the next. For a few seconds I could really believe in a Helen who was waiting for me to join her; but I couldn't sustain the belief, I didn't have what it took to reshape a life on the basis of that simple idea. I felt as if I was being taken further than I wanted faster than I wanted, so I stepped back, afraid to commit myself too far. I don't know if Signora Giorgini found that 'maybe' a disappointment or if she was upset by the persistence of my secularity. But it was the most positive word I could honestly use. It was only when she rose to leave that I felt another surge of faith.

'Signora?'

'Yes?'

'Your neighbour who was murdered, Signor Tardelli.'

'Pietro?'

'I knew him. Not very well, but I knew him. I'm not happy about him – something came between us and I didn't love him as I should have. Could you tell him I'm sorry too?'

She went white, understanding me with terrible precision, and took a step backwards. I realized then that, even for God's chosen ones, there are labours of love too mountainous to undertake.

'No,' she said. 'I think you must tell him that yourself.'

7

Half an hour later, the police arrived: two uniformed *carabinieri* and a man in a grey suit looking like a bank manager who boxed in his spare time. Conti, he said his name was. The *carabinieri* turned the flat upside down and Conti waved a warrant in my face. It was undated and unsigned, but I didn't quibble. In Italy, if you query details like that, you're assumed to be an intellectual. Italians don't like intellectuals.

'Meester Barham?'

'Yes, that's me.'

'You a friend of Meesus Giorgini? Yes no?' The man's style of interrogation was as clumsy as his English. He stood foursquare in front of me like a bulldog guarding its bone. After the sophisticated operator who had tailed me the day before, he was a big disappointment.

'A very new friend. I met her for the first time this morning.'

'Why she come see you today if you never met her before?'

'We both knew a woman called Mrs Danes who was drowned last Sunday in a boating accident. We were commiserating with each other. Excuse me: could you ask your men to be a little more careful?'

'Paolo! Gianni!'

It was no good. Paolo growled and carried on smashing my typewriter. Gianni turned the clothes out of my drawers with the same unquenchable gusto. I seethed. Nothing convinces a guilty man of his innocence as quickly as police brutality. In my newly deepened remorse, I could have confessed Tardelli's murder to a priest without thinking: with this lot, I felt like making a fight of it.

Conti paced the room in silence, trying to think up some penetrating question. I asked him to sit down. He said no. I asked him if he minded if I sat down. He said no. I asked him if he smoked. He said no. I asked him if he wanted a drink. He said no. It was like a course in basic English: you didn't learn 'thank you' till the second lesson.

Finally his brain creaked into action. 'You knew Meester Tardelli?' he barked.

'Tardelli? The journalist who was killed? I believe I met him at a party once. That's all.'

He whipped out a pocket notebook. 'A party given by Meester Newton on April 30? Yes no?'

'It may have been.'

'You talk to him about the white shirt he was wearing. After the party you follow him to his car and say something to him. Yes no?'

'Was *that* Tardelli? I didn't realize. And to think he's dead now. Goodness.'

'What you say to Meester Tardelli on April 30?'

'I'm sorry, I don't remember. If I'd known he was going to be *dead* within a week, well, of course, I'd have remembered every word. Do you know the really funny thing?'

'Funny?' He scowled.

'I mean funny odd, of course.'

'Funny odd?' The scowl turned to bewilderment.

'As opposed to funny ha ha. I'm sorry, I've lost you, haven't I? Funny meaning strange or peculiar. *Strano, bizzarro, eccentrico.*' I made sure I rattled off enough synonyms to make him wonder why the hell we were talking in English. 'Mr Tardelli and Mrs Giorgini were neighbours. They lived in the same house. Did you know that?'

He shifted. 'Maybe I know, maybe I not know.'

'Mrs Giorgini told me that this morning. The house is in the Via Foraggi, near the Teatro Marcello, which is also rather funny, I mean strange. You see, I know the Via Foraggi well. I often walk down it.'

'Stop.' He turned back a page in his notebook. 'On April 26 you talk to Meesus Manzi at No. 36 Via Foraggi. You wear blue jeans, white shirt and smoke American cigarettes. You talk about Meester Tardelli. Yes no? On April 27 you talk to Meesus Manzi again. You wear blue jeans, blue shirt and have not shaved. You talk about Meester Tardelli. Yes no? On April 28 you talk to Meesus Manzi again. You wear blue jeans, red shirt and look as if you very unhappy about something. You talk about Meester Tardelli. Yes no?'

'Yes to all three days. I'm impressed.'

'You a friend of Meesus Manzi?'

'Only an acquaintance. We've struck up a conversation once or twice. We don't send each other Christmas cards or anything like that.'

'Why you ask her so much about Meester Tardelli?'

'She had a lot to say about all her neighbours. He seemed to be the most interesting man on the street. That's all.'

'No, that is not all, Meester Barham.' He pulled himself up to his full height and stuck out his chest. The buttons on his shirt looked as if they could pop off at any minute. It was all too ridiculous: I couldn't have felt guilty if I'd tried. 'Final question. Do not answer if you not want to. Where were you at midnight on May 1? Yes no?'

'In bed, probably.'

'Your bed?'

'Yes.'

'Alone? Yes no?'

'I don't remember. Why are you asking me this? Was May 1 when Mr Tardelli was killed? Oh *really*, Mr Conti. You don't think I did it, do you? That's so *funny*.'

'Funny odd?'

'No, not funny odd. Funny ha ha. Ha ha ha!' I laughed till the tears streamed down my cheeks. It must have been terribly convincing. I had thought I would have to fake surprise and do it badly, the way the villains do in books. ' "Surely you're joking, Inspector?" he said nervously, dabbing his forehead with a handkerchief. "On the night of the murder we were playing bridge with the Leveson-Gowers from seven-thirty till midnight." ' But my laughter was totally genuine. Conti's pomposity may have given my ribs the final tickle, but it triggered something far more fundamental, something which welled up from the depths of my being, demanding to be expressed. The merriment obliterated everything else: remorse, compassion, bewilderment, religious awakening, the whole cauldron of emotion into which Signora Giorgini's visit had thrown me. I suddenly realized what He must feel like, the cruel, capricious God who strews my path with banana-skins. Signora Giorgini's God could never have seen the funny side of bumping off Tardelli like that: He would have thought it very bad taste. Conti didn't see the joke either. He stared at my heaving shoulders and looked slightly sick: a Catholic, no doubt. But it was funny. It was, it was, great balls of fire, it was. I laughed till my whole body ached.

In the bedroom, Paolo gave a grunt of excitement. Gianni snuffled in to see what was going on. A few minutes later they emerged grinning all over their faces. Paolo was holding one of Vanessa's bras in his hand. They showed it to Conti and conferred. Conti jotted something down in his notebook. I was mesmerized. Did they think it was the murder weapon?

Conti came across to me sternly. 'Is this yours? Yes no?'

'No, of course it's not mine. It's a woman's. What do you think I am? A pervert?'

'Maybe a pervert, maybe not a pervert.'

'I thought this was a murder enquiry. What does my sex life have to do with anything?'

'You tell me, Meester Barham, you tell me.' He smirked arrogantly. Paolo and Gianni were beside themselves with glee. I took the bra and ran my fingers over it. It was delicate, soft to the touch: I remembered cupping my hands over it while Vanessa was inside it and believing, for a brief sweet moment, that I was back with Helen. Conti was warmer than he knew. If I'd never known the sweetness, would I have cared so much about Tardelli?

'It belongs to a friend of mine,' I said sharply. Their absurdity was starting to rankle. It's a sick world when the police are madder than those they hunt. 'She's called Vanessa Jansen. She is English and she is above the age of consent. She seems to be a size thirty-four. I don't know what that is in Italian. There is a reference to St Michael on the label which may puzzle you. Let me explain.'

'Never mind that, Meester Barham. You sleep with Vanessa? Yes no?'

'Yes.'

'You enjoy sleeping with her? Yes no?'

'Yes, it's all right.'

'You sleep with her many times. Yes no?'

'Not many times, no.'

'Five times? Ten times? This very important, Meester Barham. Think before you speak.'

'I really can't – ' I stopped and stared at him. He was close to bursting. As he leant forward to catch my answer, a little trickle of saliva made its way down his chin and on to his shirt-front. There is something hypnotic about unrestrained lasciviousness: it takes you by surprise even when you half expect it. I had seen the sensualist in Conti the minute he walked through the door: the full lips, the jaunty walk, the sly, roving eyes. He might have appeared in one of my books as the frustrated husband, keeping the beast at bay by running his eyes up women's legs on the underground. Now that the lid had been taken off, the character ceased to be comic. We justify our own madness by its individuality: other people's excesses are far less glamorous. I even felt a little twinge of pity, as if Helen was tugging at my sleeve and reminding me about love.

A voice behind me broke the silence. 'It was eight times, wasn't it, Mark? The ninth didn't count: we tried too hard and did it badly.'

I spun round and saw Vanessa standing in the doorway, smiling mischievously. Conti's mouth dropped open and he tried to regain the appearance of dignity by patting the top of his head. He didn't mind getting excited about a bra, but the real thing . . . what would Mrs Conti say? Paolo and Gianni stood rather ludicrously to attention. Vanessa beamed. It was quite an entrance.

Conti fumbled with his notebook. 'Vanessa Jansen? Yes no?'

'Yes, that's me. Mine, I think.' She took the bra out of his hands, folded it ostentatiously and put it away in a drawer. 'Now what's happening, Mark?'

'The police are here to question me.'

'What about?'

'A murder enquiry. A journalist called Tardelli was killed in the Via Foraggi last week. They think I did it.'

'You're *kidding*!'

'No, it's true. Ask Mr Conti.'

'Conti? *Conti!* Mark, this is too ridiculous. And the bra? I suppose they think you *strangled* him with it? How *funny*!'

She creased herself, she absolutely creased herself. Her waist buckled, then she went at the knees, then she knelt on the sofa and started kicking the floor with her feet. It was quite a sight. When twenty-year-olds let themselves go, they have it over thirty-eight-year-olds every time. You couldn't blame Conti for reacting as he did: any more unbridled ridicule and his self-importance would have suffered permanent damage.

'I wish you good morning, Meester Barham,' he said, standing stiffly to attention. 'Good morning, Signorina. This is no laughing matter. I shall return. I *shall* return. Paolo! Gianni!'

They trooped out and clattered down the stairs. I fell gratefully into Vanessa's arms.

'Bedtime? Yes no?'

'Definitely.'

In the night, as Vanessa slept, I slipped out to the living-room to have another look at the photograph Signora Giorgini had brought. My fingers trembled with excitement: it was like clutching a religious relic, a receipt for something extraordinary that had happened long ago. Helen's face smiled merrily up at me, its vitality undiminished, its joy frozen in time, its mystery safe for ever.

It was 3 A.M., not an hour when people act altogether normally. I struck up a foolish conversation with the celluloid, as if it had power to answer. 'Why didn't you tell me, Helen? Why didn't you try to *explain*? Were you frightened, dearest? You didn't need to be. I'm selfish and I'm greedy, but I'm not a monster. I would probably have fought Signora Giorgini for you tooth and nail, the way I fought Geoffrey for you, but I wouldn't have won because you wouldn't have let me win. And whatever took you back and back to that woman, I would have wanted to understand it and be part of it because it meant so much to you. I'm a cynic and a sceptic, but that doesn't mean I'm spiritually dead, that I'm without possibility. Please, please tell me you don't think that little of me.'

She smiled back, but said nothing. The love in her eyes was transparent, for the camera had kept perfect faith with what we were to each other in those so-transient days, but it wasn't enough for me. I wanted to know how much of those feelings had lasted and what had taken their place, to ask Helen why she had stuck so doggedly to Geoffrey and what she had seen in Signora Giorgini – so many questions. Her silence infuriated me, as it had always infuriated me, and my grip on the photograph tightened. 'Talk to me, damn you, talk!' My anger obscured the fact but, for the first time in thirty years, I was praying.

Still the picture kept its secrets. I waited tensely, too cocooned in emotion to be conscious of the absurdity of what I was doing. Finally I shut my eyes and whispered, without anger: 'If you can't talk, give me a sign. Prove that you still love me and want to comfort me. Let a bird settle on my balcony in the next five minutes.' My heart pounded, my forehead ran with sweat, my eyes swayed metronomically between the clock on the mantelpiece and the window leading to the balcony. A long way off, from the direction of the Forum, a woman let out a single low cry of protest – but no bird came. And then I think despair must have set in, because I did the craziest thing: I snatched a coin from my desk, gripped it tightly between my forefinger and thumb and threatened Helen with it. 'All right then, I will *make* you give me a sign. I will give you a free choice, but I won't let you run away from the choice. You will have to decide once and for all. Heads you love me and care about me, tails you don't. Show me which it is.'

I spun the coin high in the air, pinning all my hopes on a primitive act of faith, determined to drag Helen into my world, a world without mystery or complexity, a world of yes or no, not yes and no, a world in which chance was the only arbiter. But she wouldn't let me. The coin hit the ground, bounced once and rolled into the kitchen: there it lodged in a crack in the floorboards, in a perfectly upright position. And with that sign, if it was a sign, my senses returned.

8

Come the final dress rehearsal, nobody was sane. It was like a lunatic asylum outing. Eyes twitched. Hands fidgeted. Bodies writhed. Armageddon was upon us and we had nowhere to hide. People's neuroses tumbled out uncontrollably, like lemmings over a cliff.

'I just *know* my make-up's going to run.'

'These tights are killing me.'

'I'm feeling too tense.'

'I'm feeling too laid-back.'

'I'm feeling sick.'

'My cue! I've forgotten my cue! Walter, quickly: what do you say just before I come on in the trial scene?'

'Who's taken my wig?'

'Where's Geoffrey? I've got to talk to Geoffrey.'

'Oh Christ.'

'Oh shit.'

'Oh bugger.'

'Oh fuck.'

It was Paparelli's turn to move into centre stage. He stalked among us like a Roman emperor revelling in the acclaim of the populus. Now that he had screwed Geoffrey for his money, he was all smiles, only too delighted to have his house taken over by benign English eccentrics. He welcomed us warmly and put all his services at our disposal. No trouble was too much for him. There were flowers in the dressing-rooms and bottles of brandy discreetly to hand for frayed nerves. The great living-room itself, where the performances were to take place, was a minor masterpiece of the Baroque. Painted stucco cherubs chased each other up the walls and across the ceiling. White fleecy clouds punctuated an azure sky. Saints with golden haloes looked down on us with arms outstretched. It was a sublime setting, crying out for real actors. No wonder nerves started to jingle.

Geoffrey himself was more agitated than I had ever seen him. He bustled to and fro like a pantomime dame, interesting himself in every detail of the production. 'Are those shoes all right, Tony?' 'You'll need a bigger bow than that, Margaret.' 'Where are the scissors? Scissors, scissors, scissors.' At the eleventh hour, he had suddenly realized that Shakespeare wasn't enough: the nuts and bolts had to be in place or the iambic pentameters would go down the drain. That little concession to sanity kept us all alive.

Before the rehearsal, he called us all on stage for another homily. You would have thought there was nothing new to say, but he spoke eruditely and fluently for nearly twenty minutes, not just about the play but about the human feelings it expressed. He talked about love and the pain of love and the misapprehensions of love as if he had spent his entire life in a confessional or as an agony aunt – as if *nothing* could surprise him. I used to resent it, that assumption of familiarity with matters of which he knew nothing: it sounded the same false note as a millionaire talking socialism. There is something heretical in the idea that one can learn as much about life from books as from life itself. But Geoffrey sanctified that heresy. He talked about Leontes' jealousy with such understanding that my eyes smarted and my arms shivered with goose-pimples. Perhaps if you read the right books, not the wrong ones . . . After meeting Signora Giorgini, I wanted more than ever to despise Geoffrey, to hate him for driving all that was best and sweetest in Helen underground. But the hatred got stuck in my throat. And this time it was Shakespeare, not Helen, who stopped it.

The Tobins were again our only audience. They sat in gilt armchairs in front of the makeshift stage, completely dwarfed by the splendour of the room. Mr Tobin had a face of stone. His wife smiled nervously, trying to contribute to the occasion.

'It's very good of you to come,' I whispered to her, in a brief hiatus while Geoffrey was making adjustments to the lights. 'There was no need to trouble yourselves.'

'It's quite all right, Mark: you don't have to thank us. What else is there to do?'

'It's a very long play, I'm afraid, and probably not your sort of thing.'

'Well, you can't have everything. The costumes are nice. And I did like your scene as the Bear.'

I smiled. 'I'm glad. Most people like that. You don't expect a bear in Shakespeare, do you?'

'Exactly. It was just like a pantomime. Helen *loved* pantomimes.' Her eyes misted and she dipped into her handbag for a tissue. I put my hand on her arm and she gripped it thankfully, as if it was all she had to hold. Should I tell her about Signora Giorgini, I wondered? It seemed such a strange, incoherent message to pass on that I wasn't sure it would be a comfort. There was something solidly secular about Mrs Tobin: she seemed to draw her goodness from the earth, not the heavens. But then hadn't I thought the same about Helen? Perhaps it was only me who found the life of the spirit so unfathomable.

'You'll be all right after tomorrow,' I said, not believing my own platitude. What difference would Helen's funeral make? We would bury her and be glad it was over, but we wouldn't be healed: our griefs would outlast her mortal remains as surely as winter followed summer.

229

'Will there be many there?' she asked.

'Just the two of you and Geoffrey. And me. Geoffrey didn't want a crowd. He said, if everybody came, it would be too much.'

'Too much for what?'

'I'm not sure. You know what a private man he is. Once this play's over, he'll go right back into his shell. At least you've got each other.'

'That's true.' Her left hand slipped into her husband's right hand, electronically guided to its target. The instinctive precision filled me with dumb envy. Was it for this that Helen had held out so long against me? The reassuring familiarity of a long-loved, long-lasting relationship? Even in a passionless marriage, there is an arcane beauty at once impressive and baffling to the outsider. Sometimes I think of my relationship with Helen as a tragedy of mischance, a hard luck story. If we had met five years earlier . . . But then suppose I had got there before Geoffrey, with all my passion and all my commitment? Could I ever have given her what she wanted in a husband? I doubt it. I'm greedy. I ask too much. I don't understand the value of dispassion. Ten years of me would probably have driven her into Signora Giorgini's arms as surely as ten years of Geoffrey.

The dress rehearsal – of course – went badly: not quite as badly as the first dress rehearsal, but pretty bloody badly. Mildly excruciating? Depressingly third-rate? I've run out of adjectives for that rabble. How do theatre critics do it night after night?

In the middle of the third Act, the lights went. One minute Joanie was massacring her big speech, trilling her 'o's and manoeuvring coyly into the centre of the stage like an elephant in ballet-shoes, and the next there was total black-out. Geoffrey shouted 'Hold it!' and everyone on stage giggled nervously, not sure if they were allowed to find it funny. I tiptoed out of the wings in my bear costume to see what was going on.

'Fuse by the look of it,' said Tony.

'Damn shame,' said Joanie. 'I was feeling really into the part just then. Hey-ho.'

'Any electricians in the cast?'

'Do you want a hand, Geoffrey?'

'Who's in charge of the lighting anyway?'

'Trust Italy. This country's so bloody inefficient.'

'Bad light stopped play?'

'Anyone got a candle and a pack of cards?'

A door slammed at the back of the room and Paparelli appeared with a torch. The flickering beam of light finally picked out Geoffrey, who was looking particularly apoplectic.

'*Scusi*, Signor Danes, *molti scusi. Un' accidente sfortunato.*'

'I didn't get a fucking word of that. *Mark!* Where are you?'

'Here, Geoffrey.'

'Ask this joker what's wrong with the lights. Tell him I want it sorted out immediately. Not in five minutes, not in ten minutes: *now*. Tell him, if there are no lights on that stage by the time I count to ten, I'll sue him for every penny he's got. I'll have the shirt off his back. One. Two. I'm waiting, Paparelli. Three. Sod you, you fat woppish idiot. Four.'

'Hold on, Geoffrey. I think it might be more diplomatic –' I moved forward to intervene. Unfortunately, Paparelli hadn't been warned there was a bear in *The Winter's Tale*; even more unfortunately, the shaggy head I was wearing was a masterpiece of the taxidermist's art. As his torch lit up my face, he gave a horrified yell. I said something calming in Italian, but it was fatal: after all, an Italian-speaking bear is far more terrifying than a bear-speaking bear, if you think about it. He gibbered at me not to come near him and made big shooing gestures with his arms. I had to pull the bear's head off before he was reassured.

'Ah, Signor *Barham. Scusi, molti scusi.*' Then he got the giggles: you couldn't blame him. There is something funny about a bear with a detachable head, whichever way you look at it. The trouble was, Geoffrey didn't see it like that. He was a bit protective about Shakespeare's Bear at the best of times: as much tragic as comic, he would insist, a metaphor for the irrational violence which ran through the play in counterpoint to the theme of love … To see an Italian wine-merchant laughing at one of the Bard's masterstrokes was even more infuriating than a blown fuse. His face went purple and he lunged towards Paparelli like a frenzied child.

'Geoffrey, stop it. This is madness. Do get a grip on yourself.' I pinioned his arms and he struggled to free himself, tearing strips of fur off my costume.

'I won't,' he screamed. 'I won't. I'm not having that slimy Italian bastard making a fool of me. I'm going to kick his balls into next week. Let go of me, Mark, let go of me.'

I kept my grip. Paparelli pulled himself together. Mrs Tobin said: 'Really, Geoffrey.' There were murmurs of disapproval from the actors blacked out on stage. Then, with merciful suddenness, the lights came back on. We froze like figures in a tableau, blinking and looking uncertainly around us. The light shamed Geoffrey into moderation, but it did more than that. Before they could pull apart, I saw Peter and Margaret standing together in the corner of the stage, holding each other furtively like children playing hide-and-seek in the cupboard under the stairs. Not everyone noticed, but those who did wore broad grins as the rehearsal ground back into motion. Something surely, some human act of dignity, would be salvaged from those dark days in our lives.

9

In all the chaos, I didn't talk to Geoffrey till the following morning. We drove out to the cemetery together, crawling in second gear behind the hearse while the Tobins followed in a hired car. Geoffrey wanted it that way. I think Martha Tobin's constant tears had unnerved him: they probably reminded him of what he should have been feeling himself. His own heart – I suppose you can call it that – was in its usual place.

'I do think last night went better than the night before,' he announced, as we came to rest at a traffic light. He sounded like a man comparing two vintages of claret. 'People were much quicker on their cues and I thought the pastoral scene came across well. If it hadn't been for that fiasco with the lights, I would have been reasonably pleased. What did you think?'

'It could have been worse.'

'Do you think we'll pull through?'

'Maybe.'

'You sound doubtful.'

I watched the wind rustling the wreath on the top of the hearse and remembered the same wind – there's only one wind, it's as indivisible as the sun – billowing Helen's blouse as we walked in Hyde Park.

'It's hard to be an optimist, Geoffrey. There are other things . . .' I couldn't have finished the sentence if I'd tried, but Geoffrey was on a different wavelength. His eyes followed mine to the hearse and it took him a full thirty seconds – thirty seconds and they'd been married twelve years – to work out what I meant. Then he just nodded and said: 'Ah yes.' After that he maintained a respectful silence, the sort of propriety one observes upon the death of distant relatives or minor international statesmen. My hatred blazed and attained a sudden white-hot purity. If I could have believed that Helen was with me, if I could have hated Geoffrey with her blessing, I would have attacked him as I attacked Tardelli. I would have strangled him with that redundant black tie and consecrated the death to God, my God, the cruel, laughing God of the Via Foraggi. But my hands stayed on the steering-wheel, tense, sweating, itchy. The more I understood of Helen, and her quirky search for goodness, the more I wanted to be a part of that search and to follow where she led. But how hard it was, loving my enemy. I had thought it would become easier with time, like giving up smoking, but the pressure never slackened. We were only ten minutes from the cemetery, and it seemed like a lifetime, a long road of charity and forgiveness with no apparent end.

'Oh really,' said Geoffrey suddenly. He had noticed what I had seen all along: the police car bringing up the rear of the funeral cortège. 'You'd think they had better things to do. Do they always do that?'

'I don't think so.'

'Then why are they following us? Just because we're foreign, I suppose. It's a bit bloody much. Can't you do something about it?'

'At this speed?' I indicated the speedometer, wobbling between twenty and thirty kilometres an hour. 'Come on, Geoffrey. Just try and forget them. We're nearly there.'

The hearse turned off the road into the cemetery: a sprawling modern development tucked in between a department store and a football pitch. My heart sank. Non-denominational, Mrs Tobin had asked for, somewhere simple and unpretentious. She was probably wishing she had gone for a crematorium or chucked the body into the Tiber in a garbage bag. You expect at least a few trees in a cemetery, leaves fluttering down among the headstones, branches creaking overhead. This place was as bare as an archaeological dig: it was depressing beyond words. Mounds of freshly turned earth were everywhere, as if a colony of moles had been at work.

A priest was waiting for us beside the grave with a prayerbook in his hand. He looked so utterly non-denominational it hurt. His front teeth jutted out in a goofy smile and he wore brown suede shoes under his cassock.

'Mr Danes? How are you? Mr Tobin, Mrs Tobin. How are you both? I'm sorry, I don't think – '

'Barham. Mark Barham. Friend of the family.'

'How are you, Mark? I was reading one of your books last week – isn't life funny? Michael Windsor-Clive by the way. I'm on the Embassy list. Shall we walk this way?'

At least he was English, I thought, clutching at straws. The Tobins would be grateful for that. I just hoped they didn't mind the occasion being treated like a British Council cocktail party. What vicious lottery had landed us with one of those priests whom only God can love?

I watched as the coffin was unloaded from the hearse and carried to the graveside. There were only two pall-bearers, but they weren't straining: even in life, Helen had been a frail woman, as weightless as a bird. Once I had carried her myself, single-handed . . . but I couldn't bear to remember. I glanced over my shoulder and saw the police car pull up next to the hearse. Conti, Paolo and Gianni got out and sauntered to within a hundred yards of the grave. My blood boiled. Even at Helen's grave I was not going to be allowed to forget Tardelli.

'Would you excuse me, please? I'll be back in a second.'

I strode angrily towards them. They leered and kept their hands in their pockets. Conti looked particularly smug.

'Nice day for a funeral, Meester Barham.'

'What the hell are you doing here? Don't you have any feelings at all? Go away and leave us alone.'

'Police business, Meester Barham.'

'Not now it isn't. We are paying our last respects to someone very precious – but I don't expect you'd understand that. Talk to me later if you have to. This is *not* the time.'

'Sorry, Meester Barham. You see, we talk to Meesus Giorgini this morning. Very interesting lady.'

He smirked, enjoying every minute. Priests, policemen: who could be trusted in this city of madmen? You would have thought it was him, not me, who had sinned, who had committed the great evil for which the world would demand retribution. So Signora Giorgini's conscience hadn't allowed her to remain silent. I felt bitter, betrayed.

'*Later!*' I shouted, with such savagery that he took a respectful step backwards. 'Let us bury this woman in peace and then I'm all yours. Where's your humanity?'

I stormed back to the graveside and muttered my apologies to the others. Out of the corner of my eye, I saw Conti and his friends get back into their car and drive slowly off. My shoulders untensed. My heart stopped pounding. My outrage turned to gratitude. Perhaps I really was getting slowly humbler: it was certainly taking smaller and smaller mercies to console me. But it couldn't last.

'Heavenly Father, we give thanks for the life of Thy servant, Helen Danes. For thirty-eight years she laboured under Thy gentle yoke, happy in the hope of the resurrection, loved and respected by all who knew her . . .' The priest read a few paragraphs from a typewritten sheet folded into his prayerbook and again my blood boiled. It sounded like a press release, a scissors-and-paste job by the consular section at the Embassy. How did he *know* she was loved? She might have been a slag, a drug-pusher, a murderess. She might have spent her whole life denying God, spurning His gifts, kicking off His gentle yoke, never sparing a thought for the resurrection but living greedily and selfishly for the moment. Why did the dead have to be embalmed in this sickly sentiment? Hadn't we grown up enough to celebrate the other Helen, the real Helen? The Helen who writhed and moaned in my arms while her husband was out at the theatre? The Helen who lied and cheated and ran away from everything that mattered? The Helen who sought sanctity only in the last months of her life – and still lied about it? In my bitterness, I felt more than ever alone. Mrs Tobin wiped a tear from her eye. Her husband fumbled in his pocket for a handkerchief. Even Geoffrey blinked with emotion. How could they be so affected by the plaster saint the priest had invented?

The coffin was lowered into the grave, the flowers thrown on top, the last tears wiped away.

'Thank you, Father,' said Mrs Tobin, wringing his hand in both of hers. 'You said just the right things.'

'Thank you, Father,' said her husband, clumsily pressing a ten-thousand-*lire* note into his palm. 'You've done Helen proud.'

'Thank you, Father,' said Geoffrey, surreptitiously looking at his watch. 'I'm sorry if we've been a burden on your time.'

'Thank you,' I muttered, not bothering to shake hands. There was a brief, confused silence, one of those moments of perfect but painful equilibrium. Behind us, the grave gaped like an ugly wound too deep to heal. Overhead, a flock of birds changed direction and wheeled away towards the football pitch. The sun streamed down, burnishing the bonnets of the cars. We couldn't have said how or why, but we were not the same four people who had arrived in the cemetery half an hour before.

'Interesting chap,' Geoffrey commented as we turned back on to the main road. 'Could have been a Catholic, could have been C of E, could even have been a Methodist. What do you think?'

'I've no idea. I'm not an expert on the differences any more than you are. Didn't you ask in advance?'

'Martha said non-denominational, so that was what I told the Embassy. But what does it mean exactly? All priests have some denomination, however woolly their beliefs. I think she just wanted Low Church rather than High Church, which is what she got. Still, what does it matter? Helen wouldn't have minded.'

My hands clenched tight on the steering-wheel. 'Are you so sure of that, Geoffrey?'

'What do you mean?'

'How do you know Helen wouldn't have minded? How can you judge what mattered to her and what didn't? You've no idea how arrogant you sound sometimes. I'm no more a Christian than you, but I could never speak like that about – about someone I loved.'

'I was her husband, Mark. We were married twelve years.'

'If you call that married.'

'Oh don't start that.'

'Why not?'

'It's not – it's not the time.' His voice fell, sounding a

false note of piety. He probably thought he could claim the respect due to his bereavement, but he had forfeited it long ago – the day he married Helen and loved her with less than his whole heart. I tried to soften the hatred in my voice, but it was hard.

'Listen, Geoffrey. I know this will sound absurd and you won't believe me when I say I knew Helen better than you. You'll probably think I'm just acting like a jilted lover. But I did know her better. I found out more about her because I was more curious than you ever were. I didn't love her, I adored her. And I wasn't interested by her, I was fascinated. Even now she's dead, I'm still finding out more about her. And you can take my word for it: she was religious, very religious. Did you know a Signora Giorgini?'

He snorted. 'That witch? I warned Helen off her straightaway. She was an out-and-out crank. You're not saying –'

'Yes, I am saying that. She didn't let you warn her off, Geoffrey. She visited Signora Giorgini many times, secretly, behind your back, pretending she was going to the cinema.'

'Are you sure?'

'Positive. I talked to Signora Giorgini yesterday. She and Helen were obviously good friends. They became so close you couldn't have kept them apart if you'd tried.'

'I didn't try any such thing.'

'No, but you made damn sure Helen knew you disapproved of the relationship. You made her feel guilty and furtive and disloyal – the way she was with me all those years ago. Only this time something bigger than love was involved. Don't ask me what it was: I'm not sure myself. But it was there, Geoffrey. You couldn't stifle it any more than you could stifle her love for me. You thought you had her where you wanted her, but you didn't. She may be dead now, but she still won that battle and you lost. Why not admit it?'

He said nothing. I glanced to see if my message had got home, but it was impossible to tell. There is something dangerous and unpredictable about people with very thick skins. You can make no impression at all, then a single word will provoke a violent response. Geoffrey normally reserved his violence for Shakespeare, but these weren't normal times. His wife had cheated with me, then with God. Wouldn't any man feel bitter at that lurching between two extremes, the search for something, anything, to feed the needs he couldn't satisfy?

When he did speak, he wasn't angry. Perhaps he'd felt the anger and waited for it to subside; or perhaps he had more generosity than I allowed. It was the voice of someone more serene than complacent.

'I'm not a religious man, Mark. I had the chance when I was at school, but it made no sense then and it makes no sense now. Probably you're the same. When Helen got involved with that crazy woman, I just thought she was running away. We'd arrived in this marvellous city and all I could think was how many better things she could be doing with her time. We didn't talk about it much: perhaps that was my fault as much as hers. We didn't talk about lots of things. But you shouldn't think I was a tyrant about it. I'm a reasonable man, Mark.'

'Are you? Are you reasonable?'

'About most things, yes. I don't say about Shakespeare because that's something altogether special. You say Helen was looking for God, but she wasn't looking in the right place. Christianity's an illusion. There's only one God and He was born in Stratford-on-Avon on April 23rd, 1564.'

I gave an involuntary shudder. The blasphemy didn't strike at my own beliefs, but it still shocked. 'Don't talk like that, Geoffrey.'

'I will talk like that. Why do people have to have a trinity and a virgin birth and all that claptrap when everything that matters in life can be found in His plays? Is the Bible a better book than *King Lear*? Or *Macbeth*? Or *The Tempest*? Of course it isn't. I don't care what you think, Mark, and may Helen forgive me if I'm wrong, but I have to say it because it's what I believe. Shakespeare is God – not metaphorically, not figuratively, but actually. He talks to us, He cares for us, He loves us, He consoles us, He raises us up to the high places on earth. What more can a God do? You don't believe me, Mark. You're looking nervous as if I was delirious. But I'm not delirious. I'll say it again. Shakespeare is God. Why am I the only person who sees that?'

He started to cry. I pulled over to the side of the road and took his head on my shoulder. I knew it would only provoke him further, but I couldn't stop myself saying it.

'You poor mad fool, Geoffrey, you poor mad fool.'

And then, for the first time, I felt it, as if Helen or God or even Shakespeare – and it didn't seem to matter which – had breathed it into me with all their strength and all their love. I felt pity. Not the synthetic, everyday version – the twinge of sympathy, the flicker of compassion, the tic of guilt – but the real thing. It swept over me like a wave, carrying all my doubts and frailties away with it. It galvanized me with a sense of power, the same power I'd sometimes seen in Helen, the power to change and to be changed. It wasn't the same as love, but it excited just as much as love. The day I buried my dead love, I started to live again.

10

My next duty was obvious. If I owed it to Helen to be kind
to Geoffrey, then I owed Vanessa something too. I meant
it kindly, but she just looked hurt.

'Why now, Mark? I don't understand.'

'Because I can't go on pretending.'

'Yesterday everything seemed fine. We had a really good
time. We were so *close*, Mark.'

'That was yesterday.'

'Do things change that quickly?'

'Yes, they do. Not always, occasionally. Sometimes life
moves so fast you can't keep up. I'm sorry, Vanessa.'

'I'm sorry too.'

We looked at each other miserably. Two 'sorries' but
how totally different: a sorry-guilty and a sorry-sad, as
unrelated as a funny-odd and a funny ha-ha. It was going
even worse than I feared.

Geoffrey had wanted me to have lunch with him and the
Tobins after the funeral: he didn't say so, but I imagine he
was nervous of handling them alone. Instead I had a pizza
with Vanessa in the Campo dei Fiori. The impulse to give
had become as strong as the impulse to take: I wanted
desperately to give her back the freedom I had pilfered
from her. But she didn't see it like that. She baulked, she
bridled. There was a painful directness in her questions.

'But do you love me, Mark?'

'I don't really feel I do, no.'

'Did you ever love me?'

'Not exactly. I was very fond of you, obviously. But love?

I'm not sure it was ever that. And, to be fair, I never said it was, did I? We were lovers, but that didn't mean – oh, come on, Vanessa, you know the rules.'

'What rules? Whose rules? Your rules. That's what you're saying, isn't it?'

'Maybe.' I picked an anchovy off my pizza and spent a long time eating it. I felt as if I'd been here before and yet not been here before. We've all done it, haven't we? Fired our lovers, given them their cards, told them it had been fun while it lasted, but . . . And we've all had it done to us: don't imagine Helen was the first or the last to tell Mark Barham his time was up. The score's about ten-all by now, so I'm as much sinned against as sinning, or almost. The situation was familiar: I was word-perfect already. 'We've got to be realistic about this.' 'Let's not get sex out of proportion.' 'I'm really thinking of you more than me.' The lying, the fudging, the self-interest posing as philanthropy, the desperate attempts to keep emotion to a minimum: I knew every trick.

And yet something about this bust-up was different. I used the same lines, but my feelings ran with them, not against them. I really was being realistic, I really was putting her interests before mine – for what would have been nicer or easier than to have her keep my bed warm a few weeks longer, until the worst of my pain had passed? If anything, my hunger for her companionship had sharpened with each passing crisis. She was becoming more confident with me, less grating. The relationship was on the upward slope, a long way from the top. With another woman, I would have given it more time, seen how much further it would go, waited till I had nothing to lose before calling a halt. But I couldn't do that with Vanessa. I felt too sorry for her. Was if fair to go on pretending to love her on the off-chance that one day I might? Was it fair to share my

243

outer life with her when my inner life was so bound up with another woman who was dead? And was it fair to keep her tagging along if I was about to be arrested for murder? To each question the answer was obvious. She deserved better than I could give her and I should set her free to look for it. Helen would have done the same, I told myself. Helen *had* done the same. I needed no higher authority.

But that still left Vanessa. How could she be made to see it my way? It had taken Helen eight years and her own death to convince me she was right to say 'enough'. How could I possibly do the same over a pizza and a carafe of wine? Gloomily, I pushed the last mouthful round the plate with my fork and waited for the right words to come. They didn't come.

'You're still very young, you know, Vanessa.'

'Oh don't give me that.'

'It's true. I'm not being patronizing. In a year's time you'll see things quite differently. I know it's easy to say this, but there are thousands of men out there far more suitable than me, who'll give you what you need better than I ever could. I'm thirty-eight. I'm old enough to be your father. I'm a selfish, ingrained bachelor, quite incapable of sharing my life with anyone. I'm yours as long as you want me, but don't expect what you feel for me now to last. Love doesn't last: it isn't like that. Once it becomes one-sided, once one partner wants out and the other wants in, it's no good. You see – '

'Go on, Mark.'

'You see, the thing is – I don't know how to say this, Vanessa, it will sound so simplistic, but the thing is – '

'What's wrong, Mark? You're crying.'

'It's nothing, just a speck of dust.' I wiped my face with a napkin, but my anguish only deepened. I had thought I was doing well, developing a solid, compelling line of argument, but the final link in the chain was fatally flawed. 'Love doesn't last': isn't that what parents have told their teenage children since time immemorial, as a salve to their heartbreaks? But shouldn't they say something else? 'If it is love, it will last. It won't be conditional. It won't accept being rejected. It won't heal with time. It won't be cured by separation. It won't disappear with death. It will either save you or destroy you . . .' Why settle for the cosy platitudes of the agony columnist?

I took a deep breath and started again, attacking the problem from a different angle. I argued, not that love was fragile, but that I was fragile; that she should pour her feelings into a stronger vessel or she would waste them. The new logic was no more successful than the old.

'You're doing it again,' she said angrily, after a few minutes listening impatiently to my self-pity. 'You're telling yourself you're a failure as a human being, just as you tell yourself you're a failure as a writer. Why can't you believe in yourself? Why can't you let me help you believe in yourself?'

'Because it's too late.'

'Don't be so silly, Mark. It's never too late. Life's there to be lived, not despaired of: I wish you could see that.' It might have been Helen talking: the vitality, the confidence, the youthfulness, the chance repetition of an aphorism I had heard on Helen's lips. Again the sense of continuity overwhelmed me, as if far less had drowned in Lake Bracciano than I realized. Mechanically I said: 'Of course it's too late', but I didn't believe it. Nothing seemed irretrievable any longer.

'How can you say that?' she said, growing in confidence the whole time. 'You've got thirty, forty, fifty years to live. There's all the time in the world to recover from failure, if that's what you want. Give yourself a chance. Don't let despair take a grip on you. Be positive.'

'I am being positive.'

'Not about you and me.'

'Especially about you and me. I'm getting out of your life because I don't deserve to be in it. You shouldn't throw yourself away on a third-rate hack, Vanessa. You need someone younger, someone kinder, someone more generous than me.'

'And where do I find him?'

'I don't know. You won't have to look far. There are thousands, literally thousands . . .'

'Are you sure?'

'As sure as I'm sitting here.'

'Baloney.'

She grinned affectionately and our hands met in the middle of the table. Who taught her to say 'baloney' like that? It was one of Helen's words: I could hear her rolling it playfully off her tongue like a phrase of a song. That was twice in as many minutes she had stolen Helen's lines. Could she do it again, I wondered? Could she do it four times, five times? Could she go on doing it for the rest of her life? The echoes of Helen frightened me, as Signora Giorgini had frightened me with her wild tales. That the dead should talk through the living so eloquently . . .

'Listen,' I said quickly, twisting and turning in my mind, wanting to escape and yet not to escape. 'I do need someone to love me and believe in me, and don't think I'm not grateful to you for doing that. I think you'd be better off without me, but I'm far less sure I'd be better off without you. I just can't convince myself I deserve you, Vanessa. That's all. I haven't loved you properly because I loved someone else.'

'Helen?' She said it so quickly I blushed.

'Yes. How did you know?'

'Did you think I was stupid?'

'I thought I was clever. Geoffrey never saw. I didn't think anyone saw.'

'Oh Mark.' She lowered her eyes and started stroking the back of my hand with her fingers. The sudden shyness, and the sudden sense that I had underestimated her, moved me almost equally. Who else had stroked the back of my hand like that? Helen, of course. I started to retract the hand, then left it where it was. I felt confused, apprehensive. In popular psychology, bereaved people are supposed to rediscover the person they have lost in another person. They fall in love with the same physical type and encourage their new partner to dress and behave like the old one. What isn't meant to happen – for there is no reason in psychology or logic why it should – is that the new partner, instinctively and without prompting, should ape the speech and mannerisms of the old. My careful plans were being shot to pieces. I had come in a spirit of pity, with the sincere intention to redress my wrongs to another person, and I was feeling love instead. I had known the two emotions would overlap, but not so totally, not so sweetly.

'Vanessa, there's one other thing,' I stammered, then dried. This was to be my final card, the one which would convince her, if all else failed, that she should leave me. Now I wished I didn't have the card at all. Tardelli's ghost was beginning to throttle me.

'What is it, Mark?'

'You know those policemen yesterday? They were right, you know. I did kill the man they said I did.'

'I don't understand.'

'I murdered him because I thought he was having an affair with Helen. He wasn't, of course, but I was too mad and blind and stupid to get my facts straight. You tell me to believe in myself, but you can see why I find it so hard. If that isn't failure, I don't know what is.'

'No,' she whispered, her voice cracking in disappointment. 'That's failure all right. Oh Mark.' Again her hand snaked across the table towards mine. Again she held it and tried to let her fingers express the love that stuck in her throat. And again, for the third time, Helen spoke in her: the last despairing word at Lake Bracciano.

'Patience.'

I used to find the two women's voices very different. Helen was an alto and Vanessa a light soprano. Helen had a lilt, Vanessa had a tang. Helen sparkled, Vanessa gushed. Helen soothed, Vanessa grated. Helen was music, Vanessa muzak. Now, if I shut my eyes, it was the same voice. The miraculous transformation was almost complete.

In one of my early novels, I had a character just like Vanessa. She was young and naïve and had spent her first twenty years within a taxi ride of Harrods. She said 'yah' and wore designer clothes which nobody else could afford. Her friends had double-barrelled names and mothers called Hetty or Mo: they went off to the country at weekends and killed foxes after church on Sunday. By such subtle pointers, the reader was encouraged to dislike the character.

Having set her up nicely, I had her fall in love with a swine, a cad. His swinishness was indescribable, his caddishness was out of this world. He treated her like dirt and had a gold tooth which glinted when he laughed at her. He beat her up, he forced her to have an abortion, he also lived near Harrods. The reader's loathing was whipped to a crescendo as the story unfolded.

I don't remember exactly how the book ended: no doubt both characters got their come-uppance in some grisly way. But I remember thinking, as I inflicted more and more misery on Reggie and Lucinda (yes, even their names were subtly chosen), how good it must feel to be God: my God, you understand, the inveterate practical joker with the malicious grin on his face. How I enjoyed exercising that unlimited power over my creatures: judging them; punishing them; manipulating them; putting words into their mouths; afflicting them with coarse vowels and crooked noses; striking them down with thunderbolts from a cloudless sky; letting them stray in unexpected directions, then recalling them capriciously to my bidding; doing to them all the things I had wanted to do to similar people in my life, if only the courage had been there . . . It was a young writer's arrogance and I later saw it for what it was. But it did give me a tremendous kick at the time.

Looking at Vanessa now in the Campo dei Fiori, I was reminded of Lucinda. If God wrote with as much cynicism as I, she would have been written out of the script long ago, condemned to be a loser the moment she opened her mouth and betrayed that she'd been to a public school. I had done my bit to consign her to the also-rans, wanting her to survive the pain of falling in love with me and make a new start. But did it have to be that way? Wasn't she entitled to survive on her terms rather than mine? If, by some ludicrous accident, I had become her Helen, the love she couldn't let go in any circumstances, who was I to reject that love? I had wanted to sever the relationship for both our goods: I now knew I couldn't do that. She deserved more than me, but she also deserved no less. There was nothing for it: until her madness had run its course, I was all hers.

11

And now the opening night was upon us. For days it had been louring darkly on the horizon: now it was above our heads, as menacing as a school exam for which one hadn't revised properly.

Geoffrey wore a white rose in his buttonhole to mark the occasion. The flamboyance was out of character, for he normally dressed with the awkward self-deprecation which is the English hallmark: grey suits, black shoes, shirts so anonymous you had to look hard to see what colour they were. I thought it might have been Mrs Tobin's idea, but apparently he bought it himself on the way to Paparelli's house. White for innocence, I thought. Yes, he was certainly that. White for after the funeral, to show that the time of mourning was over. White for the blank page on which a new life had to be written.

'You know something, Mark?' he said, drawing me aside. I had become not just his right-hand man, but his closest confidant. How Helen would have laughed. 'I'm feeling quietly optimistic about tonight. Now that it's for real, I think everyone will make a special effort to give of their best. There's something in the air: can't you feel it?'

'Not really, Geoffrey, no.'

'Oh it's there all right.' His eyes ranged around the room, taking in the baroque frescoes, the great gold candelabra, the cherubs scurrying up the walls. He looked at the white-robed God in the middle of the ceiling and smiled. 'I feel as if someone's taking care of us tonight, as if William Himself – '

'You're mad, Geoffrey.'

'Not mad, Mark. Inspired.' He strolled off and, for some reason, I found myself glancing at his feet: it wouldn't have surprised me if they'd been six inches off the ground.

In the next room, a champagne cork popped. I went to investigate and found Paparelli fêting some of the cast.

'*Saluti, signori, signore. Molti saluti.* To Shake-speare.' He raised his glass and everyone clapped. Vanessa was there with her father, Margaret, Walter, Tony, one or two others. After more jollity, Tony leapt up on a chair like a man of twenty and clapped his hands.

'Ladies and gentlemen, one moment *please*! I have an important announcement, a very important announcement.'

Everyone stopped talking and looked at each other nervously. A speech from Tony seemed sure to be an embarrassment: he had the sort of genius for going over the top which you see in Englishmen a thousand miles from home. We needn't have worried.

'Peter, Margaret, let's see you now. Don't be shy. You've taken us all by surprise, but well done, jolly well done. This beats Shakespeare any day.'

'What's going on?' I whispered to Vanessa.

'They've got engaged.'

'When? Today?'

'This afternoon. Daddy told me when I got back from seeing you. Isn't it wonderful?'

'Wonderful.' I watched as they stepped coyly into the limelight, hardly daring to hold hands. Margaret was crimson. Peter tried to stammer his thanks, but they were drowned in the applause. Yes, I thought, it was wonderful. The winners had been winning for too long: it was time for the losers to have their day. If there was hope for Peter and

251

Margaret, then even I . . . I congratulated them as if they were my oldest friends.

'We didn't want it announced till after the funeral,' Peter whispered. 'I hope we did the right thing.'

'I'm sure you did.'

'You young things' – he took in Vanessa and me with a magnanimous gesture unthinkable a week before – 'must think we've taken leave of our senses.'

'Of course we don't. It's the best news for a long time.'

'I'm forty-one, you know,' Margaret said cheerfully, as if she was telling me she'd won the football pools. What normal forty-one-year-old woman tells *anyone* her age? But wasn't that the beauty of it? If she wasn't doomed to be single, then nobody was doomed to be single. By the law of averages, only one man in her whole life was ever going to want her. But there he was, as if he'd been waiting all along, as if he needed her just as badly. And Peter did need her just as badly: that was the marvellous thing. He needed hope as much as I did: something, anything, to free him from that long, sterile struggle to keep his twenty-year-old daughter a child. I smiled at them happily. They were the least glamorous couple I'd ever seen, but there was still a harmony to the relationship, a symmetry which seduced the onlooker like a perfect painting. For someone used only to inequalities – loving too much, being loved too much, never finding the true balance – it was an enviable sight. There it was again, that glittering shop-window into which I peered so forlornly, for ever excluded from the warmth inside. Vanessa put one arm round me and the other round her father and an odd, wild dream – inconceivable when I woke that morning – took root in my mind. If only . . . More than ever I regretted my moment's madness in the Via Foraggi.

'Er, can we get a move on please?' Even Geoffrey was

touched. Champagne corks flying around half an hour before curtain-up, something other than Shakespeare being celebrated . . . I'd seen him go berserk over less. As zero hour neared, he showed an unexpected serenity. Instead of dragooning people, he shepherded them: asked them if they were sure what they had to do, dealt patiently and politely with any problems. It was as if he really did believe that his own role had become superfluous, that Shakespeare would look after things from now on. I expected a final, climactic oration: in fact, what he said was terse and to the point.

'Don't rush. Don't shout. I want to hear every word Shakespeare wrote. Let the play develop in its own way and at its own pace. Act with feeling, but don't overdo it. Be careful about the mechanics of the production. Make sure you know where your props are. Try not to trip over the furniture. And *don't* be put off by the audience. Oh yes, and there's one final thing.'

He stopped and scratched his ear, then looked at the floor as if having difficulty finding the right words. We held our breath. It wasn't like Geoffrey to be bashful about Shakespeare, but he suddenly seemed crippled by shyness, a last-minute access of humility. He spoke his great truths like a lover whispering in the dark.

'Whatever happens in the rest of your lives, none of you will ever have as big an opportunity as you've been given tonight. Not to be famous. Not to win other people's applause. Not to enjoy the sound of your own voice. Simply to be *alive* in His great works. Nothing else matters, nothing else has any significance. If you realize that, you'll go home tonight on fire with joy. Yes, Paparelli, what is it?'

Paparelli had appeared in the doorway looking flustered. He gesticulated that he would rather talk to Geoffrey alone and I followed them out of the room to interpret. I imagined there was some technical hitch or a problem with the lighting. The supply of electricity in Rome is notoriously random: voltage is allocated on the same basis as prizes in a national lottery. In the event, no interpretation was needed. The sight that greeted us was self-explanatory: it spelt catastrophe in any language. Our mouths fell open in horror. A hundred and fifty chairs had been squeezed into the hall and, with five minutes to go, not a single one was filled.

'Shit,' said Geoffrey.

'*Merda santa*,' said Paparelli. Italian can be so expressive.

'Where – ' began Geoffrey, trembling with rage.

'*Dove* – ' began Paparelli, equally apoplectic. I got in between them like a boxing referee.

'Cool it, Geoffrey. *Calma*, Signore. There has obviously been an unfortunate misunderstanding about who was supposed to be selling tickets for this production. Someone, Geoffrey, seems to have slightly overestimated Shakespeare's popularity in Rome this year: that is *entirely* understandable. This has been a very trying time for us all, Signore: it's no good holding an inquest now. The time for recriminations is later, *dopo*. All we have to decide now is what to do next. Do we carry on as if there was an audience? Do we cancel? Do we wait ten minutes? Come on, Geoffrey. You're in charge.'

He gnawed anxiously at his lower lip and stared at the empty seats. 'I'm not performing without an audience, Mark. That's for sure. Shakespeare would have been horrified. He was a working dramatist, a man of the theatre.'

'Well, cancel then. Let's hope a few people turn up tomorrow.'

'And I'm not cancelling either. That's just defeatist. Shakespeare would turn in his grave.'

'Geoffrey, it's two minutes to eight. We've got to be realistic. There'll be no audience at all if we start on time.'

'Then we'll *get* an audience. It's simple.'

'Are you crazy?'

'No, listen, Mark.' He gripped me feverishly by the arm. Of course he was crazy: there was no point in asking. 'We'll postpone the start by an hour, then we'll go out into the street and get on the telephone and hustle and chase until we've filled every one of those bloody seats. Every single one, Mark: a full bloody house. We'll make Shakespeare proud of us.'

'Geoffrey, I don't think – '

'There's no time to argue. Go and get the cast.'

The cast trooped nervously on to the stage to receive instructions. Geoffrey barked out his instructions like a drill-serjeant, his eyes gleaming with the excitement of a new challenge, an evangelical mission. Everyone was to be personally responsible for finding ten people to watch the play: friends, relatives, acquaintances, strangers, any nationality, any age, anyone. Nobody was to come back until they'd got their quota and nobody was to come back later than five to nine. Was that clear?

'You don't mind us going out on the streets in our costumes?' asked Joanie.

'Of course not. Actors didn't have that silly hang-up in Shakespeare's day, so why should we? Anything else?'

'Do we charge people the full rate?'

'No, no. Give them a discount or give them free tickets. We're not here to make money. We're here to perform a great play and bring something special to people's lives. Is that all? Then get on with it.'

We tumbled out of the house and fanned out in all directions. One or two people headed for telephone kiosks: the rest took our chance on the street. Vanessa and I started hustling for business among the cafés on the Piazza Rotonda. Tourists turned and stared, waiters looked contemptuous. A middle-aged American couple were our first victims.

'*Winter's Tale?* Is that a tragedy?'

'Sounds like a tragedy to me, Woody. I'm staying right here.'

'Actually, madam, it's a comedy, a sort of a comedy. One or two people do die in the first half, but after that it's a gas.'

'I'm telling you, Woody. Don't take those tickets.'

'My wife has a migraine, sir. I'm afraid – '

'Bloody philistines.' I stormed off. Vanessa followed, giggling.

'You're beginning to sound like Geoffrey.'

'I'm beginning to feel like Geoffrey. Shakespeare may not be everyone's cup of tea, but he should be some people's cup of tea. It's disgraceful. Ah, this looks better.'

A crocodile of Japanese tourists – well, a baby crocodile, there were only four – was heading straight towards us. I blocked their path and bowed.

'Speak English? *Parla italiano? Parlez-vous français?*'

They shook their heads. One of them whipped out a camera and took a photograph of Vanessa in her Perdita costume. I fished four tickets out of my cod-piece and brandished them in the air.

'Shakespeare, Shake-speare. Yes? *Si? Oui? Ya?*'

'*Ya.*' One of them stepped forward hesitantly and took the tickets. I pointed in the direction of Paparelli's house and tapped my watch to indicate nine o'clock. They nodded. I bowed. They bowed. Vanessa gave me a little squeeze of excitement.

'We're winning, Mark, we're winning. Only sixteen to go.'

Immediately a man behind me tapped my shoulder. 'Excuse me. Did you say Shakespeare?'

'Yes, that's right.' English, I thought, English: as English as apple crumble and Fortnum & Mason's and three slips and a gully. He was wearing socks with his sandals and trousers so baggy you could have put an army of ferrets down them. No salesmanship was necessary.

'How much are they?' he asked, pointing at the tickets.

'Nothing, my friend, nothing. As free as air.'

'I say, that's awfully decent of you. Do you mind very much if I take two? My wife – '

'Two, three, as many as you like.'

'No, two's fine. I feel awfully guilty not paying. You see, I love Shakespeare. We did *The Winter's Tale* at school. I played – '

'Don't tell me.'

' – Camillo. You're playing Camillo yourself, aren't you? You look like a Camillo. I say, that is incredible. The best of luck, the very best of luck.'

He shook hands and trotted off, clutching the tickets for dear life. I watched him skip happily through the crowds around the Pantheon and my heart soared. Never, in eight years, had I felt such nostalgia for England. If he was the only person in the audience, who would dare say the performance was wasted?

Fired by our success, we roamed the streets and offloaded the remaining tickets. A family of Germans took four, an English priest two, a bemused bus-driver one. We had only five left when we ran into Judy. An old flame, you might say, an extremely old flame: the sort of old flame you wish had never been ignited. It would have been an awkward encounter at the best of times.

'Mark.'

'Judy.'

'Hi.'

'Hi.'

'How are things?'

'Fine. You?'

'Fine.'

'Good. Judy, this is Vanessa.'

'Hullo, Vanessa.'

'Hi.'

'Are you two off to a fancy dress party or something?'

'No, we're acting in a play. It starts in half an hour. Why don't you come? No charge for the ticket. On me. How about it – for old times' sake?'

'Oh all right. What's the show?'

'*The Winter's Tale.*'

'Oh God, Mark, isn't that Shakespeare?'

'Afraid so, Judy. Don't worry, it won't hurt: there are some jokes in the second half. See you at nine.'

We sped on. I heard Vanessa mutter 'You shit,' but I took no notice. Never, not even when I stabbed Tardelli, was I less of a moralist than between eight and nine that evening. A single ambition filled my head: to get a hundred and fifty bums on a hundred and fifty seats. Nothing else mattered, nothing. I felt like Geoffrey and I *enjoyed* feeling like Geoffrey. Who could have predicted that?'

We got back to Paparelli's at five to nine with no tickets left. The others had had mixed fortunes. Joanie had struck lucky with a busload of nuns, Walter had found a dozen impoverished archaeology students, Tony had enlisted the help of the ambulance service. The rest still had tickets unaccounted for. Geoffrey gave them to Paparelli and told him to distribute them among his neighbours. Curtain-up would be at ten past nine and no late-comers would be admitted till the interval. He was too rude to thank us

258

directly, but the relieved smile on his face was eloquent enough.

Elated we returned to the dressing-room, laughing, joking, slapping each other on the back, swopping taller and taller stories about how we'd disposed of our tickets. A sense of comradeship passed between us like an electric current: even if we were doomed to fail, we would fail gloriously and fail together. I'm no sort of actor, but I never looked forward to anything as much as I looked forward to that performance. It was a nasty shock when Conti made his entrance, with Paolo and Gianni behind him.

12

'Meester Barham? Yes no?'

He was simpering, positively simpering. I thought, you know bloody well who I am, you smug bastard, and refused to answer. He whipped an important-looking piece of paper out of his inside jacket pocket and showed it to me.

'What is this, Mr Conti?'

'Arrest warrant, Meester Barham. The game is over. Come with us please.'

'I think you mean the game is up and, no, I'm not coming with you. I have more important things to do. Come back later.'

'Not later, Meester Barham. Now. Gianni, Paolo.'

His henchmen moved forward in uncompromising mood. Gianni pinioned my arms and dug his knee into my kidneys. Paolo jerked my neck back and spat in my face. The rest of the cast watched open-mouthed. The whole thing had happened so quickly that nobody had time to protest. I heard Vanessa sobbing and Tony muttering 'This is a bit thick', but knew it would take something sterner to save me. The something sterner arrived in the nick of time and from a predictable quarter.

'What the *hell* is going on here? Let go of my Camillo immediately. My name is Geoffrey Danes and I am a British citizen.'

His anger carried authority, as it always did. Conti gave a surly grunt and gestured to Gianni and Paolo to release me.

'*Scusi*, Meester Danes. We are arresting Meester

Barham.' He waved his warrant again, less confidently than before.

'*Arresting* him? Are you mad? What's wrong with this bloody country? Do you know what this is all about, Mark?'

'More or less. They think I've murdered someone. A journalist called Tardelli.'

'*Murdered?*' he whispered, his voice dropping in horror.

'*Murdered?*' gasped Tony. 'Good God.'

'*Murdered?*' yelped Joanie, practically popping out of her costume. From Shakespeare to Agatha Christie in seconds: the descent into farce was much too funny not to laugh about. And, with the onset of laughter, my will to resist suddenly buckled, like a boxer's legs going. I could no longer pretend to the world because I could no longer pretend to myself. Tardelli's ghost had finally broken me.

'Yes,' I yelled, '*murdered*! And do you know what, Geoffrey? Do you know what, everyone? I *did* murder Tardelli. I stabbed him in the back with a kitchen knife because – I'm sorry, it's far, far too complicated to go into. It was only a joke really, a sort of joke. Not my joke, you understand: someone else's. He thought it was frightfully funny. He spends His whole life playing pranks like that. Did you get that, Conti, you bastard? I only killed Tardelli because someone up there thought it might be rather amusing: that's all. What's wrong? You don't look happy, Geoffrey. You don't look happy, Vanessa. Nobody looks happy. You're all staring at me as if you think I've gone off my head. Well, maybe I *have* gone off my head, but don't just stare at me like that. Somebody help me – please.'

Tony caught me before I collapsed and Vanessa thrust a glass of water into my hand. I had dehydrated badly and my head was throbbing. Then I must have blacked out completely. When I came to, Geoffrey's face was pressed into mine and he was slapping me none too gently with the back of his hand.

'Are you all right, Mark? Wake up, for Christ's sake, wake up! We're starting in five minutes.'

'Starting?' I murmured, then saw the motley crowd of people in Elizabethan costume gathered around me. 'Oh yes: Camillo. God Almighty, is it really only five minutes. My lines, what are my lines? I've forgotten my lines, Geoffrey. No, it's all right. "I think this coming summer the King of Sicilia means to pay Bohemia the visitation which he justly owes him." "Beseech you." "You pay a great deal too dear for what's given freely."'

'That's it, Mark, well done. I knew I could rely on you. Now get up and walk around and try to clear your head. Concentrate on the character of Camillo and what motivates him. Imagine you're a loyal Renaissance courtier who suddenly finds his allegiance to his master called into question.'

'Yes, yes, I remember the drill. Thank you, Geoffrey.'

I stood up shakily and looked around. Vanessa held me tight by the arm. Everyone stared at me nervously, averting their eyes in embarrassment when I looked them in the face. Why were they treating me like an outcast? Then I remembered. In the corner, Conti was still holding his officious bit of paper. He coughed.

'*Scusi*, gentlemen. *Scusi*, ladies. This performance cannot take place. I am arresting Meester Barham. Gianni, Paolo!'

'GET your hands off my Camillo!' Never had I heard Geoffrey roar so loud: they must have heard it on the other side of the Tiber. Gianni and Paolo stopped in their tracks and turned to Conti, who shifted nervously.

'Meester Danes, please. Be reasonable.' He couldn't have chosen a worse word if he'd tried. Geoffrey went into the stratosphere.

'Reasonable? *Reasonable?* Do you call it reasonable to sabotage this production at the very last minute by dragging off one of my leading actors? Do you call it reasonable to keep a hundred and fifty people waiting to see a performance of *The Winter's Tale* and then tell them there'll be no Camillo? Do you know *The Winter's Tale*, Mr Conti? No, I didn't think you did. Camillo, if you must know, is an absolutely vital character. He's like Kent in *King Lear* or Menenius in *Coriolanus*. Take away Camillo and that whole perfect, beautiful, delicate structure collapses. *Collapses*, Conti: do you understand that? You can arrest Mr Barham at midnight on Sunday after the last performance. Before then, he's mine: mine, mine, mine! I'm warning you, Conti.'

'All right, Meester Danes, all right. *Capisco*. You are feeling strongly on the subject. Tonight maybe, we see. But Sunday? No, definitely no. The law is the law.'

'And Shakespeare is Shakespeare, you idiot. When are you going to get that into your fat head. Get your men out of here immediately.'

'Impossible, Meester Danes.'

'Then I'll throw them bloody out. I'll show you impossible.'

'Geoffrey, listen.' I could hardly stand up straight, but my brain was starting to function again. A final compromise had occurred to me, a last triumph for Mark Barham, mediator and peace-maker. God willing, Shakespeare willing, Helen willing, the production could still be saved. I spelled out my terms meticulously, with the confidence of a master diplomat.

'Let's carry on with tonight's performance with me as Camillo. Mr Conti can have his men guard the exits, then arrest me after the show. Tomorrow night, and the other two nights, you'll need a new Camillo. It's all right,

Geoffrey, don't worry, I've got just the man: Vanessa will point him out to you. He's in the audience tonight: a small man with glasses and baggy trousers. He played Camillo at school and he's keen as mustard on Shakespeare. He could mug up the part again in no time and do it far better than me. Is that all right, Geoffrey?'

'Oh very well.'

'Mr Conti?'

'I am happy.'

His grasp of English idiom failed him again, for he looked more miserable than I had ever seen him, defeated and confounded by the mad *Inglesi*. Whatever would his superiors say? But, if he wasn't happy, I was. My shoulders slackened as the deal was agreed and I felt a great power surge through me. I could hardly get on the stage fast enough.

'Come on, Geoffrey,' I said, doing up the buttons of my doublet. 'It's ten past nine. What are we waiting for?'

13

And then, finally, it happened. The word had trembled on my lips more than once during those extraordinary days that followed Helen's death. Something was in the air, as Geoffrey put it: nothing seemed quite normal. A more spiritually aware man might have read the signs sooner: now the most hardbitten cynic had to say it. At ten past nine on May 10th 1985, in a small *palazzo* in the centre of Rome, a miracle took place.

I don't know how that word is defined by people who use it professionally – priests, I mean. They would probably say that it has no definition: that a miracle is something which cannot be limited, cannot be categorized in everyday language. Among laymen you often hear quite little things described as miracles: holes-in-one at golf, people escaping uninjured from car accidents, the sun shining on the day of a wedding. And I suppose, for people who are confident that someone up there is looking after them, those little reminders are enough. But I'm an agnostic. I'm greedy. To be convinced, I need more than a lucky break, an unexpected stroke of fortune: I need a total reversal of the natural law. The odds against my winning the pools may be a million to one, but I wouldn't call it a miracle if I did. Somebody has to win, after all. It's when the impossible happens, something for which science, logic and history provide no explanation, that I begin falteringly to talk of the miraculous.

And that performance of *The Winter's Tale* was impossible: impossibly good, impossibly real, impossibly moving. We reached heights of acting which weren't just beyond us, but beyond any actors. We confounded normal expectations as surely as a man flying or running a one-minute mile. The spirit of Shakespeare blew like a hurricane through every word.

I was in the first scene, so I was one of the first to notice it. Walter delivered the opening speech like a man inspired. Gone was the lisp. Gone was the lacklustre manner. Gone was the habit of holding his right arm out like a washing-line to emphasize a point. He spoke the lines clearly and simply and the audience listened. No coughing, no whispering, no programme-rustling, nothing. Then it was my turn.

'I think this coming summer the King of Sicilia . . .'

It was my voice and yet not my voice. The words came out with a strength and a purity which a trained opera-singer couldn't have bettered. My body trembled, but it wasn't stage-fright. The enormity of the transformation left me thunderstruck.

'Well done,' whispered Vanessa, as I came off stage. 'You were terrific.'

'I know I was terrific. I don't know what got into me.'

'And Walter was acting out of his skin. What's happening out there?'

'I'm not sure.'

We watched from the wings as the first Act unfolded. The second scene had the same lucidity as the first, the same confidence, the same authority. We held our breath. How long could it last? Surely our amateurishness would catch up with us? Surely Rupert would lose his nerve or Joanie lapse into her customary banality? But there was no falling off, no diminishment. Every actor treated every line as if it was too precious to throw away. It ravished the ear like perfect music. It *was* perfect music.

I glanced from the stage to the front row of the audience

and saw Geoffrey wiping away a tear. Behind him, receding into the darkness, was row upon row of unmoving faces, held spellbound by the authority of the performance. I saw my English friend – tomorrow's Camillo, though he didn't know it – leaning forward in his chair as if willing himself closer to the stage. Judy rested her chin on her hand, not missing a word. Even the Japanese were hooked. They sat there totally absorbed, as if no language-barrier existed, as if Shakespeare had suddenly become the universal poet we were told he was at school, but never quite believed. It was impossible to remain unmoved.

By the time my second scene came up, I had total confidence. Acting no longer seemed like walking a tight-rope, with the abyss yawning beneath: I now knew I would reach the other side, as surely as Sunday followed Saturday. I acted my heart out and the others did the same. We didn't need to squint at the furniture to avoid bumping into it: we moved about that rickety wooden stage as if it were our own home. As I made my exit, my eyes began to water. It seemed cruel that there were only four Acts left.

'Is good,' Conti announced, escorting me to the dressing-room. 'Very good. Well done, Meester Barham.'

'Thank you.'

'I think you very fine actor. Such a pity about Meester Tardelli.'

'Quite.'

He watched bemused as I changed from Camillo to Bear, with Vanessa helping me squeeze into the costume. It was normally a time of great merriment, of giggling and leg-pulling and silly ursine noises. But the solemnity of the occasion embraced even the Bear. In that immaculate performance the smallest cameo had to be right. I got gingerly into my costume and preened myself in the mirror till not a fur was out of place. Conti ushered me back to the stage and whispered 'Good luck!' in my ear. There were no neutrals left, no agnostics: the performance was afloat on a sea of universal faith.

The Bear provides the first light moment in *The Winter's Tale*, the first indication to the audience that a tragedy is ending and a romantic fairy-tale taking its place. I wondered if our audience would pick that up. Having been silent for so long, would they dare to break the spell by laughing? I needn't have worried. They *howled*. They roared their delight as soon as I appeared and applauded thunderously as I chased Antigonus off the stage. Until then I hadn't believed there was such a thing as a good Bear or a bad Bear: it seemed the most actor-proof part in Shakespeare. Now, for ten seconds, I had been a great Bear. What could be sweeter?

On the stage I had vacated, Tony and Walter launched into a scene of rustic comedy, a vaudeville-type double-act between an old shepherd and his son. Nothing seemed more certain to flop with a Roman audience than Shakespearian rustic: nothing seemed less capable of weathering the great divide of time and place. But there was no sense of culture shock. A contented chuckling filled the audience as if they were watching their favourite TV sitcom: they laughed in all the right places and at the most erudite jokes like a roomful of dons. I had thought it was only us, the actors, who had been touched with superhuman gifts. The extent of the miracle was only just emerging.

In perfect unison, the chuckling stopped and silence descended again. It fell to Tony – and how I would have wished it was me, if such egotism hadn't become an irrelevance – to speak the great lines on which the whole play pivots.

'Heavy matters, heavy matters! But look thee here, boy.

Now bless thyself: thou met'st with things dying, I with things newborn.'

Still in my bear costume, I put my arms round Vanessa and started to cry. Five minutes later, the curtain fell for the interval. The audience clapped deliriously, but I scarcely heard them.

Geoffrey put in only a brief appearance in the dressing-room during the interval.

'Keep it up, everyone. Don't lose your concentration.' There was no need to say more. Looking at his serene, confident face, it was hard to believe that this was the Geoffrey who had castigated us so savagely for our short-comings. When he'd said it would be all right on the night, had he known just how all right that meant? And how had he known? In his hour of triumph I felt as remote from him as ever, but I couldn't resist one last effort to bridge the gap. As he was leaving to go back to his seat, I slipped my arm quietly through his.

'You've worked wonders, Geoffrey.'

'Not me, Mark. Him. When are you going to understand that? If the play's good enough – '

'I know all that, Geoffrey. But are you still not surprised how well it's going? We're only amateurs. Did you really believe we had it in us?'

He shook his head. 'No, I suppose I didn't, not deep down. You're right about that. I didn't dare to hope for such quality, such panache, such – perfection. I knew I had the faith, but I didn't think any of you would have the faith. It's been a revelation.'

'Of what?'

'Of something I should have known all along.'

I wanted to question him further, but he wouldn't be drawn. The same beatific look returned to his face and it was still there when the performance resumed. Throughout the whole of Act Four, he sat in the front row with his arms folded and his head swaying gently from side to side, like a man listening to his favourite symphony. Some of us were superstitious that the interval would have broken the spell, but there was no deterioration. If anything, the acting grew stronger and stronger as the final curtain approached.

The last scene of *The Winter's Tale* is, in a dramatic sense, ridiculous. It gives ammunition to those who say that, however great a poet Shakespeare was, his stories are too silly to be taken seriously. It takes some swallowing, even for the initiated. For people bred on the rigours of TV psycho-drama, it must seem like sentimental pap.

What happens, briefly, is this. The hero Leontes is still in mourning for his wife Hermione, who died sixteen years before as a result of his vindictive jealousy. He is then reunited with his daughter Perdita, whom he tried to have destroyed at birth, also sixteen years before, but who miraculously survived and is now betrothed to Florizel, the son of Polixenes, the cause of the original jealousy (but you won't want to hear about *him*). To assist the celebrations, Paulina, an old crone, widow of Antigonus who was killed by the Bear, also sixteen years before (is everything falling into place?), produces a statue of Hermione. Great admiration all round at the quality of the sculpture. Only it *isn't* sculpture (well, of course it isn't: any pantomime buff could have told you that). On cue from Paulina, and with the help of a little music, the statue comes to life as Hermione. Far from being dead all those years, she announces blithely, she has really been alive and well and waiting for this very moment, the moment when her daughter would reappear. She didn't actually tell anyone she hadn't snuffed it because an oracle told her not to (well, that's her story and she's

270

sticking to it). Oh yes, and Camillo picks his nose through-out the scene – until Shakespeare dreams up something even more corny to happen to him . . .

It's a bit rich, isn't it? How can you suspend your disbelief when the author kills off a character in Act Three and capriciously resuscitates her in Act Five? The greenest hack would have been ashamed of such chicanery. Was it arrogance or senility that made our national poet flout the rules?

And yet *the scene works*. Suspend your disbelief – and that night everyone suspended their disbelief – and the power of Shakespeare's vision is overwhelming. He wrote happy endings before, but never such a bold one, never one which expressed so clearly the joy beyond joy on which the happiest endings are founded. At a literal level, Hermione's resurrection is ludicrously far-fetched: at the level of myth and metaphor, it is entirely coherent. I watched Joanie come to life as that statue and saw only Helen. It was lucky Camillo didn't have many lines: even now that acting was easy, I don't think I could have coped.

I said Shakespeare had something corny in store for Camillo. He did, oh God he did. Not content with bringing a dead woman back to life, not content with reuniting her with her husband and the two of them with their daughter, he attempted one final tug on the audience's heart-strings. Paulina, as I say, is a widow and Camillo one of nature's bachelors. The two old trouts are just asking to be married off, so Shakespeare obliges. It's pretty peremptory, mind you: the whole thing's over in ten lines and Camillo isn't even consulted. A hard man, Shakespeare, a hard man: a bit autocratic sometimes, like Geoffrey. But I never felt more keenly the rightness of that little sop to the audience's sentiment. If great plays don't end like that, what chance is there in life?

So Margaret and I kissed as Paulina and Camillo. Joanie hugged her Leontes. Vanessa held her Florizel by the hand. The lights faded. The curtain fell. The audience started to clap. I had thought Helen was my only experience of Life with a captial 'L', that everything that followed would be a shadow of that great passion. How wrong I was. Never had I felt so totally, unquenchably, irreducibly alive as I did at that moment. Conti put a restraining hand on my shoulder, but he held no terrors for me.

avoiding me at all? Suppose she really did have alternative engagements night after night? She had always enjoyed socializing and, when women who enjoy socializing marry madmen who fill the house with morons massacring Shakespeare, don't they have to do their socializing somewhere else? Aren't they *entitled* to look for other entertainment?

And there, in a phrase, a different doubt loomed in my mind. What kind of entertainment was she looking for? Wouldn't a woman who'd been unfaithful once tend to be unfaithful again? Suppose some new lover was filling the vacuum which I had once filled? Where was she night after night when she was avoiding me – if she was avoiding me? Did I actually matter to her at all?

Within seconds, I was on fire with jealousy. What lover escapes those flames? Jealousy is no more than the instinct to hang on to what you've got. 'To have and to hold': even the Christian marriage service acknowledges that the two concepts are inseparable. I don't like knocking a fellow professional and I mustn't criticize the dead because they can't answer back, but for me Shakespeare got jealousy arse about face in *The Winter's Tale*. He had this strange wheeze – I remember Geoffrey calling it a 'dramatic masterstroke', but then he would, wouldn't he? – of presenting jealousy as an *irrational* emotion. A man suddenly gets it into his head that he is being cuckolded and, without any evidence to support him, takes it out on his wife in a hasty way. Violent rows, baby-battering, long speeches about what happens when he realizes the glass of decent-tasting wine he's just swallowed had a spider in the bottom . . . It's all very sad (whoops, I mean tragic: sorry, Geoffrey), but it's not true to *life*, not to life as I know it anyway, here in Rome in 1985. Obviously jealousy can get out of hand sometimes: William hit that nail squarely on the head and all credit to him (he was an old man when he wrote *The Winter's Tale* and going a bit gaga judging by some of the speeches). But I can't go along with his idea that jealousy is something rootless, an emotional aberration which attacks people out of the blue like a coronary. Jealousy isn't rootless. Its roots are all too obvious: need, longing, insecurity, all the old pains. And it isn't irrational. When I'm jealous, my mind examines different hypotheses with logical coldness; in the pain of my doubt I look everywhere for certainty. As soon as I'd postulated that Helen had another lover, what mattered wasn't revenge, but finding out if I was right. Did such a man exist? What was his name? Where did they meet? I didn't turn into a monster the minute the thought entered my head, as Shakespeare's hero does. I turned into a private detective, a more civilized animal altogether.

In one of my early novels, the ones that nobody but the critics read, I had a scene in which a husband realized his wife was being unfaithful just by looking at her face in the dressing-table mirror. I had toyed, I remember, with a car-key, an earring, a man's wristwatch: one of the physical devices writers use to show closely guarded secrets being betrayed by a moment's carelessness. But then I thought, no: it doesn't need a stage-prop to achieve that effect; if he'd known her that well for that long, he would be able to read her mind anyway. I must have been rather naïve, for I'd never been able to mind-read women that fluently myself, however well I knew them, and I can only suppose that I invested marriage with magical powers which I expected to understand better if I ever got married myself. It's that face peering into a shop window again: to an outsider, married couples operate with a certain confident smoothness which convinces you they must be telepathic. But I don't now think they are. You can tell some things from a human face, but not everything, not the things you

76

most want to know. If I wrote that scene again today, I'd use a car-key like everyone else.

And yet the myth of the face persists. When you love someone well enough, or badly enough (how apt that those phrases should be interchangeable), you hope against all experience that what will be inscrutable to the rest of the world will be legible to you. When Helen got home at quarter to twelve – I stayed on specially after the rehearsal to wait for her and was engaged in a rather dusty conversation with Geoffrey about Shakespeare's flower imagery – I stared at her face like a rattle-snake, expecting it to reveal whether she had indeed been seeing Luigi or Carlo or Giuseppe. (In my mental picture it was already Giuseppe: there are several well-known Roman studs called Giuseppe.) But the sphinx guarded her secret well. Our eyes never met – I never expected they would – and she sat down next to Geoffrey on the sofa with the nonchalance of someone returning from the cinema. Perhaps I was a mind-reader after all: she *had* been to the cinema.

'Good film?' Geoffrey asked, with supreme indifference. I imagine he thought the cinema rather vulgar, the way some people find one-day cricket vulgar.

'Not bad. It was that one about the Polish family arriving in New York after the War. *Strange Dawn.*'

'I think I've just about heard of it. Where was it on? The Pasquino?'

'Yes.' The Pasquino is the only Roman cinema showing films in English. Everywhere else the films are dubbed, because Italians don't like subtitles: for some reason the most civilized country in Europe is also the most illiterate.

'No violence, I hope?' He turned to me and explained: 'Helen hates violent films.' I said: 'Yes, I know,' and immediately wished I hadn't. Geoffrey knew I'd been to the cinema with Helen in the past, so it wasn't a fatal give-away; but a man in my position prides himself on observing the demarcation lines scrupulously. A woman's attitude to cinematic violence is rather a personal matter: it falls within her husband's domain. Perhaps the eight years that we hadn't been lovers had made me careless about such niceties. Or perhaps I was just trying to attract Helen's attention. I did notice she flushed slightly when I made my interjection.

'No, it wasn't that sort of film at all,' she said quickly. 'There was a lot of petty crime among the Polish community because everyone was struggling to survive, but there was no actual violence. It was more like a documentary than a drama: there were birthday parties and train strikes and funerals and a big wedding in a church. It was quite moving really.'

'Yes, darling.' Geoffrey patted her hand like a father and an old hatred flared in me. If she'd married me, I would *never* have patted her hand like that: I would have treated her as an equal because I cared for her as an equal and we would have related like real human beings, not acted out a Victorian pantomime. How simple life seems when you're on the outside looking in. Angrily I left my coffee unfinished and rose to leave.

'Oh Mark, there's one other thing.' Geoffrey sounded embarrassed and I thought: Let him be embarrassed. If he's going to harp on about my sleeping with Vanessa being unprofessional, I'll tell him to get lost; I'll tell him there are professional virgins all over Rome just *aching* to play Camillo in his crappy production and see if he believes me. I was spoiling for a fight but, when he finally came out with it, it was too banal to fight over.

'It's about Walter, Mark. He says he doesn't feel he can play the Bear any more.'

'Why on earth not?' Immediately I smelled a trap. The